# THE JOLLY
# FARMERS

# THE JOLLY FARMERS

*A Gay Odyssey*

Robert Hurst

ISBN:        Softcover            978-1-6641-7489-4
             eBook               978-1-6641-7488-7

Cover Design and Artwork © Nancy Clearwater Herman

Print information available on the last page.

Rev. date: 05/21/2021

**To order additional copies of this book, contact:**
Xlibris
844-714-8691
www.Xlibris.com
Orders@Xlibris.com
828314

# Contents

As always, for my husband, John, for thirty years of love and support

And for Father Bob in gratitude

# Book One

## ANDANTE MOSSO

# Chapter 1

He had heard it all before. Shifting uncomfortably on the hard wooden pew, he recalled the other occasions he had come under the scathing attack of Father Sullivan. Now he had to sit through it again, enduring the slurs and accusations that he could acknowledge in his heart but never respond to publicly. Tom's mother nudged him gently; she had noticed his restlessness but attributed it to the unusual length of the sermon. He attempted to sit still because he did not want her to suspect. He turned his attention to the red glow of the stained glass window against the stucco walls of the sparsely decorated Roman Catholic church that looked like every other one built in the 1950s. At least, he thought, it would be better if he could sit through the diatribe in a more attractive setting.

"Every day the immorality of this land increases. The bookstores are filled with pornography, our movies contain only filth," the good father proclaimed in his heavy Irish brogue. Tom thought he would sound more natural if he had a Southern accent. His message seemed more akin to that of Jimmy Swaggart's—why should not his way of speaking. "Sex, drugs, and alcohol are the themes of our television shows. Old men shown lusting after scantily clad girls is the constant fare." Tom remembered the rumors when he had attended the parish elementary school about Father Chauncey, the previous rector, chasing after some of the schoolgirls and getting a thrashing from one of the fathers. Tom was also fairly certain that Sullivan himself was a hypocrite. "Homosexuals are openly carrying on their disgusting lifestyle. They now march in so-called pride parades. How can they be proud of such debased conduct?"

Tom knew that it could not be long before he got to his favorite topic. "They call themselves gays, but they are the scourge of God and won't be gay when they burn in the fires of hell, I can tell you that." It was more than Tom could stand.

After Mass he walked into the warm June morning with his parents. The great trees of Brookline were now heavy-laden. It seemed just a short time before they had been bare and the streets covered with slush. The school year was almost over, and Tom looked forward to summer break. He longed for the prospect of freedom that lay before him. He hoped that the new job and the new location would free him from the oppressiveness of his life thus far. He loved his parents dearly, but he also was eager to get away from them even though it would only be for a few months. As he rode home in his parents' Dodge, the light filtered through the leaves of the great trees created a dappled effect on the windshield and on Tom's face as he peered longingly out of the side window.

Tom's father had been a mail carrier for almost forty years and was set to retire in a few months. For the two years preceding, Mike and Clara had been examining different retirement prospects. They had thought about Arizona because of the dryness, but like California, it was too far away from what they regarded as familiar. His father finally decided to retire and, at Christmas, announced they had finally settled on Florida to get away from winter. They urged Tom to join them; for one thing, they knew their Tommy could probably get a good teaching position there. "Your mother has a cousin who lives down there. Probably could find you a job," Mike assured his son. "Lives in Orlando. We should look for places near there, don't you think, Clara?" He honestly tried to consult his wife even though he never expected contradiction, except perhaps occasionally a subtle dissent.

At first, Tom thought the decision to move was ill-advised. His mother was forty-two when he was born and his father forty-seven. His father was now seventy and not in robust health. Tom knew his mother was not capable of caring for her husband if he became ill. For that reason he had at first pleaded with his parents to remain in Boston. He had done some research and found the Florida health system lacking. It was with good reason that Florida was called God's waiting room. For that reason he urged his parents to reconsider their decision, but they were adamant. "That's what old people do—they retire and move

2

to Florida." Then she would show him a full-page ad in *Look* showing happy retired couples playing croquet shaded by palm trees.

In fact, Tom never much thought about not going with his parents. He briefly considered remaining in Boston; then he felt the pangs of familial obligation. After all, he was their only child. That in fact had been one of the great tragedies in the family. Not that they did not love Tommy, but they felt strongly that their brood should have been much larger. His parents had had difficulty having children, and his mother had suffered a series of miscarriages before Tom appeared. Clara's hysterectomy ended all hopes of having more children. Tom therefore felt a great deal of obligation to his parents. To think that they would move away without him was never really seriously considered by any of them. Moreover, Tom wanted to get out of Boston. He found the place stifling, although the constrain of living at home with his parents was primarily responsible for his distress. He felt that he could not really experience life as he wanted under his parents' solicitous gaze, even though many Bostonian homosexuals seemed to live happy and free lives there. He never really considered getting an apartment of his own. Living with his parents proved just too convenient.

When they reached their modest bungalow on a quiet side street in Brookline, Tom disappeared into his room to listen to music. He turned on WGBH and lay on his back in bed listening to Mozart. His mother busied herself in the kitchen, and he could hear the pots rattle as she prepared Sunday dinner. His reverie ended when he heard her calling rather sternly, "Thomas O'Mally, get down here now." He knew that he must have committed some serious crime since his mother only used his full name under the most dire circumstances. He rushed into the kitchen to find her standing by the open washing machine. "You left your wet clothes in here all night. They should have been put in the drier."

"Sorry, Mother," he muttered and began to transfer the clothes to the drier.

"If you would only allow me to do your laundry for you, you wouldn't have these problems. I'd be more than happy—"

"Yes, I know, Mother. But I can look after my dirty clothes myself. I don't want you to fret over them."

"It's no problem at all," she protested.

"Then who would do my laundry when I move?"

"I thought you might mail it home to me just like you did when you were in college."

Tom at first almost laughed until he realized that his mother was quite serious. All during his four years at Kenyon College, he had sent his laundry home. It was the least he could do to placate his mother, who was upset enough that he had decided to go away to college and not attend a local Catholic school. "And what is wrong with Boston College?" she had protested. Boxing up the laundry each week seemed little enough penance even though his fraternity brothers kidded him endlessly about receiving back his ironed underwear.

As Tom moved his wet clothes to the dryer, his mother then added, "And please pick up your room. It is getting somewhat disorganized." That left Tom rather befuddled because in reality his room was exceptionally neat. He had neatly folded his clothes, the clean ones that is, and put them in his dresser or hung them in his closet. The dirty ones he placed in a wicker hamper in his bathroom. His LPs were carefully stored in two containers, and his books on the brick and board bookshelf he had brought home from college. He had added considerably to his book collection, which required an addition to his bookshelf since he refused to throw any of his old books away. He even retained his dog-eared copies of *Atlas Shrugged* and *The Fountainhead* from his brief love affairs with Ayn Rand in high school.

His mother continued to chatter as she completed the dinner. She still had a hint of an Irish lilt to her voice even though she had left County Down when she was five. His father had been born in America but was fiercely loyal to the Irish cause, sending money to a friend who assured him that the cash would reach Sinn Fein. Tom had often argued about that with his father but to no avail. Finally he stopped trying to dispute with his father. He also never mentioned that once he had voted for a Republican in a local election.

As they sat down to supper, his mother observed, "Wasn't Father Sullivan's sermon exceptionally good today?"

"Personally, I thought it was reprehensible," Tom muttered.

"I don't know what you have against that dear man. He has been such a friend to you over the years. You never seem to be able to explain why you feel so strongly against him."

"I think he's a bigot and a hypocrite. I've said that many times before. Now please can't we get onto a cheerier subject." Tom could certainly not articulate his full feelings about the priest. And his mother never accepted the stories that had circulated about him and other priests. There had been talk in the parish about Father Sullivan's proclivity for the altar boys when he first arrived. Some of them had even told their parents about sacerdotal hands that had roamed in the sacristy, but their parents chose not to listen. Tom himself had fortunately been spared that; he had often served as an altar boy, but when he heard rumbling about what was going on, he took early retirement.

The remainder of the supper was quiet. Tom's parents continued to muse about retirement and their travel plans. Mike in particular wanted to return to Ireland. He hoped it might be possible to meet one of his IRA heroes. He fancied himself running guns through the British lines to his comrades in Belfast. Clara always calmed his reveries with more practical talk of perpetual sunshine and walks on the beach. Yet on this warm June afternoon, both Ireland and Florida still seemed a long way off.

Dinner conversation did not return to the offensive sermon. Clara knew when her son meant business. Instead she chatted idly about doings in the block, bringing sweet Dorothy down the street to Tom's attention. It was not too late, she mused, for Tom to take an interest in her before he left for Orlando. After all, she could follow later after the wedding. Clara never gave up hope that her son would marry a good Catholic girl like Dorothy and present her with a string of grandchildren, making up for her own lack of fecundity. Tom caught the drift of his mother's chatter, but quietly ignored it.

After supper, Tom retired to his room again, this time to listen to his old scratchy recording of Tchaikovsky's *Swan Lake* ballet suite. A pile of term papers sat neglected beside the bed as Tom slowly began to drift off to sleep. Only the clanging of the telephone startled him out of his rest. His mother called from the foot of the steps to tell him that his friend Tony was on the line. Tom knew instantly what he wanted.

Tom rushed downstairs, held a brief telephone conversation with his friend, and then informed his parents he was going to Tony's house to listen to some new LPs. "I wish you would just stay home and watch TV with us," his mother sighed.

"I'll try to get home early," Tom rejoined. But his mind was on Tony.

Tony was two years Tom's senior. He could not be regarded as good-looking, but they shared many interests together including classical music. They often took themselves off to the Esplanade in the summer to hear the Pops Concerts and see the sights along the Charles River. They would swap LPs and argue which performance of Tchaikovsky's fourth symphony was best: Ormandy at Philadelphia or von Karajan at Berlin. They also shared more intimate interests.

When he arrived at Tony's, his father opened the door and directed Tom upstairs to Tony's bedroom. The visits had become routine. Tony's father, a burly man of Polish descent, wondered why his son hung out with Tom, whom he regarded as not quite a suitable friend for his son, and speculated even more intently why his son liked listening to classical music. In fact, the classical music served as a cover for that other shared common interest, although Tony had to admit that while at first he disliked the music, he had come to appreciate some of it.

Tom followed Tony up the stairs to his bedroom. Unlike Tom's room, Tony's was a complete shambles. Dirty clothes were scattered around the room; and a pile of records, many not in their sleeves, surrounded his record player. Tom's LPs were scratched because of considerable use; Tony's because of negligence. The thought often crossed Tom's mind when he enters Tony's bedroom that it represented the Platonic ideal of clutter.

"I got a new LP at Tower Records of Tchaikovsky's sixth. Thought you might like to listen to it." He carefully placed the disk on the turntable and turned the volume up. He then walked over to his bedroom door and shut it quietly. Even more discreetly, he turned the lock, the noise of the click hidden by the music. He smiled at Tom. "You know I've actually come to like this symphony."

"Well, I think this is your third version of it. Don't you already have the recordings by Ormandy and Klemperer?"

"Yeah, but this one is a new release by Leonard Bernstein." He paused for a moment. "I wish Tchaikovsky had reversed the order of the movements. Why did he have to end on such a downer? It'd be much cheerier if he had used the third movement as the last instead. You know he committed suicide shortly after he finished the sixth. Perhaps if he had composed a cheery ending, he won't have been depressed and killed himself."

Tom laughed. "But that would miss the whole point of the *Pathetique*. Life is generally grim, but there are some happy times, and even some real joy. But it always comes back to the morose."

"The what?" Tony had only finished high school and now worked in his father's auto mechanic shop. Words like *morose* rarely came up in conversation.

"*Morose.* That means 'gloomy' or 'somber.'"

"Oh, I see. Well, I think he should have been less moruse." Tom thought about correcting him, but by this time, the music had become a cover. They had removed their clothes and lay on Tony's bed, soon becoming intertwined. The noise of lovemaking was shielded by the music. The triumphant climax of the third movement covered the blissful noise from the bed. They dressed while the New York Philharmonic played the "morose" final movement. They kissed just before Tony quietly unlocked his bedroom door, and they descended into the living room where his parents were watching *Columbo*, the volume turned up very loud.

"I wish you wouldn't play that music so loud. We can hardly hear the TV." Tony explained that they had to listen to it that loud because that is how it sounds in a live performance. The fact that his parents had to turn up the volume was just another means of covering the noise their activities in his bedroom might emit. "Well, we could hardly hear Glen Campbell sing because of that noise you listen to. Had to turn on *Columbo*."

Tony walked out of his house to see Tom off. "Can we get together Wednesday night? My parents will be out, and we don't have to rush?"

"Sounds good to me. I can't stay too long because I have to get ready to teach my little ones something about Shakespeare. They probably have all read *Richard III* from Cliff Notes." Tony gave him a quizzical look. "Oh, it's just a plot summary so they don't have to read the whole play."

"Sounds good to me," Tony repeated, laughing. "I had to read *Romeo and Juliet* in high school and hated it. Why do they have to take so long to die? Not the way it happens on *Bonanza*. They just fall over dead." Tony almost forgot himself and started to kiss Tom goodbye but fortunately Tom stopped him.

Tom turned and started walking toward his house, which was a few blocks away. "See you Wednesday," he said over his shoulder.

He realized he was applying late. His final decision to move to Florida had only occurred recently. He knew that most vacancies had already been filled; he only hoped that someone had dropped out, and he could take advantage of it. He had an impressive resume and strong letters of recommendation from the administration at Cardinal Cushing. He had applied to Orange County Schools, but since he did not have a teaching certificate from Massachusetts, he knew his chances were slim. But he had found any number of private schools. Two—Trinity Prep, an Episcopal school, and Lake Highland—sounded very appealing, especially since their beginning salaries were better than some others. They still were not impressive compared to salaries in both private and public schools in Boston; but he thought the cost of living would be much less, and he could get by. He knew, however, that his best chances lay in one of the Catholic schools to which he applied.

Tom's choice of job hunting distressed his mother. "We found this lovely bungalow in Clermont, Florida," his mother explained. "It's a retirement community called The Ridge. It's about as big as our house here, so you could have your room there."

"But, Mother, I do want to be close to you, but the only job opportunities are in Orlando."

"I did some research," she countered. "You could live with us and commute. It is only a forty-minute drive. And they are just completing an expressway, which will cut the travel time in half."

"But that still adds time onto my day. If I get an apartment in Orlando, I would be five minutes away from work."

His mother scowled but said nothing more. Tom had already contracted his cousin Eddie Turner to see if he could room with him until he found an apartment. Eddie had left Boston at the first possible moment after he had completed his law degree to get free of his overbearing parents. Helen, Clara O'Mally's sister, did not share her submissive temperament. Her loud commanding voice caused her sister to wither, as Helen explained to Clara just how wrong she was in just about everything. She had treated her children with the same stridency, which encouraged them to move far away from Boston at the first possible moment. In fact, Eddie stayed close to home in comparison to his brother who moved to California and his sister to London. They successfully had prior engagements when their parents threatened a visit.

Tom could not have felt more differently. He parents always supported him, often at a high price. When he received his acceptance at Kenyon College, his parents remortgaged the house to pay the tuition not covered by the scholarship. His decision to look for a new teaching position in Florida was not any form of flight; he really liked his colleagues at Cardinal Cushing. On the other hand, he felt somewhat stifled in Boston living with his parents. He knew, however, that he had to follow his parents even though he was not particularly keen on moving to Florida. And even ten miles away would give him the freedom that he did not have currently. Eddie had a good job as a lawyer in the family division of Orange County and had no interest in leaving, but he told Tom that he actually hated living there. "I was originally in private practice, but savagery among private law firms is cutthroat here that I took with the job with the county." He said he was happy to put up with him while Tom apartment hunted. Now all Tom needed was a job. He would be close to his parents if they needed help, but not too close.

In July, he finally got word that Catholic High School had a position for him. He was actually shocked by the offer. He knew that a private school paid less than the public system. They did not have to give hazard pay for working in some schools. And he also knew that Florida salaries in general were far below those in the Northeast. He never imagined the differential would be that great. As he hunted for apartments, however, he found, to his surprise, rents also were much lower.

He was excited about having a place of his own. Finding a guy able to host was often a problem, and at twenty-four still living with parents did not help his reputation. Not that men found him unattractive. He was tall, had pitch-black straight hair, which he had styled regularly, and piercing blue eyes. He was often told he had Paul Newman eyes. Unfortunately, from a gay perspective, he was not clearly muscular, although he did have a good chest, he thought. His busy schedule, however, did not give him time to work out at the gym except during the summer. He would return to school the picture of fitness, but that quickly disappeared as the school year progressed. He was always embarrassed to take off his shirt at the pool in June. By August, it was almost too late.

He therefore looked forward to having his own place. Then he could entertain whenever he wanted, just as long as he was discreet. Moreover, he could keep a set of weights to work out with when he could not get to the gym. And he had a stash of porn magazines he kept locked in a trunk hidden in the attic. One day his mother found the trunk and tried to open it. When she asked him about it, horrified he told her he had lost the key, and it only had some of his old college papers in it.

The other issue he craved to escape was the constant questioning by his mother about why he did not date more often. "You always have your nose in a book over the weekends. You need to get out and have fun. You need to find a nice girl to go out with." She would always pause and then continue. "Maybe you'll find one that will give me lots of grandchildren. Several of every variety," she laughed.

"Oh, Mother," he would reply. But he knew she had her heart set on completing the task she had been unable to complete herself. Perhaps God would forgive her for failing at her marital duties if her daughter-in-law finished the duty for her. A few times, Tom considered telling his mother he was not the marrying kind, but he thought she would not understand and would see it as an act in ingratitude for all the sacrifices they had made for him so that he could attract a suitable spouse.

In some ways Tony was a good match. He shared many of Tom's interests, especially classical music; he had no intention of settling down, and the sex was great. Tom never worried that even if Tony's parents were downstairs, they would interrupt them. The loud music annoyed his father, but it served a good cover for any sounds of ecstasy. Tom really desired to sleep with a man, to wake up the next morning holding or being held by someone with whom he had shared. Yet he did not see how he could arrange that. Tony had actually suggested that he stay overnight. They would pretend that each had had too much to drink, and they thought it best that Tom would remain. Sleep on the floor, of course. It was hardly believable since neither Tony nor Tom were heavy drinkers; and Tom knew that, once he called, his mother would order his father to drive to Tony's house and transport Tom home to sleep it off in his own bed. It would be even more difficult with someone Tom had picked up at a bar. Sleepovers were out of the question.

That is why Tom was in part enthusiastic about the move to Orlando. He would have a place of his own not under the gaze of his parents, some thirty miles away in Clermont. Yet he would be close enough to take care of them in an emergency. He would just make certain his trick did not answer the phone.

He had had a series of conversations with his cousin about where to find an apartment. The Catholic High was in west Orlando. He did not want to be so close to the school that his comings and goings might be observed. So he looked for a place in nearby Winter Park, a very tony neighborhood. He could not afford the apartments there, but he found some apartment complexes on the outskirts. He intended to settled for one off Semoran Boulevard.

In mid-June, classes ended at Cardinal Cushing. Tom announced that he would not be back the next year—he held off as long as possible. When he met with the school head, Father Andrews expressed deep regret that Tom had decided to leave. "I certainly understand your desire to be close to your parents. You are a very dutiful son. But Florida's gain is our loss." He then smiled. "And I'm sure Lucy Tillman will be especially aggrieved."

"What do you mean by that?" Tom said quizzically.

"Why, everyone expected that you and Lucy would someday marry."

"Oh, I'm very fond of Lucy . . . but as a colleague. We worked very well together. We were really a team so that we planned our tenth- and eleventh-grade syllabi to have the one build on the other. We tried to show how American and British lit dealt with the same issues but with very different answers."

Clearly Andrews had little interest in a lecture on pedagogy and quickly changed the subject. "When do you intend to move?"

Feeling rather cut off, Tom replied, "Very soon now. I have a job interview at Orlando Catholic next week, and I plan to check out apartments when I'm down there. If all works out, I guess I'll move mid-July."

"Well, I wouldn't worry too much about the job. I was contacted by the headmaster there, and I gave you a glowing review. Told him you were probably one of our finest teachers, and we were sorry to lose you."

So at least the principal knew about Tom's plans. He wondered who else in the school did. That afternoon at a meeting of the English department, Tom announced his resignation. No one actually looked surprised, which indicated to Tom that everyone was privy to his news even before he had made a final decision. He also noted that Lucy looked rather downcast. After the meeting, he stopped by her classroom. "It seems that everyone in the department, perhaps even the whole school, knew that I was thinking of leaving even before I had fully made up my mind."

"I was really hurt that you hadn't even mentioned your thoughts to me," Lucy said plaintively. "We've worked so closely together I thought at least you'd let me know."

"I'm sorry, Lucy, but I really didn't want to tell anyone until I was positive. And really, my parents hadn't decided definitely to move to Florida until recently." He tried to shorten the decision-making time.

"So you'd still be living with them?" There was a tone of mockery in her voice.

"No, I'm not actually living with them. I'll be in Orlando, and they'll be somewhere out in the sticks. But I really need to be somewhat close to them since they are getting older, and my father is not in the best of health."

"Oh, I see," was her only reply. For the first time, Tom realized that Lucy had feelings toward him that went beyond just that of a colleague. In reality, Tom was often rather tone-deaf to the feelings of others, especially women. There had been a number of girls in college and afterward who found him very attractive and attempted to intimate their admiration. Those signals seemed just to bounce off him. Tom's radar about glances from men was, on the other hand, rather finely tuned. Tom had the science of flirtation with other men finely developed, although it rarely led to any sort of fulfillment.

"I'm really sorry, Lucy, but I really need to help out with them. I have no siblings, and frankly, I don't trust the social services in Florida to be adequate. But I have to say I'll really miss teaching with you. You have helped me a lot to develop as a teacher"—Lucy was five years older than Tom and therefore had more teaching experience—"and I doubt if anyone at Orlando Catholic will be the same."

Lucy smiled, but inside she knew Tom just tried to soothe her, but perhaps not with a great deal of sincerity. She had long thought that Tom returned her affection, but it became very clear now he did not. He respected her as a colleague, but nothing beyond that. Once Tom had moved, he did send two letters to Lucy, apprising her of his new life in Orlando. When the second letter remained unanswered for a month, Tom did not compose a third.

The next day, as Tom began cleaning out his desk and packing some of his books, Bill Fisher, another member of the English department, slipped into his office. He was smiling a Cheshire Cat smile. "Lucy's pretty bummed out about your leaving."

"I know. I feel really sorry, but it can't be helped."

"Well, I tried to warn her about not getting emotionally involved with you."

"What do you mean by that?" Tom was irritated.

"Of course, I didn't fully explain, but I just told her you didn't reciprocate?"

"Huh?"

"It was obvious to everyone in the department that she had the hots for you. But you and I know you aren't much interested in women."

"What do you mean by that?" By this point, Tom had begun to turn red.

"I mean that you are like me. We both are interested in men and not women."

Red had turned to white. Tom could say nothing.

"Come on, Tom. I've known ever since you arrived you were a homosexual. You can pass for straight very easily unless you know what to look for."

Tom continued to be mute.

"It's the way you treated Lucy. She was always just the colleague. But it's also been clear that you certainly admire the baseball coach with his well-defined muscles, really attractive face, and a really cute rear end. I must admit I lust after him myself."

Tom relented. He obviously had not been practically good at hiding his attractions. "So we have some interests in common?"

"Like men's bodies. Guess so. At one point, Father Andrews thought I should warn you to be more discreet. I think most of the staff figured you were homosexual, that is except Lucy. Her own lust must have blinded her," he laughed.

"Andrews guessed?" Tom had no idea he had been that obvious. He always believed that no one would guess his attraction to men.

"Sorry, Tom. Remember that the South is far more conservative than we are here in Boston. You'd best keep your roving eyes in check." Then as an afterthought, he added, "I often thought of inviting you over for dinner and jumping your bones. But then I judged it was not a good idea to be involved with someone at work. But I wanted you to know I thought long and hard about it."

Tom paused a moment and replied, "I'm very flattered." But he didn't add that he was equally interested since he wasn't. Bill was a nice guy, but Tom did not find him at all attractive. Unfortunately, he knew the baseball coach was totally straight.

Bill was correct about one thing. Florida was far more conservative than Massachusetts. When he interviewed at Orlando Catholic, the headmaster, Father Humphrey, assured him that the job was his if he wanted it. "I've known Father Andrews for many years, and his recommendation carries a great deal of weight with me. And he spoke of you in glowing terms. We would love for you to become part of our team in September." Then, however, came the warning. "Now I want to make certain you understand the behavior we demand of our faculty outside of school. We are a conservative Catholic institution, and we expect our faculty to uphold our standards. And that includes how we comport ourselves outside school in the community. You're not married, are you, Mr. O'Mally?"

"No, sir, I'm not."

"Then you need to be very careful about your public appearances. We don't tolerate our faculty being involved in sexual activities outside of a Catholic marriage." At this point, Tom almost stood and walked out. Only the fact that his parents had already signed the sales agreement on their home in Brookline stopped him. "You live alone?"

"I do. If I get a two-bedroom apartment, I might get a roommate to help with the rent."

"Well, make certain that he's a male and that you have separate bedrooms. We won't condone any gossip about our faculty. It is one of the main selling points of our school. A one-bedroom might be more expensive but less liable to lead to innuendos."

Tom walked out in a daze. His interview had not consisted of any discussion of his educational philosophy, examples of his teaching techniques, books he would like to include on his syllabus. No, he was lectured on his sleeping arrangements. The headmaster did not seem concerned if he had robbed a bank or murdered anyone, just as long as he only had sex with a woman he had married in a Catholic ceremony. He wondered if a civil ceremony would count. What convinced him to take the position not only included that his parents were scheduled to move in a week but that two of his future colleagues in the English department and a guy named Toby from the History faculty impressed him. They invited him out to lunch at a small sandwich shop called the Lunch Basket. He had a meatloaf sandwich and good conversation. His female colleague in a department was a rather large woman by the name of Barbara—she would be said to have big bones—who placed her tray next to Tom and began talking. She was as brassy as her hair, which was a startlingly shade of red. "Did old Humphrey give you the sex lecture?"

"Well, yes."

"I think he's only interested in what goes on between your navel and your knees," observed Hank Smith. "Prurient interest with a vengeance. I bet he goes home and writes down his fantasies." Everyone at the table laughed, which made Tom feel a little better.

The only faculty member who gave him pause was the chair, Sister Alice. She never seemed to smile, and it appeared that she had a glass left eye. He found her looking straight at him with her left eye, but scanning the room with her right. It was quite unnerving.

When he returned to his cousin Eddie's apartment, where he was staying, he repeated the events of the day, especially his interview with the headmaster. "You got to remember that you're in the South now. If you think the Catholic Church is conservative, you should meet some Baptists. Personally I've joined the Church of St. Wilfred the Doubter. I can do as I please without any of the guilt."

"Do your parents know about this conversion?"

"Don't know and don't care. I have as little contact with them as possible anyhow. I'd advise you to keep your own distance."

"Oh, I intend to. They'll be in Clermont, and I doubt if they'll drive over to Orlando very often. I'll visit on Sundays for lunch. But they aren't at all like your parents. They don't interfere much at all."

"But I bet they do ask when you're going to get married and settle down."

Tom wondered if even cousin Eddie, whom he had not seen in years, had also guessed about his perversion.

The next day, he looked at some apartment complexes and settled on a one-bedroom apartment at the Carlton Arms, so as to avoid suspicion. The apartment overlooked an undeveloped marshland through which he was told ran a train known as the Dinky Line. He had many second thoughts about his decision to move. Although his future colleagues seemed nice enough, he had reservations about the administration. And the ability of Sister Alice to look in two directions at the same time, he found disconcerting. Finally, his beginning salary was pathetic. But he thought it was the best thing to do.

15

The week before he left Boston, he made one last visit to Tony's. The sex was as good as ever, and they chatted afterward. Tom was very fond of Tony; it was certainly not love, but he did have a sense of sadness in leaving. In fact he promised to visit and to stay the entire night. He was not sure if that would happen, but it was very nice to think about. When he left, he gave Tony a very passionate kiss. When they moved apart, Tony gave him a very quizzical look and then a big smile. There was no mention of love, but something passed between them.

# Chapter 2

Rather despondently, Tom walked out of his tenth-grade English Composition class. He had been impressed that the school required all tenth graders to complete a course that strengthened writing skills and emphasized correct grammar and punctuation. The students so strenuously resisted learning anything that he quickly became discouraged. Moreover, the skills they had brought with them from the Lower School were remarkably abysmal. He knew that most Florida public schools were inferior to those in the Northeast. A friend told him about all the ninth-grade classes in one school had to share the biology textbooks so that the students could not take them home. And the books were in such a bad condition that transporting them out of the school would have destroyed most of them. His cousin Eddie had a friend who moved his family to Pennsylvania and found that his children were almost two years behind their new classmates. Yet Tom had anticipated that private school education would be considerably better. At least in the Catholic system, it was not. Yes, the kids had decent books, but that was because the parents had to purchase them.

Today had been particularly frustrating. Tom tried to teach his class the difference between transitive and intransitive verbs, particularly *lie* and *lay*. He knew the topic was not particularly scintillating, so he tried to make a game of it. The attention of the class, however, shifted away from the game to the boys on the back row who were rather loudly arguing if "getting laid" made one transitive or intransitive. Tom dutifully wrote them up for detention, which did not increase his popularity.

Tom walked into the teachers' lounge and poured himself a coffee. Fred Higgins sat at one of the tables, marking some papers. "Should have done these last night, but the beer got the best of me."

"Wish I could get a drink right now." In fact, Tom was not much of a drinker; he generally had a glass of white wine, while he watched the *CBS Evening News* before his dinner. "I just had one of the most memorably awful classes in my entire teaching career." He told Fred about the transitive verbs, but they both laughed when he mentioned the conjugations of "getting laid." "I had the hardest time trying to look disapproving."

"I bet they actually learned something today. If we could teach all our classes on their level, they'd get more out of it."

"I doubt if the bishop would approve."

"Listen, from what I've heard, he knows a good deal about getting laid."

Again they laughed until another teacher, with strikingly red hair, entered the lounge. "Morning, Barbara," Fred greeted her.

"What's so funny?"

"Oh, nothing much. How's your day going?"

"Oh, I just had the best discussion about *Tess of the D'Urbervilles.*" Barbara's classes always seemed to go better than her male colleagues'. Her students always excelled because they were exceedingly bright and just absorbed all that she had to convey. She constantly criticized her male colleagues when they complained about their students. "You just don't try hard enough. You got to put more effort in." She then proceeded to explain all the marvelous techniques she had used to draw the students into Tess's sins and her just punishment. The Hardy Tom learned about at Kenyon, Barbara had transformed into a Catholic moralist.

After she left, Fred commented, "I understand the students hate her classes, but if they suck up to her, they all get As for doing practically nothing. They could turn in the most banal essay, and she'll gush over it."

"I try to teach them something, and they seem to resent it. I had a much easier time at my last school."

"I think anti-intellectualism is a component of the water. And their parents are no different. All they want is that their children get good grades so they can get admitted to community college and get a good job at Disney waiting tables"

"Oh, I think you're being a bit harsh."

"You obviously haven't had enough contact with the parents. You've only been here two months. I've taught here four years and am completely jaded."

"The Catholic school where I taught in Boston had much better students. They all had their eyes of Notre Dame or even Harvard. If any one of them got a C, they would run in to see me, ask how they could improve their grade, and if they could do the paper over again. I often let them after they convinced me with tears, and by golly, the paper was significantly better. While the paper might now be a B+, I would give it an A just for the effort."

"Half the students here should thank their lucky stars if they get a C. And actually I don't give many because the administration doesn't like it. They don't want to hear from the parents who are paying $2,000 a year for little junior to be 'edumacated.' That means an A." Tom could only roll his eyes at that observation.

The English faculty consisted of three younger members: Tom, Fred, and Barbara. The other six were teachers who had been with the school for decades. Two were nuns. Fred said that Sister Alice had a mustache, probably a glass eye, and smelled of mothballs. "She assigned the same essay at the beginning of the school years to her class: what did you do on your summer vacation? Students get copies from previous class, remove the title page, and submit it as their own. You would think the old dear would recognize that every year at least one student spent their vacation in the Amazon collecting specimens for biology classes."

Tom laughed heartily until another faculty member entered the room and frowned at such frivolity. "I thought her left eye looked strange," he whispered. "She seemed to be able to look in two different directions at the same time." Fred tried to stifle a laugh.

Most of the faculty had taught there for a long time; there were few his age. Only Toby Anderson in the History department was in his mid-twenties. He had joined the faculty a few years before. He would often sit with Fred and Tom in the faculty dining room for lunch. They often talked politics since they were all Democrats, frustrated with the thought that Nixon would probably be re-elected despite the fact that the war he had promised to end continued. "Thank God I had a high number," Toby grinned. Fred was over thirty and out of danger, but Tom also praised the lottery gods that he was in the low three hundreds. "Two of my fraternity brothers at UF were killed right after they had graduated. But for the grace of God and the numbers tumbler go I."

Tom had only partially unpacked all his books. Boxes remained stacked in the corner of his living room waiting for his attention. Preparing for class or grading papers had consumed most of his time. He liked his apartment, which was near the center of Winter Park, a very wealthy small town, and far enough away from Orlando Catholic, from the prying eyes of administrators and inquisitive faculty. The apartment seemed solid enough until he noticed that he could hear his next-door neighbor doing dishes. Obviously the walls separating the apartments were not as rock-solid as he originally thought. A few days later, he heard loud voices emanating from next door, eventually followed by some very loud lovemaking. This pattern repeated itself on several other occasions, until finally Tom went to the manager's office to complain. The manager brushed him off, observing that apartment walls were suitably thick enough that he had to be imagining any noise. Tom seriously thought about finding a new apartment even though that might mean losing his security deposit. Nevertheless, Fortuna seemed to smile on him because during the next altercation of the battling duo, shouts were followed by the sound of smashing crockery, and finally the decisive slamming of a door. Thereafter all that, he heard nothing but the sound of the dishes and the television, which he successfully blocked by turning on the PBS radio station or playing some of his records. He knew, however, if he ever had a houseguest that he would make certain he had several LPs handy, music that might help set the mood, at that same time masking the accompanying moans and groans.

On the weekends, he drove to Clermont to help his parents get settled in their new home. As he came to the entrance of The Ridge, he drove through an impressive gatehouse with a room for a guard and an arm that was raised that allowed him to enter. Obviously, the guard had taken a break and left the entrance open, Tom thought. The gatehouse was far more impressive than the houses it guarded. They were all modest cinderblock houses painted various garish shades of pastel. Each had the mandatory palm tree in the front yard surrounded by what the natives called "Spanish bayonets," which look perilously dangerous.

Tom told his parents that the guard was not in his booth. "Oh, there never was anyone there. It's strictly for appearances. Makes the estate look impressive," his father laughed.

The house had been left in a state of disrepair, which Tom helped his father rectify: windows that would not close properly or would not open, a leak in the roof over the kitchen, and some electrical outlets without any power. "The home inspector must have been the cousin of the realtor. 'The house was in perfect condition!' he claimed." Mike thought about contacting an attorney, but his next-door neighbor told him not to bother. They all had dealt with issues involving shoddy contraction, and efforts to get compensation had universally failed. "They told me not to waste my money."

"And the houses are so close together I can hear our neighbors eating their Rice Krispies," his mother grumbled. "And flushing their toilet!"

"I feel your pain. I have the same problem in my apartment." He did not explain exactly what he had heard.

His mother also complained about the bugs that had invaded her kitchen. "They call them palmetto bugs, but I know a cockroach when I see one. They fly and make a snapping noise when they do." Tom slept uneasily in the spare room thinking about an invasion of the palmetto bugs taking over his room. As he drifted off, he composed a screenplay depicting the approach of the carnivorous cockroaches. He thought it should be titled "Vermint," a combination of *vermin* and *varmint*. Harrison Ford would play him . . . and Nixon would portray the bug. All in Cinemascope and Technicolor . . .

Tom helped his father find contractors to fix the various problems and also help them unpack. He even located a pest control company that provided emergency calls. Even though their house in Brookline was small, the new house had even less storage space to accommodate years of collection. His mother did not want to throw anything away, so Tom spent every Sunday finding spaces for items that "we can't possibly part with."

Another topic of conversation centered on Tom's diet. Each time he arrived, his mother would look at him suspiciously. "You seem to be losing weight," she would always comment.

He assured her that he was not and in fact was working hard not to gain weight. "I can't get to the gym the way I did before, so I have to be careful." He realized, of course, that his consumption of chardonnay and Tanqueray did not help.

"Are you learning to cook? You always had healthy home-cooked meals in Boston. I wonder if you are actually eating properly." Again he assured her that he was and mentioned that he had purchased a copy of *The Joy of Cooking*. He was not lying, but he had rarely opened it. He had discovered the joy of frozen entries.

Finally, in mid-October, Tom informed his parents he could not come over every weekend because he was getting behind in his work, and he had not even finished unpacking himself. "Oh, but you are such a great help," his mother pleaded. Finally they reluctantly agreed that he would come over every other weekend to assist them. By November, it would become once a month with telephone calls in between if an emergency arose. To Tom's frustration, the "emergencies" remained rather frequent. He realized that he had become the parent. He purchased an answering machine, which he used to filter his calls, explaining—when he did not immediately return a call—that he had an evening meeting or special event at school. These meetings also became more frequent.

He spent the first weekend in December at home; the weather finally broke, and it was cool enough to sit outside. The constant assault of humidity had also subsided. He sat on his balcony overlooking the scrub grass field and watched for the first time the Dinky Line train pass by.

Tom also now had the option of some sort of social life on the weekends. Yet he had no idea where any sort of gay life existed in Orlando. He stopped by a bar in Winter Park called Harper's, but it was filled with students from a nearby college, most underage with fake IDs, and none apparently gay. He finally mustered the nerve to go to Orange Avenue News to buy some magazines, slipping a copy of *The Advocate* in the pile of news magazines. Even so, the clerk looked up when he added that magazine to the total. At least at Orange Avenue News, Tom was no longer closeted.

He found the section of the Pink Pages, which listed venues in the Orlando area. He saw listed a gay bar called the Silver Hammer, a most peculiar name, he thought. Then there was Southern Nights, which he thought should have been spelled with a *K*. The biggest venue was Parliament House on the Orange Blossom Trail. He drove past it and found an old motel that apparently had been retrofitted. He wondered what went on in those motel rooms. He decided it was too large and public to chance. He did not dare be seen in a place like that considering the admonition he had received from his boss. He therefore decided to risk the Silver Hammer, not only because of his curiosity about the name but also it was a small spot. The first Saturday in November, he put on a rather tight pair of jeans, a polo shirt, and his best gay attitude.

The place itself was quite small with the requisite pool table in one room and a small bar area in the other room. He walked confidently to the bar and ordered a gin and tonic. "Sorry, sir, we only serve beer and wine, no hard stuff."

Totally deflated, his confidence gone, he meekly ordered a white wine and stared down at the bar. It was only then that he realized it was covered with pictures of naked men, many engaged in explicit sexual activities. It appeared that the photographs had been decoupaged onto the bar. "That's my favorite one," said a man who had just walked up next to him. He pointed to a picture of a couple involved in rimming. "So you're new here?" And without taking a breath, added, "Can I buy you a drink?" Fortunately the bartender walked over with his glass of chardonnay.

"That'll be $5."

"Oh, thanks, but I already have one." He grabbed his wallet and pulled out a bill and handed it to the bartender, almost in shock about how expensive the drink was. The bartender looked annoyed, probably expecting a ten-dollar bill and being told to keep the change.

"Watch out. They water the drinks here. That's why I always order a bottle of beer," his new friend said. "So are you new here?" he asked again.

"Yes, I just moved here a few weeks ago. And I really don't like beer, so the water-downed wine will have to do," he laughed.

"First time in the Hammer?"

"Yes, just beginning to explore."

"So where do you work?"

"I'd rather not say." Tom was determined not to provide any information that could subsequently be used against him.

His new companion tried to continue their conversation, but Tom's curt answers convinced him that Tom was not interested in continuing their romance. Tom actually wanted to know the origin of the name of the bar but did not want to encourage the man further by asking questions.

Tom had noted that the crowd at the Silver Hammer was on the older side. Most of them did not really interest him. He did receive two more offers of drinks to which he replied by showing them the glass of wine he nursed. They obviously took the hint. He wandered around the bar some more, seeing a side room that was occupied by a group that obviously always sat there. His intrusion was clearly unwelcome by the looks he got, especially from the older man with a heavy white beard who seemed to pontificate and clearly served as doorman as well. Tom next walked into the poolroom and watched some guys playing. One of them was particularly good-looking, and his tight jeans beautifully highlighted his delightful rear end. Tom tried to make eye contact, but evidently the young man was more interested in his game of pool. Disappointed, Tom thought that the only really hot guy in the bar was more engrossed in the game than he was in an evening of amusement with him.

Tom saw a door next to the pool table and walked over to see if it was unlocked. He opened it and started to walk out onto a fenced patio when he heard the unmistakable sounds of lovemaking going on in a dark corner. Just then a hand reached out the door and pulled him in. "You better not linger out there. The Orlando Police raid this place regularly, and if they find anyone out there, they immediately make an arrest. They don't come in the main entrance but through that gate into the patio," pointing to the partially ajar wooden entrance. "They say it has to remain unlocked for a fire escape, but they only want it open to catch guys with their pants down."

Tom thanked him for the warning.

"Can I buy you a drink?" the man offered.

"No, actually I have a bunch of work to do tomorrow and planned an early night. But thanks anyhow." He walked out of the bar, feeling like he had actually been in a butcher store, and he was a piece of fresh meat. Ironically, he forgot that he himself had been regarding a piece of meat holding a pool cue. Nevertheless, he did go back to the Hammer, as it was affectionately called, and actually became friendly with some of the patrons, especially Peter, who had saved him from imminent arrest on the patio. The patrons had come to realize that Tom was not available, at least to them. The man with the white beard who pontificated in the small back room always looked disapprovingly at Tom whenever he saw him.

On Sunday morning, Tom prepared to go to Mass. When he had been travelling to Clermont, he attended church with his parents as he always had. Now that he stayed most weekends in Orlando, he slept in a few Sundays. One day, the headmaster cross-examined him about the regularity of his church attendance. Tom explained that he visited his parents on most weekends and attended there. "But when you stay here?" came the rapid-fire question.

"Well, I've been shopping around, but I haven't found one that really attracts me yet." It was clearly the wrong thing to say.

"Faculty at Catholic High are expected to set an example of regular church attendance. You are supposed to attend the church in which parish you reside. Where do you live?" Tom explained that his apartment was between Winter Park and Goldenrod. "Well, you need to find which parish you reside and attend regularly." The implication was that the Reverend Father would be tracking his attendance.

After some research, he discovered he should attend Saints Peter and Paul in Goldenrod. He twice attended Mass there, but was unimpressed by the priest and found the gaggle of little children in this obviously fecund area annoying. He then busted out of the parish limits and attended Margaret Mary in Winter Park. Although the throng of children seemed almost as enormous, he found the priests there gave rather more intelligent sermons, including some oblique expressions of disapproval of what was happening in Vietnam, which gave Tom hope. Also a number of faculty from the local college attended, which significantly lifted the intelligence quotient.

Saturday nights, however, were reserved for explorations of local gay watering holes. He had come to like the Hammer, but there did not seem to be any sexual outlet available. Therefore, he decided to broaden his parameters. In early December, he drove to Southern Nights but had serious reservations about entering. At the entrance to the parking lot sat an Orlando police car, its headlights burning and a blue light threateningly visible inside. It did not appear that a raid was in progress, but Tom frankly did not like the looks of it. He was nervous already about being discovered in one of these places, and the police car was sufficient reason not to try here. He therefore drove on and stopped again at the Hammer. He had a few drinks, chatted with several who had in reality become somewhat like friends, but concluded the night retiring to his apartment alone, sleeping in a cold and lonely bed. Despite his conviction upon leaving Boston that his days of sleeping alone were over, he had yet to notch his gun in that regard.

The Parliament House proclaimed itself the Gay Mecca of Central Florida. When Tom had driven by before, the large number of cars in the parking lot alarmed him. What if he ran into someone he knew? Did only gay people go there, or is it an attraction for straight people out to "slum it"? He could not imagine his headmaster going to a place like that, and heaven forbid that Sister Alice would slip on her sequence habit and disco the night away. Still it was a scary thought.

Again donning the slightly tight jeans, the chest-defining polo shirt, and his leather jacket, he climbed into his Honda and drove to the Parliament House. The parking lot was as usual quite full, and he had to walk quite a distance to the entrance. The complex was huge. He walked into a small bar area with a theatre through one door and a large dance floor through the another. He boldly approached the bar and ordered a gin and tonic, even calling for Tanqueray gin. It tasted so good. He then strolled into the dance hall and confronted an amazing array of men, some couples, some men dancing alone, some with capes or fans, most shirtless. The energy level was infectious.

Tom looked around carefully to see if he recognized anyone, but he was relieved that no one looked familiar. He did see quite a few men though whom he would not mind waking up with tomorrow morning. Church would have to wait. He noticed that some men exited the dance area, and he decided to follow. Apparently there was a nine o'clock drag show in the theatre. Most of the seats were already taken, and many men lined the sidewalls. Tom found a single seat in a row close to the stage which he claimed. He had never been to a real drag show before—Tony had taken him to one once, but it was all amateurs—and so he looked forward to the show.

The lights dimmed, and a rather disheveled drag queen entered the stage and announced that she was Miss P. She was greeted with loud applause and equally loud boos. "Shut up, you bunch of nelly queens." Again cheers and boos arose from the audience. She carried on what Tom thought was a very clever monologue. Every once in a while, an attractive young man would walk to the stage and hand Miss P a drink, which she quickly consumed. Tom thought that if she kept that up for long, she would collapse on the stage. She carried on constant arguments with men sitting in the front row. Obviously they had gone through this routine many times. Finally she asked the audience to "Put your hands together and welcome to the Parliament House . . ." the name of a drag queen that Tom could not hear over the din of applause. The act mesmerized Tom. Although he knew the performer was a male, who was not actually doing the singing, the effect was magical. At the end of her (?) performance, he stood with the others to shout his approval. He had noticed that a few lesbian couples sat in the audience, but the bulk of the crowd were all men. The sound of all those gay men cheering and applauding filled Tom with pride; he had found a home at last.

At the end of the show, Tom moved with the rest of the crowd back to the dance hall. He stopped along the way to get another Tanqueray and tonic. He looked around the room to see if he saw an interesting prospect. Tom regarded his dancing abilities as pathetic, but it never stopped him from making a fool of himself on the dance floor. He was tall, gangly, and awkward. But he made up for it with his enthusiasm. Most of the men seemed to be coupled or at least on a date, or with a large group of friends. Few seemed to be there alone like he was. But he had seen a very cute guy standing alone in the corner. He did not appear to be waiting for someone. Tom had just about decided to saunter over (to show off the best aspects of the jeans and the snug polo shirt), when he felt a tap on his shoulder.

He turned around and saw with horror Toby smiling at him. "Well, well, fancy meeting you here."

Tom could feel his face turn red. Quickly he tried to come up with an excuse: he had wandered in here by mistake, a gay friend brought him, a lesbian friend brought him. For a while, Toby just allowed Tom to stammer, trying desperately to come up with an excuse. "Don't worry, Sister Alice and the Morality Patrol aren't outside waiting to arrest you." Tom noticed another man standing next to Toby. "Oh, Tom, this is my boyfriend, Jeff. Tom teaches English at Catholic." Then to Tom, he said with a smile, "I always thought you were family. Welcome to the Parliament House."

They tried to carry on a conversation, but the loud music overwhelmed them. Toby therefore steered them onto a side patio, which was much quieter. Tom looked around to see if anyone was having sex, but it was just guys talking and smoking.

"I thought I saw you in the show. You were sitting down front. We stood on the side. Isn't P terrific?"

"She certainly was funny and certainly could down the drinks."

"That's why we come to the early show. She can get pretty incoherent by the second show. So is this your first time here? You sort of had the look of a lost child," Toby smiled.

"Yup. First time. I went to the Silver Hammer a few times, but it certainly isn't as lively as this place."

"Yes, pretty much the same crowd hangs out there. Older guys. Did they try to hit on you?"

"Frequently," Tom laughed.

"It's nice if you go with a few friends to have a drink and chat. But the action is here. Especially for someone your age." Then as an afterthought, he asked, "Do you have a boyfriend?"

"No, I'm very single. You know I just moved down here and actually only getting settled. No time for romance."

"Well, you need to make time. There's nothing like it." At that he pulled Jeff over and gave him a passionate kiss. Tom began to feel himself swell. "Is there, sweetie?"

"I should warn you," Toby continued, "that Jeff is Jewish. Jeffrey Rosen. So please don't tell anyone at school that I'm dating a Jewish boy. Oh gosh, you'd better not even tell them that I'm dating a boy. But at least he's an attorney. Perhaps the Vatican says it's okay to suck a legal dick."

"Well, technically I'm not Jewish. My father is Jewish, but my mother is a Presbyterian. Boy, did that marriage cause consternation in both families."

"But I can attest," Toby added, "that he is properly circumcised. I've examined it closely."

"I bet you have," Tom laughed.

They talked some more, and then Toby said, "Well, we'd better get going. My parents are coming over tomorrow for lunch, and I need to get an early start. I'm the chef de cuisine." At that, Jeff wrinkled his nose and frowned.

"So you're out to your parents?"

"Have been for a long time. You sound surprised. Apparently you're not."

"Not at all. They keep pestering me about finding the right girl and getting married so that they can have seven grandchildren."

"Sounds dreadful." They walked out the main entrance and turned to go to the parking lot in the rear. Toby looked up and saw a small crowd clustered in front of the motel windows. "Oh, a show must be going on. Do ya want to see?"

"What is it?" Tom asked.

"You'll see." They climbed the stairs to the second-floor balcony that ran around the building and stopped by the crowd. They really couldn't see until Toby called out, "Virgin perv voyeur here. Can we squeeze through please?" At that the crowd parted and allowed Tom to press to the front. What he saw almost shocked him. The curtain was fully open, and the lights in the room brightly lit. On the bed were three totally naked men having sex. He watched mesmerized as they committed all the homosexual mortal sins: fellatio, mouth-to-anus resuscitation, anal sex, the lot.

"Does this sort of thing go on all the time?" he asked Toby, who had clambered in behind him.

"Generally only on weekends. Mostly they are exhibitionists who crave an audience. On the weekends, there are plenty around to oblige."

"Don't the police stop it?"

"Never seen one venture up here. In uniform, that is. I bet some arrive in their civilian clothes to partake."

"When I drove past Southern Nights the other week, I saw a police car parked out front."

Toby continued his tutorial on Central Florida gay life. "He was an Orlando policeman. They patrol both Southern Nights and the Hammer. We're in the county now, and the Orange County Sheriff's Department never comes by. We're certain the management provides a gratuity to the sheriff to make certain they do stay away. Welcome to Florida." After the show had come to its climax, literally, they departed to their own cars. Tom drove home very cautiously because he feared he would fail a breathalyzer if stopped.

He woke up the next morning with a pounding headache. Even premium gin can have consequences. He thought about church and decided that Margaret Mary could just have to do without him. He knew one thing though. He would never be a performer in a second-floor window at the Parliament House.

The next weekend, he made his obligatory trip to Clermont. He had not driven over in four weeks, and he could tell his mother was rather angry with him when she telephoned that Wednesday. He explained that he had been spending his weekends grading papers and that he had not even been out. His mother pointed out that he could bring his papers with him for the weekend. They would turn down the television.

He made sure he saved a pile of papers to take with him to demonstrate to his parents the strain he was under. Normally he would have finished them during the week so that he could have at least Saturday free to play. He made sure to have the papers piled around him the entire visit whenever he came to Clermont.

He found that his parents were not particularly happy. They obviously missed having him around, but they also missed their friends in Boston. While the neighbors seemed friendly enough, Mike and Clara did not seem to be able to connect. "All they talk about is their medication, which doctor they see, and what aliments they suffer from."

"Well, have you made any friends?" Tom asked rather anxiously. He hoped his parents would not decide to move to Orlando.

"Well, Peg and Will next door are very nice. The couple on the other side are from Indiana and Republicans! And they hate Blacks, Jews, and Catholics. The other couples have not been very friendly. They gather at the gazebo in the park and start drinking at four in the afternoon. Now I do like my glass of chardonnay before dinner, but they all get drunk every afternoon. They bring in these big, gallon bottles of Carlo Rossi. I tried it once. It is disgusting. Now mind you, I don't need Chateau Lafite." Then as an afterthought, she added, "And they all dye their hair blue. I refuse to do that!"

After supper, before Tom began grading the pile of papers he still had to complete, he sat with his father in the screened patio to avoid the predatory mosquitoes. "I know what you're going to ask. No, we aren't planning to move to Orlando. She's not very happy about our move, but I can assure you when she hears about the first blizzard in Boston, she'll change her tune. And we have made some good friends, especially Will and Peg. He's a good golf partner, and Peg got your mother to start learning bridge."

"Well, that's a good thing you plan to stay here. It would be rather difficult to move in with me since I only have one bedroom," he laughed.

"No, don't worry about that. If anything, we'd return to Boston."

"After I moved down here to be near?" he said with a fake tone of indignation.

"You do like it here?"

"Well, it has taken some time to get adjusted, especially to the new school. But I really like it here." He was in fact lying. "Well, I better get back to my papers. I need to hand them back Monday."

"You really are incredibly busy. Seems you have more work to do here than you did at Cardinal Cushing."

"This school requires more written work and lots of evaluations from me." Actually the opposite was true. The headmaster complained that he assigned too much homework. "These young people say they need lots of free time. Parents have protested."

His father continued, "My only concern is the health care in Florida. We just don't have the same confidence in the doctors we've seen here. It is more like an assembly-line operations."

"I'll do some inquiries in Orlando. It might be better than out here in the boonies," he smiled. "Well, I need to get to work," demonstrating a reason he would not make the trek over there for a while.

"Too bad, I'm about to launch a full-scale war against the palmetto bugs and thought you'd like to join the brigade."

The next Saturday, Tom went to the Parliament House, knowing that Toby and Jeff were away. As he walked from the parking lot, he noticed a crowd gathered in front of a window on the second floor. Obviously another show, Tom thought. He climbed the stairs and tried to position himself in the crowd so that he could see. The effort was not worth it. The room contained three fat and ugly men, barely able to see their dicks over their stomachs, Tom surmised. He was just about to walk away when a very nice-looking guy said to him, "They should have closed the curtains long ago." Then he looked at Tom more closely. "I don't recognize you. You new here?'

"I just moved here in September." Then he added because he know the man would wondered about his accent, "from Boston."

"You don't sound like you're from around here. Now you'd never guess I'm from the South," he said in an exaggerated drawl.

"Hi, I'm Tom. Not from the South."

"I'm Al, originally from Mississippi, but now from Lakeland."

"Where's that?"

"Mississippi or Lakeland? They're both easy to miss."

"I used to play 'Game of the States,' so I know where Mississippi is," Tom laughed.

"Lakeland is in the middle of nowhere in Imperial Polk County. That's spelled with an *L*, but they don't pronounce it. So it's 'Poke.' I'm off to the show. Want to join me?"

*Sure do,* thought Tom. *You talk funny, but you sure look good.* "I'll follow you. You know, I think we met once before. At the Silver Hammer."

"Never been there. I only am able to get here on the weekends. Lakeland rolls up the streets at five on Saturday."

Miss P was already a little on the tipsy side and, as always, hilariously funny. Following the show, they retired to the dance floor and remained until about eleven. Then Al said that he had a long drive back to Lakeland and should leave. Tom, seeing an opportunity to fulfill one of his long-held fantasies, asked, "If you want, you could crash at my place and drive home tomorrow."

"I was afraid you won't ask," Al grinned.

Al followed Tom home to his apartment and, once they entered the living room, gave Tom a deep kiss. "Previews of coming attractions—spelled with a *u*." They then showered together—another fulfilled fantasy; he'd only showered once with Tony when his parents were out—and Tom, thrilled as Al, gently washed his rear end and massaged his butthole. During the shower, they negotiated the does, don'ts, and don't-even-think-about-its, so they knew what to expect. They found that they were incredibly compatible. They were fully aroused as they dried each other off and slipped into bed. They now knew what to do without any awkward questions. Tom thought it was magnificent, especially since he had not had any sex except self-inflicted since he had left Boston. Even more glorious for Tom was awakening the next morning with a muscular male wrapped around you.

# *Chapter 3*

Tom had spent the week of Christmas with his parents. They had attended the late Mass on Christmas Eve at his parents' church, Saint Alphonsus. His mother had told him that they now rarely attended because the church did not offer a traditional Mass, only ones with guitars and drums. They felt they had to go Christmas Eve and endure the poorly sung music. Tom thought it dreadful. He quipped to his mother afterward that he could play a guitar better than the man at church. "And I never took lessons."

Fortunately his mother's younger sister, Aunt Ida, was visiting for the week after Christmas from Pittsburgh. His mother apologized for forcing him home, but she had not seen Ida in several years. Tom was more than happy to vacate the spare bedroom. It would allow the sisters to gossip about the rest of the family, especially complaining about the eldest sister, Helen. The only time Tom heard his mother to refer to someone as a bitch was about Helen.

Once he got home, he called Al and asked if he wanted to come over for a few days. That afternoon, Al showed up with a week's worth of clothing. "Don't mind if I stay awhile, do you? Look what I brought you." He unloaded an electronic contraption. "It's a VCR, and I brought some tapes I think you'll enjoy."

"What are they?" Tom inquired suspiciously.

"Art films. I think you'll get a rise out of them, if you know what I mean." Tom certainly did have his suspicions. They ate dinner, and then Al hooked up his machine to the television. He then pulled out some tapes. "Let see, *Left-Handed* or *Secret Tapes*." He put one of the tapes in the machine and started it. The quality of the film was dreadful, but Tom got the point. Fairly soon they were both naked; and in a sense, life began imitating art.

At breakfast the next morning—it was more like a late brunch—Al was looking at some magazines in the kitchen as Tom cleaned up. "How come you have all this stuff about McGovern?"

"I worked very hard for his election. Unfortunately that crook Nixon got reelected."

"You voted for McGovern. He's a Communist!"

"No, he's not. He's just progressive. Isn't interested in only looking out of big business."

They started to get into a serious political argument, but finally Al agreed that Nixon was not totally aboveboard. "But certainly better than McGovern." The disagreement put a damper on Tom's regard for Al. He was a proud Democrat and had troubles abiding Republicans. Now he discovered he was having sex with one. And he did enjoy having sex watching those films.

Two days later, the sun was shining, the temperature had finally dropped below ninety degrees, and Al had a wonderful idea. "Have you ever been to Playalinda?"

"Where's that? And what is it?"

"It's over in Volusia County near the Space Center. It is generally not crowded, and it's clothing optional."

"You mean nude?!"

"Sure do. Some really fat and ugly people there. But also some really hot men and often a good deal of public sex unless the rangers are around. Oh, I don't fuck on the beach. I'm an exhibitionist to a point, but not that far."

"Perfectly fine with me. I'm a first-class voyeur, so it should be fun."

"Just cover your ass with lots of sunscreen. The burn can be excruciating."

The next day, they drove to Titusville and arrived at the beach. They drove past several parking lots carved out of the dunes until they came what seemed be the end of the road. "I take it you've been here before," Tom observed.

"Only a few, since it is a very long drive from Lakeland. No nude beaches around there in Baptist land," he laughed.

They carried their blankets and a cooler over the dunes and onto a beach that seemed to stretch forever. Al insisted they walk even farther to make sure they had some privacy. Finally they set down, removed their bathing suits, and ran into the water. Tom was amazed how warm the water was. Even at the height of summer, the water off Cape Cod was much colder, almost frigid in comparison. He would not think of going in the water there in late December. They walked back to their blankets, dried off, and covered each other with sunscreen. Even in December, the sun was very hot.

Tom began looking up and down the beach. To the north was a couple clearly fucking, with a group of bystanders watching. The men in the audience practiced self-abuse. To the south was a very fat man performing fellatio on another equally fat man. Tom wondered if they were part of the performing balcony cast from the Parliament House.

Finally he noticed a trio of naked men walking up the beach toward them. In the middle was a tall, well-built, and especially well-hung black man, probably in his midthirties. On either side walked two young white males, one tall and the other short, each perhaps early twenties. Their equipment, Tom noted, paled in comparison to the black man. They were slightly twinky in appearance but still nice-looking. They were engaged in very animated conversation, stopping few feet in front of Tom, who now boosted himself onto his elbows. Al was watching them as well. The trio turned their backs toward Tom and continued their conversation. Tom figured that the two white guys might be a couple, and either they picked up the black man or vice versa. He thought that they were perhaps negotiating where to have some intimacy. They must have reached some agreement because the tall white guy kissed the black man and put his hand on his rear end. The black man in turn patted the tall white man on his rear several times.

At that point, Al said rather loudly, "Oh crap," and rolled over. "Wish they'd take that somewhere else."

The three then continued on. Obviously something had been decided because the short guy was now slightly hard. They walked down the beach with their arms around each other. They stopped again by some towels on the beach. The black man now was clearly hard. Tom wanted to look away, but the appeal of that erection was too attractive to miss. It looked like all three were fondling each other, but because their backs were to Tom, he could not actually tell. Then the black man and

35

the tall white guy kissed again. They turned toward Tom, and he could see the tall guy starting to get hard. They then put their arms around each other and began rubbing each other. The short white guy got hard himself. As they turned away, he lightly grabbed the erection of the tall white guy with a smile. They picked up their towels and started toward the parking area. Tom followed them all the way, wishing he could join them whatever they planned to do.

"What gave you that boner?" Al demanded.

"I was watching those three guys, and it really turned me on. It was really hot watching them. Guess I was fantasizing about what they were planning."

"You mean that nigger with those other white guys. That was disgusting. They let him kiss them."

"What's wrong with that?" Tom said, getting angrier by the minute.

"White guys don't have sex with niggers! It's sick."

Tom realized that Al was not only a Republican but also a racist of the worst sort. That ended it for him. "Listen, I think I'm getting a bit burnt. We should be getting out of the sun."

Al protested that he liked to take a walk on the beach to see the action, but Tom insisted. As they walked toward the path leading over the dunes to where Tom had parked his car, they passed the three guys who had drawn Tom's attention. The tall one was giving the black man a blow job. Al looked at them and said very loudly, "Oh, how gross!" They got into the Honda and drove home in silence. When they got to Tom's apartment, he announced that he had promised his mother that he would come over again before school started. So Al would have to leave. Al realized this was a brush-off, but he gathered his stuff and started to depart. "When can I see you again?"

"Oh, it will be soon. Let me give you a call once I get the semester started and get settled down." That call would never be made.

Tom in fact had no plans to go to Clermont again so soon. He did, however, want to return to Playalinda as speedily as possible. He was like a little boy who had just discovered a candy store stocked with unlimited sweets. Tuesday, the day after New Year's, Tom pulled on his bathing suit and drove to the same beach. He walked down the beach, which was much more crowded than when he had been there with Al a few days ago. He looked in vain for the trio he had observed so carefully. If they were there, he had all intentions of walking up to them and asking to join them. Instead, he ambled along the beach, watching the various activities. Few were actually involved in sexual activities, but there were plenty of hot male bodies for cruising. Finally he came across a crowd of men watching two gays first engaging in fellatio and then anal intercourse. Most of the guys standing around had themselves become hard and were stroking themselves. Tom joined them, and when another guy placed his hand on Tom's erection, he did not stop him. He was in gay heaven. What really surprised him was the woman standing there also watching and stroking herself. Before he could stop it, Tom ejaculated, for which he received a round of applause from his fellow voyeurs.

As he drove home, he took stock of his life as a gay man. Really for the first time he could admit without hesitation that he was gay, that it was not going away, and that he was proud of who he was. He had read a good deal about Stonewall and the subsequent gay pride parades, and he had hitherto wondered what there was to be proud about. For the longest time he felt a self-loathing about it and could not understand the joy on the faces of the parade marchers he had watched on television. He always hoped his attraction to men was just a passing phase, and he would grow out of it. Even when he fooled around with Tony, he thought it was a stage in his life that would eventually vanish. Now that he had turned twenty-five, he came to accept that it was not merely a period but a permanent fixture of who he was.

The cracks had begun to appear once he was on his own in Orlando, not under the solicitous watch of his parents. The visits to the Silver Hammer had not helped much since there was a sense of furtiveness that hung over the patrons. At the Parliament House, however, he witnessed a *joie de vivre* that he had not previously experienced himself or observed in other gay settings. Yet strangely at Playalinda, the full conversion experience hit him. He found that standing on the public beach, totally naked and aroused, with other naked and aroused clearly gay men, admiring the other men around them, and being admired by others exhilarated him. The applause that greeted his personal climax seemed as if he had been welcomed into a fellowship.

Tom decided to return again, but suddenly the weather turned cold and rainy. He had not thought that Florida actually had something resembling a winter. Obviously trips to Playalinda would have to wait for warmer weather. He wondered if he would even meet any of the trio again. They became a constant fantasy for him for several months.

Commencing school after New Year's agonized Tom. The day before the students returned, the teachers had to endure something called "teachers' workshops." For the most part, it consisted of the headmaster lecturing the faculty. This time the message seemed directed right at Tom. Father Humphrey complained about how some faculty graded students so hard that they were being driven away. "The parents are paying $2,000 a year, and they expect their children to become excellent. That means not receiving Cs."

Tom wondered about how parents could complain about paying so little. Cardinal Cushing charged $10,000 per year, and some very exclusive private schools in the Northeast cost a great deal more. And he had given Cs and even Ds at Cushing without reprimand.

To drum in the point that the complaint was directed primarily at Tom, the headmaster called Tom into his office and showed him a paper that a parent had sent. It was a paper written by Joe Higston, perhaps the dumbest and laziest student in Tom's Modern Lit class. He had turned in a paper on Medieval epics, which he had obviously prepared for another class. Tom wrote that the paper was incoherent, poorly written, and filled with mechanical and grammatical errors. He had given Joe a C– for the paper, which he regarded as generous. The problem, of course, was that the Higston family were incredibly wealthy and major donors to the church and the school. "I read this paper," the principal announced, "and I thought it was excellent, one of the best I've read in years."

"But, Father, it has nothing to do with the theme of the course. I suspect he actually turned it in before."

"Did you specify the time period?"

"Of course, I did."

"Then the boy needs even more credit for being so inventive. Now I want you to reread this paper very carefully and give it the grade it truly deserves." Tom thought then he would then have to flunk it but understood the headmaster's drift. Yet it did determine him to do something else: begin looking for a new job.

During lunch, he sat with Toby and told him about his private meeting with the headmaster. "Unfortunately, some of us—like you—have integrity, while others—like me—will sell out to keep things quiet," Toby observed.

At that point, Barbara joined them. "Wasn't that a wonderful session this morning? It is good that we were reminded how to take care that our students feel appreciated."

*Or their parents' money appreciated*, Tom thought.

"Isn't that the pep talk we get every year after midyear grades come out? Remember how much these parents are paying."

"Oh, Toby, you're such a cynic. We don't want to discourage our students by giving them unnecessarily low grades."

"What if they're stupid?"

"Our students aren't stupid. They would never pass our entrance requirements if they were."

"Barbara, I just love your boosterism. So you don't think the size of the wallet, or which part of Winter Park or Windermere they live in, has any bearing on the admissions process?"

"I have served on the admissions committee," Barbara retorted, "and I'm not aware of any time where the parents' income mattered. They were selected on the basis of merit."

They continued to bicker until Toby finished his lunch and returned to his classroom. Barbara then moved her chair closer to Tom. "Did you have a good Christmas?"

"Oh, I spent it with my parents. They live in Clermont."

"Oh, what a dutiful son," she gushed. "I don't think I ever knew. So they live close by? It must be wonderful that they can see their grandchildren so often."

*A fishing expedition*, Tom thought. "They don't have any grandchildren yet." He added this last word to throw her off the scent. "I'm their only child, and I'm not married."

"Oh, what a pity. You should get married soon then. You don't want to deprive your parents of that joy."

"They never pester me about it, so perhaps they don't care." Of course, he lied since his mother nagged at him all the time about bringing her grandkids. He did not want to play any more than necessary into Barbara's scheme. She clearly knew he was not married—she had made it her duty to find out once handsome Tom appeared in the school. He was the first man to begin work at Catholic High that held any interest for her. She suspected Toby was a faggot, and most of other male teachers were either priests, married, or ugly and boring. So she fixed her sights on Tom, always commenting on how good he looked, how a student had complimented his teaching, how administrators claimed they were so happy that they had hired him. She understood that she could be too aggressive and attempted to make her advances subtle. She therefore made her approach as subtle as it was in her nature to be.

Tom, for his part, was always gracious, listened attentively when he could not avoid meeting her at school, and twice turning down invitations for some weekend event by claiming to be on his way to Clermont. Only once was that true. Toby once placed a note in Tom's mailbox volunteering to be the maid of honor at Tom and Barbara's wedding. He asked if she would wear a red wedding dress to match the large red baubles she always displayed around her neck, which matched her bright-red lipstick, which matched her hair. *Doesn't she have any other color than red to wear?* he wondered. Tom and Toby actually avoided being too friendly, instead exchanging notes, because neither wanted to raise suspicions. For that reason, they rarely communicated at school, which meant that Tom had not been able to tell him about Al.

Tom had not been involved with his cousin Eddie to any extent either. When he came down to look for a job and a place to live, he had stayed with Eddie. But once he had settled, he had only seen Eddie twice, then he was invited to dinner with Eddie and his wife, Annette. Now Tom sought him out to see if he had any ideas about getting another job; Tom had even considered leaving the teaching profession and thought Eddie could help him. His English degree had limited application other than teaching or perhaps editing. But Eddie had a great deal of familiarity with Central Florida—he had a good position with the county in their family division—and so Tom supposed he might have some suggestions. Unfortunately, he did not. "Have you thought about teaching in the public schools?"

"I'd like to, but I don't have a teaching certificate."

"Well, how do you get that? Buy it through the state?"

"No, I'd have to go back to college and earn enough education credits to qualify."

"Well, get to it."

"It's not that easy. First, I'd have to find out where to go that I can afford, and secondly, I'd have to take education courses, which everyone tells me are stultifying boring. How about a job as an editor? Some publishing house that does, say, commercial stuff."

"I'll make some inquiries, but I won't hold out much hope since I imagine you have no prior experience." Tom had to admit that he did not. "Then I suggest you try to get that certificate. You can either go to FTU, which is pretty far out of town, or Rollins in Winter Park, near where you live. But it won't be cheap."

The next day after school let out, Tom drove to Rollins and found the Education department. He picked up an application from the secretary who informed him that spring classes would begin at the end of January so that he had plenty of time to register. Tom reacted with horror when he saw the cost of tuition.

That weekend, he went to his parents and told them about his latest experience at Catholic High. "So I've decided to go back to school and get my teaching certification. Then I could get a job at a public school where the pay is a good deal better." Of course, he realized that even then, his pay would be a lot lower than what he had earned in Boston. In the end, his parents offered to help him with the tuition. He refused at first but in the end accepted their offer. He had a twinge of guilt; they had been paying for his education now for many years, although he did have a very handsome scholarship at Kenyon.

His first class in the program was held in what must have been an old schoolhouse across the street from the campus. A retired principal taught the course, Sociological Foundations of Teaching. Although the course content was mostly common sense, the stories he told—war stories really, first about his time in the classroom teaching history and then as a principal—inspired Tom. They made the very steep price of admission totally acceptable. He tried to deal with the vague overgeneralizations of the textbook; but when heads would begin to nod, he would launch into an anecdote to illustrate. At one point he did suggest that education textbooks were deliberately made as dull as possible to weed out only those most dedicated to joining the profession. Tom only hoped the remainder of his courses would be as interesting.

Tom had not ventured out to the Parliament House for several weeks, fearing he might run into Al again. Finally, exhausted from grading too many papers and horny, he decided to risk an encounter. He avoided the balconies, dreading Al might be wandering on one of them. He got there in time for the show and ran into Toby and Jeff, and they sat together during the show. When it ended, they walked out onto the side patio. "Where's Al?" Toby asked.

"I certainly hope he's not here."

"Oh, something is amiss. What happened?"

"Well, beyond being a bigot, a racist, a Nazi, I'm not sure." He then explained the views Al had expressed about Nixon and interracial kissing. In passing, he mentioned the trip to Playalinda.

"Ah, so you've been to our local nude beach. Naughty boy."

"Twice. I went by myself a few days later."

"And did you participate in any action?"

"Just watched." He did mention that he had masturbated while two guys went at it.

Then Toby turned serious. "Actually you'd better be careful over there. The rangers don't do anything about nudity, but they do arrest folks for public sex."

"I didn't see any around either time I was there."

"That's because they hide up in the dunes. Normally they watch out for people going into the dunes to have sex. It's illegal to climb on the dunes. They used to go down on the beach as well but pretty much have stopped that. A year or so ago"—Toby could not help starting to laugh—"one of the rangers climbed down from the dune where he was watching to arrest a couple fucking. Well, some guy was hiding in the dunes and stole the ranger's ATV. The ranger had left the keys in his hustle to arrest some fornicators. The guy drove it down to the end of the park, and hid it." By this time, tears streamed from Toby's face. Even Jeff, normally rather taciturn, had a broad smile. "The ranger tried to persuade any of the drivers to take him back to the ranger's station, and they all refused. So he had to walk about three miles in the heat in his uniform. Now they either come in pairs so that one of them can guard the bikes, or the ranger only arrests the guys in the dunes. But I'd still be careful if I were you. If the school found out you've been screwing on the beach, you'd be out of a job. I say that knowing that at least two of our priests have been seen over there."

The weather still did not invite naked romps on the beach, but Tom knew that given the opportunity, he would return again. He would not, however, venture into the dunes. While he intended to find another teaching position, he could not afford to be fired.

Toby also told him that one of the elder priests at Catholic had wondered about Tom's "sexual preference." After all, he was strikingly handsome, but not married, and certainly did not seem to have a steady girl. When there were social events when spouses were invited, Tom always came alone.

Tom's graduate work made him too busy to worry about trips to Playalinda or the Parliament House. Teaching and writing term papers left him with no leisure time. He actually gained some respect for his students who juggled six courses with writing assignments in most of them, especially when he had a stack of them to grade in addition to completing his research paper on inner-city schools in Philadelphia and the impact of race.

Nevertheless, he decided to attend the Founders' Day Dinner at school when all the faculty attended with a large number of graduates, mostly from decades past. (The recent graduates, it seemed, wanted nothing more to do with their alma mater.) To silence rumors, Tom decided to invite Barbara to attend with him. She ecstatically accepted his invitation, thinking that this represented the beginning of a wonderful romance. Tom regarded her as only his beard. They sat at a table with Toby, who had come alone, and two older graduates who waxed eloquent about their experiences. They told tales about Sister Alice as a young nun. Toby later whispered that Sister Alice had never been young. She had been born half blind with that mustache. Tom had imbibed a good deal of the wine, which tasted dreadful at the beginning but slowly morphed into a better vintage. Tom blasphemously thought of the miracle during the wedding at Cana.

He drove Barbara home to her apartment in Audubon Park. She invited him in for a nightcap, and foolishly Tom accepted. She had a very nice apartment, very tastefully decorated. It surprised Tom since he expected it to be as brassy as Barbara. They sat on the sofa and had a glass of wine, which tasted even remarkably better than the ones at the banquet. Barbara moved closer to Tom, who became somewhat alarmed.

"I really want to thank you for inviting me this evening. I had a wonderful time. I hope this won't be the last occasion."

"Not at all. I really enjoyed myself as well. It was wonderful getting to know you better," he lied. At that point, she placed her hand on Tom's leg. He was totally flummoxed but did not dare remove it.

"Perhaps we can get to know each other even better." A squeeze on the leg as the hand moved northward.

"I really should go. I have a term paper sitting on my desk at home waiting for brilliance to descend upon it."

"Oh, I think that can wait a little while. You need to get some relaxation. You have looked very tense of late."

Tom was trapped. If he turned down this invitation for sex, Barbara would likely spread rumors to the right people that he had rejected a sexual offer. They in turn would conclude that he must be queer. He knew she certainly would not admit to the priests or Sister Alice that she had almost engaged in illicit sex, but to the staff secretaries always eager to spread gossip. The administration would know soon enough.

"Well, I guess I can stay a little longer." At that, Barbara almost mounted Tom as she pressed her lips to his. Somehow Tom ended up in her bedroom; he attempted to block out the experience.

They lay on her bed as she started to rub his groin area. It did feel good, he thought, as long as he did not think about what was at the other end of that arm. He knew he had to reciprocate and so began massaging her rather ample breasts. He never did understand why men where turned on by those mammaries, but it was part of the script. Barbara then slipped off her dress, and Tom understood that he must begin to disrobe as well. She began to massage his chest, observing she always liked men with hairy chests.

At this point, the trouble began. She asked him to remove her bra. Tom knew the basic steps; he had gone to a porn movie theatre in Boston to watch straight films. He had no interest in the women whom he found disgusting because they all seemed to wear high heels while they fucked. Actually he went to watch only the men; the women were a distraction. He had seen *Deep Throat* just before he left Boston. He was particularly impressed with Harry Reems' equipment. He had also watched *Behind the Green Door*, where he learned a good many heterosexual techniques that now seemed to come in handy. He knew he needed to remove her bra, begin to caress her breasts, and finally begin to suck on them. The thought of that last act revolted him.

He attempted to undo Barbara's bra but fumbled with his hands behind her back trying to figure out the secret of disengaging it. Finally, with a sigh of exasperation, Barbara completed the task. She was obviously well-endowed, but when she removed the bra, her breasts flopped out and sagged rather obviously. Tom looked with alarm at them, as Barbara cupped them with both hands, obviously wanting Tom to be impressed with them. He was more startled than impressed.

He now knew the next required step. He fondled them as Barbara moaned quietly. He then approached them for the next assault. He blanked that entire process out of his memory. All this time, Barbara was fondling Tom. Unfortunately nothing was happening in his nether regions. He remained as flaccid as ever.

"What's wrong with you? No action."

"Guess I had too much to drink. Perhaps if you sucked it, that might help. It usually is a big turn-on for men."

"What do you mean suck it?" There was a tone of horror in her voice.

"Give me a blow job." Still a puzzled look. "Fellatio."

"You want me to put your thing in my mouth?"

"That's the general idea. Makes me hard."

She looked as disgusted as he had when he saw her breasts. Nevertheless, she did move down toward his happy spot. She took it in her hands as if it would bite. She held it with just two fingers, like it was some dreadful object. She took the tip in her mouth and made a gagging sound. "How's that?" she asked.

"You got to put it all in your mouth and move it in and out. Here, I'll help you." He started to get up so that he could move back and forth.

"No, just stay there. I can cope." Tom thought that a strange word to describe what she was doing.

She really never got into it, but it really did not matter. Tom was not going to get hard. And it was not because he had too much to drink. The whole episode was a huge turnoff. He was not sexually aroused in the slightest. In fact quite the contrary.

"I'm really sorry I can't get it up," he said. "I obviously had too much to drink tonight. And you're a really hot girl. I really wanted to make love to you." The lies kept pouring out. "We'll do it when I'm sober."

Barbara tried to console Tom. She assured him that she would be happy to "what did you call it?"

"Blow job." Tom put on his clothes, gave Barbara a kiss, and drove home. Immediately he stepped into his shower and washed every part of his body several times. He thought about masturbating, but even that did not seem to interest him.

The next day, he saw Barbara in the hall. "I'm really sorry about last night," he said quietly.

"Oh, I understand."

"We'll go out again soon, I promise."

Later, he saw Toby in the faculty lounge. Since they were in the room alone, he took the opportunity to tell Toby about what had transpired the night before at Barbara's apartment. He did not relate all the gory details, but Toby got a clear picture of the disaster. "Are you going to go out with her again? You might have to tape a tongue depressor on your dick to keep it up," Toby laughed.

"Maybe I'll tell her I had a penile stricture and can't function any longer."

"You might tell her you met a girl and you're really serious. She'd be unhappy for a while that she's not the one, but she'd get over it." Tom thought that might be the best solution. Yet it was not needed for quite some time since Barbara obviously avoided Tom.

At the beginning of March, the weather began to improve. Toby told him it was the three days of spring before summer set in. He was on spring break from his graduate program and so decided to make some time for himself. He took a personal leave day from Catholic and packed his beach gear and drove over to Playalinda. The last car park was not crowded, but Tim hoped that there might be something going on. He walked down the beach where he saw some people gathered. He quickly passed normal collection of overweight naked men, glanced at a man and woman engaged in some mild petting, and finally came upon two younger men who were well beyond the mild petting stage. He put down his towel close to them and removed his bathing suit. He lay down and commenced to watch them. They apparently noticed he was there but continued their lovemaking without embarrassment. Finally one of them turned to Tom and asked if he wanted to join them. Tom already had an erection and eagerly agreed. They then commenced to pleasure each other in a variety of contorted body positions. They were interrupted by the sounds of motorcycles. "Rangers," one of them said as he grabbed his bathing suit. Tom scattered over to his blanket and slipped his suit on just as a ranger on an ATV rushed down from the dunes and began speeding toward the "bathers." Tom's heart was in his mouth thinking that the rangers had spotted them and came to arrest them. Instead the ranger stopped in front of the heterosexual couple and began talking sternly to them. He obviously had been watching them with binoculars from the dunes. He apparently asked for identification, since the man went through his bag to pull out his wallet. The ranger wrote down some information and then sped away.

"Why didn't he arrest us? We were engaged in far more advanced activities than that couple was."

"Oh, that's Officer Frank. He's as queer as any of us. He resents the fact that straight couples pollute our beach," one of the men laughed. The straight couple were packing up their beach gear and walked toward the car park. Tom and his two new friends resumed their activities. Tom finally felt clean of the heterosexual stain.

With the end of spring break, Tom had now to complete his final research project. He gladly heard the announcement that he would not have to endure a final examination. He had been very active in class—perhaps too active to some of the students since his pronouncements tended on the liberal side not shared by many of the conservative Southerners—so he expected that would help his average. He had already signed up for two courses during the summer and had interviewed with the local public school employment office about the possibility of a teaching job. They pointed out that he needed to complete at least eight education courses before he was eligible for a teaching certificate. Tom had already planned to complete the ten courses for a master's degree because that would increase his pay.

On the way to class, he dropped off some shirts to be cleaned. He always did most of his own laundry to save money, but when he attempted to iron shirts, they came out more wrinkled than when they emerged from the dryer. So Orange Cleaners became one of his frequent stops. Unlike the public schools, faculty at Catholic had to be properly attired. That meant, for men, a collared shirt and tie, although it was not much of a problem for Tom since he also had a jacket when he taught at Cardinal Cushing. The tie, however, became quite a burden when summer began, since the school had no air-conditioning. It was the first week in May, and summer had already raged for a month. Tom rejoiced that school had only a few weeks to go.

That Friday, he had intended to stay home and catch up on some reading. He planned an Anthony Trollope book festival this summer. He had just started *Barchester Towers* and discovered that the headmaster at Catholic greatly resembled Slope. He decided he had better run out to Orange Cleaners to have shirts for the next week. He planned to stop on the way home from school but remembered he did not have his checkbook. So he drove to his apartment and grabbed his checkbook. As he rushed toward the door, fearing that the dry cleaner closed early on Fridays, he noticed that his answering machine was blinking. Probably his mother, he thought, but then he hesitated, wondering if it might be something important.

# *Book Two*

## ALLEGRO CON GRAZIA

# Chapter 1

Tom looked at the clock; it was 5:30. Fearing that something had happened to one of his parents, he hit the play button.

"Hi, Tom, it's Toby. Listen, I'm having some friends over for a small party. Not that type, slut. Anyhow, I've made some new friends and thought you might like to meet them. Eight o'clock my place. Bring something stimulating to drink. No excuses about having schoolwork to do. They all want to hear about your fuck session with that beautiful redhead at school."

Tom thought about it for a moment, but Trollope got put away for the moment as did his clean shirts. He rushed to take a shower and put on clean clothes, including the formfitting polo shirt. It was too hot for jeans, so he donned a nice pair of shorts that he believed highlighted his muscular legs, which were nicely hairy, although not of the primate sort. He checked himself in the tall mirror, bending around so that he could check out his rear end. Everything looked fine. Perhaps some prospects would be in attendance.

He rushed out the door and drove to the nearby ABC to pick up a few bottles of wine. He worried that everyone else would bring beer. He drove to the apartment in South Orlando and was greeted at the door by Toby. Once inside, they kissed—Toby was somewhat paranoid that the neighbors would guess that homosexuals lived next door. How they could not have guessed always surprised Tom.

"Tom, I'd like you to meet Syd—short for *Sydney*, I guess. He just moved here from Charlotte, North Carolina. We met at the P House and thought we'd take the poor orphan in. And this is Josh Simmons.

51

He's an old friend who made the big mistake of moving to Jacksonville, only to find that nobody actually lives there. So he has returned."

"Like *The Return of the Native*," Josh said. Tom was immediately impressed that this guy knew Thomas Hardy.

"Pleasure to meet both of you," Tom said. Actually, Tom hoped that Toby did not have Syd in mind as a potential partner. Josh, on the other hand, was a veritable hunk. "So, Josh, you've read Hardy?"

"Love him. So you and Toby both teach at that institution of advanced superstition," Josh added.

"As you can tell, Josh is not very friendly toward religious institutions," Toby observed.

"If you had my experiences with the Catholic Church, you would feel the same."

"What happened, if I may ask?" Tom inquired.

"Don't want to spoil a wonderful evening with sad stories. But I'll pontificate next time the pope condemns some perverse sexual activities."

"Oh, yes, I know there's a story there," Toby interjected. "But I've certainly never heard all the bloody details."

"And you won't now," Josh said firmly, clearly wanting to cut off that topic. "I love Hardy, but especially George Eliot. I got hooked on her after reading *Silas Marner* in high school."

"Time for some of my special barbeque ribs, speciality *maison*," Toby interrupted. "We need some good American chow, not that Victorian drivel."

"Oh Christ," interjected Jeff, who had just entered the room. "You're not going to subject our guests to that slop?"

"I don't think any of them have had it before. So don't try to poison their minds before they've tried it."

"No, I'm more afraid of poisoning their stomachs," Jeff retorted.

"You fed that to me before," Josh observed. "That's why I moved to Jacksonville."

"You should have moved farther than that," added Jeff.

"Okay, you can all fuck off. It's the barbeque or Denny's."

"Well, in that case, I'll have the barbeque," Jeff sighed.

"Hey, what's wrong with Denny's? We often go there after the P House closed for the midnight buffet."

"You mean more like the two a.m. early breakfast," Jeff added.

"Whatever, grab a plate and fill it with my luscious concoction."

"Is that because it has cock in it?" Tom suggested.

"You wish. No, I forgot you love fucking redheads with big boobs."

This banter continued throughout dinner and into the night. Tom had developed a severe case of indigestion; he suspected the others had as well. Syd kept burping although he tried to conceal it. In other respects, the evening had gone well. Tom sat across from Josh and tried to conceal the amount of cruising he was doing. Josh obviously took good care of himself. He had almost-black hair, and a shock of hair peeked through the top of his polo shirt, which also was slightly tight fitting. He had powerful calves, which Tom greatly admired. Josh sat most of the time with his legs crossed, so it was difficult for Tom to scope out his package.

At the end of the evening, Tom walked out to his Honda, which was parked next to Josh's BMW. "So I really would like to hear what happened to you with the Catholic Church. I'm obviously Catholic myself. Couldn't teach at Catholic if I weren't. I've never had a bad experience—well, except for the dreadful sermons. Oh, and the awful music at my parents' church. But I have heard some stories about priests carrying out some inappropriate acts. Is that what happened to you?"

"I really don't want to talk about it now. But I don't mind discussing it some other time. The more I can do to destroy the Catholic Church's reputation, the happier I am."

"Oh, this one is serious. Why don't we have dinner some time?" Tom was thinking of killing two birds with one stone. At least he hoped.

"Sure. Can't next weekend, but how about the following?"

"That works for me. I'm going to school this summer, but I have a good deal of free time." He actually did not, but he certainly wanted to make time to have dinner with Josh.

"Listen. I really don't like to talk about this in public. Why don't you come to my place for dinner. I can assure you that you won't be practically poisoned the way you were tonight. I actually used to work as a chef, so I know my way around a kitchen."

"Sounds great to me. And we can also talk about Hardy, can't we?"

"As I said, one of my favorite authors. But I'd certainly like to discuss George Eliot with you as well." He wrote down his address and phone number.

"Obviously a man of literary sophistication. If we run out of church scandals, we can always discuss Victorian literature." At that point, Josh started to climb into his car, but then turned to Tom and gave him a quick kiss. "I hope Toby's neighbors didn't see that. They'd freak!"

On Monday, Tom reviewed with his students his expectations for the final examination scheduled for the next week. The groans from his students encouraged him. He had, he thought, put the fear of God in them. Perhaps they might even deem to study. After his eleven o'clock, he went to the teachers' lounge to get some coffee. Barbara came in right after him, and instead of walking out again as she had most times their paths crossed, she sat down at the table with him.

"Hi," he said almost nervously, "haven't seen you around much."

"Well, obviously I've been trying to avoid you."

"Listen, I'm really sorry, but I was—"

She cut him off. "Yes, I know you were drunk. Well, some of us think there might be another explanation."

Tom began to redden. "And what's that?' he challenged.

"Oh, never mind. Not worth getting into a quarrel about." Then she quickly changed the subject, much to Tom's relief. "So what are you doing this summer?"

"Well, I'm taking two graduate education classes."

"I didn't know you were in graduate school. How come?"

"I'm thinking of getting a teaching certificate. It gives me more flexibility."

"Well, you don't need one here. Are you thinking of leaving?"

"No, but I want the flexibility if another opportunity arises."

"Well, I can't think of a better opportunity than to teach here at a good Catholic school that upholds Christian values." Tom wondered if that was aimed at him, although Barbara had certainly violated one of the church's core teaching about fornication or—at least in their case—attempted fornication. He pondered if an attempt was as much of a sin as a success. With that, Barbara quickly changed the subject again. "So other than your courses, do you have other summer plans?"

Tom feared that she was stalking him. "Well, when I'm not in class, I'll be spending a great deal of time at my parents' house in Clermont. My father's health has been deteriorating," not a total lie, "and I need to help out with things."

"Oh, that's too bad. So I guess you won't be here much."

"Not really. If I could give up my apartment, I would, but of course, I'll need it when school starts again." Just then Sister Alice entered the lounge, which ended the conversation. The sister looked approvingly at the two, which she concluded had been sharing sweet talk. That certainly set her mind at ease since she had suspected that Tom had immoral qualities that the school could not tolerate. Fortunately it appeared her fears were unfounded, and that there seemed to be a budding romance. For the first time ever, Tom saw Sister Alice smiling at him, although he found the twinkle in her glass eye distracting.

The following Saturday, Tom got a call from Josh, telling him that dinner was still on for that evening, and gave him his address. Tom was not sure what to expect. Was this merely a dinner, or were additional benefits available? He truly hoped it was the latter. He showered and dressed very carefully so that he looked his best. Josh was a very handsome man who seemed far more sophisticated than many of Toby's other friends. Tom drove to an apartment complex in Winter Park, actually not far from his own apartment. Yet the distance between his apartment complex and Josh's could not have been greater.

Josh greeted him at the door wearing an apron.

"Glad you could make it. Can I get you something to drink? I have some beer or wine if you prefer."

"Oh, I'm an effete white wine drinker. Or a gin and tonic if you have it."

"I do. Tanqueray okay?"

"Perfect."

They sat in the living room exchanging small talk. "I know you want to hear my tale of woe with the Catholic Church, but let's have dinner first." He went out to the kitchen, and Tom heard the rattling sound of cooking utensils. Tom looked around the living room. Josh had decorated it exquisitely, or at least he had hired someone to do it for him. The furniture was obviously very expensive, not like the cheap things Tom possessed. He also noted that the walls were covered with original works of art, again not like the prints that Tom had picked up at the Louvre when he visited Paris in college. The picture window looked out over the large lake that Tom later learned was Lake Osceola. The rent must be astronomical in comparison to his, Tom thought.

"Yes, it's a beautiful view, especially at sunrise. I face east here. Did you happen to run into a collection of older ladies with walkers?" he laughed. "There are quite a few retired couples and, more often, widows. This is Florida, after all. What do they call it? God's waiting room." He laughed again. Tom remembered he had used the same expression with his parents. "And this complex is often called Whispering Widows, a play on the place's name. You hungry?"

"Ravenous."

Josh lit some candles on the table and invited Tom to sit down. The table was impeccably set—with several crystal glasses at each place; an array of silver surrounded a large plate that Josh removed when he served the first course. Tom later learned the plate was called a charger, which totally mystified him. For regular dinners when he was growing up, his mother used melamine, inexpensive plastic dishes. On weekends, however, she used better-quality china and silver plate. Tom knew instinctively that Josh's silver was pure sterling.

What followed astounded Tom. The first course was a cold soup, followed by fillets wrapped in pastry with a stuffing of foie gras (Tom had to ask later what the stuffing was) with asparagus in hollandaise sauce. The dinner ended with a fresh fruit compote with a sabayon sauce, again Tom learning the proper name after he had savored it. He recalled his mother's efforts to expand her repertoire beyond frozen foods but without much success. Tom wondered if the food he had just eaten tasted so much better because it was on china and not melamine. "I'm amazed. I can hardly cook an egg, let alone produce something like this. Where did you learn to cook?"

"Oh, I went to the CIA."

"You're a spy!?"

"No, the Culinary Institute of America. It's jokingly referred to as the CIA."

"So you're a chef?"

"Was. I originally went to Berkeley to study business administration at my father's insistence, but then decided I really wanted to be a chef. So I dropped out of Berkeley and applied to the CIA. My parents were furious. After I graduated, I worked as a sous chef at a fancy place in Miami. It was hell on earth. The head chef was a tyrant, and all the other chefs attempted to undercut me. I then learned that conditions were about the same in other kitchens, so I quit. Returned home and, after eating humble pie, took a job in insurance, and ironically I have been happy ever since. Finally completed my undergraduate degree in history. I think the choice of major was another form of defiance." He paused and took a sip of his coffee. "I make a good living, work with some good people here in Florida, am far away from my family, and enjoy life. But I don't often get to cook like this because I live alone. So whenever the opportunity arises, I pull out all the stops."

"Well, I was more than happy to help you out. Can I help clean up?"

"No, I want to sit in the living room, have a Baileys, and relate to you the horrors of the Catholic Church."

He poured two crystal glasses with the Baileys, and they settled in the living room. "So you are still a practicing Catholic?" Josh asked.

"Well, I guess I qualify. I do attend church pretty regularly. I really need to be seen in church because of where I teach. Toby does the same thing. And I always go when I'm visiting my parents. They're quite devout. But I don't accept all that the church teaches. And I suck cock whenever possible. I don't think the Holy Father would approve."

"You'd be surprised." Tom gave Josh a quizzical look. "Let me tell you a story. Once upon a time, there was a very devout thirteen-year-old boy who had aspirations to become a priest. He served as an altar boy in his small parish in New Hampshire. The old priest retired, and a new one was brought in. Apparently he had had some difficulties in his former parish and so was transferred to the boonies. Well, he took a special interest in me, very special, because I had shown an inclination about going to seminary. He began asking me to give him back rubs because he had a bad back. He also began being very touchy with me, which made me uncomfortable."

"Didn't you tell anyone?"

"I told my parents, but they just chalked it up to the priest's effort to be supportive. I only figured out later what he wanted me to support." Tom could tell Josh was beginning to get emotional. "Anyhow, it got to the point where I stopped serving with him. So then he began to come over to our house when he knew both my parents were out. I made the mistake of letting him in, and at that point, he forcibly raped me." At this point, Josh let out a sob. Tom sat transfixed. He tried to say something; he opened his mouth, and nothing came out. He was very befuddled. He wondered why Josh told him all this. They had really just met, and here Josh was spilling out his innermost feelings to a complete stranger.

"I told my parents, and they thought I was lying. They went to Father Benson, and he, of course, totally denied it. Said that I must have some mental problems. So they punished me. The church in their view could do nothing wrong. Then I called the bishop's office in Portsmouth—there was no way I could ever get there. I guess it was his secretary who asked me what it was about. I told her. There was silence on the other end, and then she said she would have the bishop phone me. He never did call me, but he called my father and told him I was spreading nasty rumors. I got punished even more severely."

They both sat there in silence. Tom did not know how to react, but he knew he had to say something. Finally, he took a deep breath. "I can see why you hate the church. If something like that happened to me, I'd react the same way." Tom knew what he had said was quite banal, but he did not know what else to do.

Then it got worse. "To this day, my parents think I made the whole thing up. I wanted eventually to tell them I'm gay, but they, of course, would claim that I had tried to seduce poor Father Benson. As soon as I could, I left home. I haven't been in a church since then, and I also haven't spoken at any length to my parents. My father died last year, and I refused to attend the funeral because it would be in a Catholic Church."

Tom got up and walked over to Josh and hugged him. Josh again let out a quiet sob. "I wonder why you want to tell me all this. You hardly know me. I feel honored that you feel comfortable enough to confide in me, but—"

"My goal in life is to persuade all Catholics that the church is evil. You seem like an intelligent man. I wanted to enlighten you about what a corrupt institution you work for. But I have to say something else. I have never lost my faith. I have come to distrust the Roman Church totally, but not God. I know something beyond me—infinitely powerful and loving—is taking care of me." That made no sense to Tom, so he changed direction.

"What does Toby think about your hatred of the Catholic church?"

"Oh, he understands and isn't very fond of the institution himself, but he's afraid to quit the church because he fears unemployment. He has no savings apparently."

"Well, that is just more incentive for me to finish my master's. I was planning on leaving anyhow." He wondered how his parents would take it if he had told them that story. He could not imagine that they would have blown him off that way. "Can I ask you a personal question?"

"What, more personal than what I just revealed?" He had a slight smile on his face.

"Well, I understand that some people who have had a traumatic experience like yours react to it by having . . ." He stumbled for the words. "Can you have normal sexual relations?"

"Oh, trying to get in my pants already."

"No," he lied, and thought, *not tonight at least*. "It just might make a person find sex repulsive."

"No, not at all. I love sex. But"—looking sternly but with a slight twinkle in his eyes—"I don't fuck on the first date."

"Well, I'm glad to hear that. Not that you don't have sex on the first date but that it hasn't had a lasting impact on you . . . Well, that came out all wrong. It obviously has had a lasting impact." At that point, Tom thought it best to keep his mouth shut.

"Don't worry, Tom, I understand what you mean."

They changed the subject and talked about Tom's interest in Victorian literature. They had mutual love affairs with the novels of Thomas Hardy. *Tess* was Josh's favorite, and *The Return of the Native* Tom's. Both found *Jude the Obscure* a difficult read. "A total loss of hope," Josh opined.

Tom finally excused himself and thanked Josh for the wonderful dinner. They agreed to get together again soon. "We can meet at my place, but I'm not cooking!" They gave each other a kiss and a hug, and Tom left. As he climbed in his car, he thought that would certainly be the last date he had with Josh. And he also knew his view of the Catholic Church would never be the same.

Exams had ended, and Tom busily graded them to meet the totally unrealistic deadline. To make matters worse, the headmaster had called a faculty meeting to review "some essential matters." The obligatory talk about being sensitive to students while grading exams, reminding them about how important it was to keep parents happy. He then explained that enrollment for next year's entering class was down considerably and that there might have to be some cuts in the size of the faculty or salary reductions. Afterward, Toby and Tom went to Denny's for lunch; after they got seated, in walked Barbara, obviously looking for them. Uninvited, she sat down in their booth.

"Those bastards. They're just trying to steal money from us." It was the first time either of the men had heard her swear. "They did a poor job of recruiting students, and they take it out on us."

Toby nodded. "I can't afford a salary cut. What they pay us is not enough to keep a household going."

"Well, you have two incomes," Tom said without thinking.

"No, there's only me," he snapped.

"Oh, come on, Toby, we all know you have a live-in *girl*friend. You've hinted enough times. I'm sure she helps you out with the bills." Obviously Toby had left enough false clues to take the scent off his trail.

"Yeah, but she has a low-paying job as well." Tom was fairly sure Jeff, as an attorney, probably made good money chasing ambulances.

Tom himself kept quiet but resolved to begin making inquiries when he could start teaching in public schools. He had already seen advertisements for teachers in both Seminole and Orange Counties. Yet he still had to gain his certificate, which meant high tuition obligations.

"You know those old nuns and priests will keep their jobs since they aren't a big financial burden. But those of us not connected will get docked or, even worse, fired." Neither men had seen Barbara so agitated. "You know it's the administration's fault because they didn't recruit enough. And they wasted all that money on the new organ for the chapel."

"Yes, I loved the way the old one wheezed," commented Toby.

"Oh, shut up, Toby."

"Barbara, what you need to begin doing is looking for another job."

"I'm not qualified to teach in public schools. And I really don't want to teach in that environment."

Tom did not want to know what she meant by that. "But there are other private schools in the area. There's that Baptist one in Orlando."

"I'd only teach in a Catholic school."

"Well, that sort of limits your choices. I think there's another in Sanford, but that's quite a drive."

Toby then interrupted. "Listen, we don't know yet what they're going to do. I agree with Tom. I'm going to begin looking for another position, even a new profession. Perhaps I'll become a male prostitute."

"That's not funny, Toby." Barbara never did quite recognize his attempts at humor.

"The point is, Barbara, if both of us leave, you have a good chance of saving your position. Also Father Bates has at least a foot and several toes in the grave. There's always hope."

Even Barbara laughed at this. Father Bates was detested by just about everyone in the department, and by every student who ever had to endure one of his classes. He taught medieval literature; the running joke was that, to Bates, it was contemporary literature.

"And Sister Alice can't be a day until one hundred. She's just turn into one big wrinkle, like a giant prune."

"Now, now," Tom said, "we must be respectful of the nearly dead."

"Will you two be serious! I'm really frightened about my future, and all you can do is make jokes."

"It's just a little gallows humor," Toby explained, which did not help to cheer Barbara up. "Well, I need to get going. My girlfriend and I are invited to friends' house tonight for a party. So I want to get finished with my grades so that I can get ready." As he walked behind Barbara on his way out, he gave Tom a big grin and a wink. Tom surmised the party would be a large gay gathering. Toby joked once that they often hosted parties of strip Trivial Pursuit.

When Tom got home, he saw the red light on his answering machine blinking. He listened to the message, which surprisingly was from Josh. He hadn't heard from Josh since they had dinner. Josh asked him to call him back as soon as he got the message.

"What's up?" Tom tried to sound nonchalant.

"Wondered if you were up for an adventure?"

"Always. What do you have in mind? African safari, trek to the North Pole?"

"Oh, nothing that exotic. Toby told me that you have been to the local nude beach. I've always wanted to go there and thought you could show me the ropes."

Tom did not know quite what to say. He assumed that since they would be going to a nude beach, they would both be nude. He hardly knew Josh, although he had not known Al all that long either. "Sure," he stammered, "that would be fine. When did you have in mind?"

"I'd rather not go on the weekend to avoid meeting anyone I know. Are you free at all during the week?"

"Actually anytime. I have graduate classes at night, but during the day, I'll either be in the library or reading really boring books on education. A trip to the beach would be a welcome break."

"Then how about Monday? I bet the beach will be less crowded then."

"It's a date. But we should go early. It will get unbearably hot in the afternoon."

So it was arranged that Josh would drive to Tom's apartment, and Tom would drive to Titusville. Josh arrived in an obviously expensive polo shirt and shorts. *Clearly some money here,* Tom thought. Tom walked into the bedroom to retrieve his bag. Josh looked at the books on Tom's shelves. He picked up one of the tapes that Al had left behind. "Ah, porn!" he said loudly.

"Oh, a guy I saw for a while forgot and left them here."

"So they're not yours? Likely story. What's this sticky stuff on the covers?"

"Honestly I haven't watched them since he was last here, which was months ago."

Tom walked back into the living room and saw that Josh was grinning broadly.

They walked down to the parking lot and climbed into Tom's Honda. It was parked next to a new BMW convertible, which Tom assumed Josh had recently purchased, since he had never seen it before. And the one that Josh was driving the night they had met to Toby's was at most a year old. *Ah, the advantages of money,* Tom thought.

As they drove, Tom began asking some questions to get to know Josh a little better. He assumed that at Playalinda he would get to know him a good deal more. Josh really was an enigma. He had a mysterious past that he revealed to Tom in a very emotional talk. Then the next thing, he asked Tom to accompany him to a nude beach. Very perplexing. "So you're originally from here?"

"No, originally I'm from New Hampshire. I moved south when I got that job in Miami. When I quit, I got a job here with my father's insurance company. He took pity on me for making such a mess of my life, so he made me manager of his office in Orlando. He has offices all up and down the East Coast." *So that is where the money comes from.* "Toby was somewhat misleading. I went to Jacksonville for a short time to deal with some problems there but then returned here. It works out well. I have a good job, which I would always have gotten if I hadn't decided to go off and become Julia Child. I think I told you my father died last year, so my mother and my older brother really control the company. They don't manage me the way he did though. My father had threatened to take me out of his will, but he died before he could change it. So I inherited one-third of the estate, but my mother and brother outvote me. Which is just fine with me. At least now, I'm not under my father's glare of disapproval. As long as I work here, I don't have to have any contact with my family, which is perfectly fine. And I can take a day off and go to the beach."

"I take it you didn't get on with your father? Please forgive me if I'm too inquisitive."

"No, we've been estranged since my parents refused to believe that I had been raped by dear Father Benson. And my father was furious at me because I refused to come into the insurance business, at least until I was forced to. I've actually only seen them in person a few times and not at all recently. We just have long acrimonious telephone conversations."

"So they don't know you're gay?"

"Oh, if my family had found out, I'd be totally on my own. That's one reason I decided to stay in Florida, so that I could be myself without them watching over me. I always wonder if they don't send spies down here to check up on my whereabouts. But I don't have to worry about that now because of the inheritance. It's still none of their business." There was a brief silence. Then he said, "We've talked a lot about me. Tell me more about yourself. Do your parents know you like dick?'

"No, it would kill them. Well, perhaps that's too strong a term. We actually have a very good relationship. I'm the only child, so a good deal of the burden making sure they're okay falls on me. But they aren't demanding or critical of me. I know they'd like me to get married, but they don't push it too often," he smiled. "My father was a postman, and my mother kept house. Very traditional middle-class family. Fortunately my father has a very good government pension, so they live comfortably. And they help pay my tuition, which is well beyond the call of duty considering I'm twenty-five."

"Sounds like a pretty normal family to me. You don't seem to have the drama that my family endures."

"Well, that's because I have always been very discreet. Although I bet if they found out about me, there would be plenty of drama. It just won't involve a lot of money." They both laughed.

Tom wondered why this almost perfect stranger had opened up to him this way. It was like they were interviewing for a long-term relationship. Tom thought that Josh was really hot-looking, but it certainly did not go beyond a little bit of lust. He regarded Josh as a bit too complicated, not a good fit for happily ever after. He pondered if Josh had vetted him through Toby. Or if Toby was doing some matchmaking. Toby was always saying that Tom needed a steady boyfriend.

By this time they had reached the far parking lot. "Well, this is it. Grab one of the bags. We have a little hike before us."

Josh got a big smile on his face. "Will there be lots of action there?"

"Who knows. I've never been here this early. But it's better than sweltering under the Florida sun."

They started down the beach, and Tom was surprised to see a number of people already there. Perhaps they all had the same desire to beat the heat. Josh said, "This looks like a good spot," and they spread their blankets out. Tom saw that they were not too close to other people but certainly close enough to see what was happening. Perhaps Josh was a shy voyeur, close enough to see, not too close to get caught.

Even at nine thirty in the morning, the sun buried into their skin, and the glare of the sun off the sand required them to wear their dark glasses. The breeze off the ocean was a hot blast. Tom started to take off his shirt and bathing suit. He then looked over at Josh to watch the show. Josh obviously worked out a lot at the gym. When he took off his shirt, he revealed a sculpted body, beautiful pecs and rock-hard abs. His chest was slightly hairy—perhaps he groomed it—and a treasure trail descended past the top of his bathing suit. He then pulled down his bathing suit and revealed the rest of his torso. He had a beautifully sculpted rear end and was nicely hung. To Tom's relief though, he was slightly better endowed than Josh. Tom wanted to pull off his dark glasses to get a better look, but the glare and the obviousness of his cruising deterred him. Clearly he had not been subtle enough.

Josh looked over and laughed. "See something you like?"

Tom looked down and saw that he had a full erection. "Oh, sorry."

"Don't worry. I take it as a compliment."

Tom quickly lay down on the blanket, facedown so that the telltale sign was hidden. For a while they discussed the moral turpitudes of Eustacia Vye. "Where did you get an interest in Thomas Hardy novels?" Tom wondered.

"Actually by accident. I checked out one of his novels, *Far from the Madding Crowd*, and became hooked."

"How old were you?"

"I think just beginning high school. I was struck how cruel fate had been to Gabriel Oak. Sort of reminded me of what I went through. Hardy believed that if there was a god, he enjoyed playing cruel tricks on humans."

"My view entirely," Tom volunteered, although he was not totally convinced of that position. He had anticipated that sex with Josh was on the agenda, but increasingly it became clear that while Josh enjoyed lying on the beach naked with him, intimacy was not in the cards. Tom had thought of rubbing Josh's ass to see if he might encourage some reciprocal action, but when he started to move closer, Josh moved slightly away, a clear indication of a barrier.

The beach conversation oddly moved on to novels by George Eliot, the particular favorite of Josh's but not for Tom. "The only one I really liked was *Silas Marner*; I found *Middlemarch* tedious."

"Oh, dear, my favorite novel. You need to give her another chance. Try *Daniel Deronda*."

Josh suggested that they take a walk on the beach. The beach was now largely empty, with a few people scattered around. They came across a heterosexual couple coupling and a few other gay men who tried to entice them into some intimacy. None of them were particularly attractive, and Tom had no interest. Josh did not even seem to notice their existence. Tom did find one guy, displaying an obvious erection, very attractive, and returned the man's smile. Josh, however, indicated firmly that it was time to leave the beach and get home.

The ride home was slightly awkward, because Tom did not know what to make of what had just happened. They had gone to a nude beach, where it was almost taken for granted some sexual activity would take place. Josh had displayed his beautiful body to full advantage and had Tom in a constant state of arousal, but obviously did not encourage any physical contact. And then Tom had made the mistake to look agreeably upon the prospect of a sexual encounter with a stranger. Josh and Tom exchanged some small talk on the way home but at times drove in silence. When they arrived at Tom's apartment, Josh grabbed his bag and put it in his car. "I really had a nice time with you today. Love to do it again some time." It did not sound sincere to Tom. But Josh did lean over and gave Tom a rather deep kiss. "Hope you enjoyed yourself as much as I did." He then got in his car and drove away. Tom was flabbergasted.

The next day, Toby called him. Obviously Josh had told Toby about their plans for the beach. "So how did it go? Did you fuck your brains out?"

"Actually we discussed Victorian novels."

"That's what I was afraid of. I had really hoped that Josh had gotten out of his funk. I know he really likes you, and I thought he was going to have some wild sex on the beach. Isn't that why you go there?"

"That's what I thought, but it was not to be."

"I've never seen him totally naked, only in a bathing suit. But I can imagine it is an incredible sight."

"Oh yes. I had a stiffy the entire time. But he never got hard once. And he kept his distance. Then I made the dumb mistake of flirting with a guy who obviously wanted a three-way. I don't know what I was thinking. But by that point, I was so horny that the prospect looked intriguing. I guess I figured that if Josh wasn't interested in me, he might go for the hunk on the blanket. Then I could play sideshow to the main event."

"No, I don't think Josh is into that scene. Something happened to him along the way which has messed up his head. Haven't a clue what it is, but I bet it has something to do with that weirdo family of his." Toby actually knew fairly well all of Josh's history but had decided that he did not want to be the one to reveal it. Tom, however, was already privy to the details.

"He said he was going to contact me again soon," Tom said, deciding not to tell Toby what he knew. "But I won't hold my breath, and I don't intend to call him. He has got to make the first move."

"Sounds good to me. He'd be a real catch: rich, handsome, rich, intelligent—did I say rich? But apparently there is too much baggage that goes with it, I'm afraid."

True to his word, Tom did not telephone Josh. And for the rest of the summer, Josh did not call him. Tom instead focused on his two graduate courses, which he found incredibly boring. He realized it was a means to an end, but the torture was almost more than he could tolerate. It did keep him busy with rather mindless projects of designing course material for high school students. Since he had already been doing it for several years, and with more sophistication than what was being required of him now, it was almost insulting. But it was, he kept repeating to himself, the pathway to a new job. He also tried to make a few weekend trips to see his parents. He took his homework with him so that he had an excuse to take a break from their incessant questions. He loved them dearly, and they had been tremendously supportive; but they could hover.

He did find time for some play. He went to the Parliament House with Toby and Jeff. On the second visit, he was cruised by a very handsome gentleman who spent the night with Tom. Tom imagined that this might become a steady thing, until he found out the man was married and his wife was out of town. But he took Tom's number in case he was free later. Tom did not hold his breath.

Tom also made another trip to Playalinda to free his loins of the constraints of clothing. Again he went early to avoid the heat and the constant threat of thunderstorms in the late afternoon. He joined a frolicsome couple that eventually drew a crowd of onlookers. One of them was the black man whom Tom had seen walking down the beach with the two white guys. He had wanted to ask what had happened with them, but the party had to disperse when they heard the sound of two ATVs approaching.

Tom had decided that he enjoyed being free and not becoming entangled in any sort of romance. Sex became his chief form of entertainment, although various other demands too often got in the way. He was young, good-looking, fit, and hung. What more could he ask for?

# Chapter 2

The school year began on the same sour note that had ended the last one. The welcome-back lecture from the principal contained a litany of faults of the teaching staff and how they must be more respectful of their students' feelings. It truly reminded him of Father Sullivan's sermons back in Boston. Yet it was more of a tirade than even one of Sullivan's homilies. Instead of having his parents prodding him to listen attentively, now it was the vice head who surveyed the teachers to make certain none were sleeping or, worse, making snide comments to each other.

The usual "celebratory lunch" followed, where the administration treated the faculty to a free meal—most of them would have gladly skipped. The departments were expected to sit together, but since so much animosity existed in most departments, faculty scattered around the tables. The younger members of the English department—Fred, Tom, and Barbara—sat together joined by Toby and a new recruit to the History department. "Hi, everyone, this is Andrew. He'll be teaching European history."

"Oh, did old Fr. Donaldson retire?"

"Oh, better than that." Everyone understood the connotation. He along with Sister Alice were some of the old-timers particularly despised by the newer faculty. "So what did everyone do for their summer vacation?"

While the others reported, Tom studied Andrew cautiously. *Yes*, he thought, *he must bat on my team. It's a shame he's on the faculty because he certainly is off-limits. But is he cute!*

"So, Mister Hardy, what did you do last summer?"

"Actually, it's Miss Eliot. I wallowed in George Eliot this summer, on Josh' recommendation as a matter of fact. That is, when I was not immersed in my graduate classes." *And other diversions*, he thought.

"Are you still pursuing your master's?" Barbara asked, a tone of indignation in her voice.

"Sure am. If I complete one course each semester this year, I'll be eligible for a teaching certification, and I can begin looking for jobs in the public schools." His voice dropped toward the end of this statement.

"Oh, you want to leave happy valley?" Toby whispered.

"As soon as possible."

Barbara overheard this exchange and frowned. Tom only hoped she would not pass that information on to higher authorities.

As he walked with Toby back to his classroom, he asked, "So does Andrew swing our way?"

"I really don't know, but if I had to bet, I would back that horse. Really cute, isn't he?"

"Toby, remember you're married. And from what I understand, it is not an open relationship."

"And you'd rat on me."

"You bet."

Tom began putting his classroom in order and mimeographed some handouts for Monday. All was set for what he hoped would be his last year at Catholic. He then drove over to register for his next education course. The same really boring professor who taught one of his courses the last summer was now teaching the next required course: Strategies for Instruction. He wished the retired principal would be teaching one of his courses again, but alas, it was not to be.

He then went back to his apartment to do some cleaning and the week's load of laundry. As he worked, he thought about his current circumstances, which in many respects satisfied him. He had developed a circle of friends who shared his proclivities. He enjoyed the various sexual outlets that circumstance afforded him. First and foremost, he had no interest in settling down the way Toby had. He loved new adventures and new bodies. While he still lived in Boston, his activities centered strictly to mutual masturbation with Tony. He was always afraid to venture out. Now that his parents lived a respectable distance away, he felt much freer. All he had to do was avoid anyone from Catholic, other than Toby.

Gay life post-Stonewall was exhilarating. Gay liberation really meant sexual liberation. Orlando was certainly not New York or San Francisco, but the police no longer raided the Silver Hammer or the Parliament House, although Tom suspected that a certain amount of bribery was involved with the latter. The Hammer did not have the reputation for sexual license that P House had.

Most of his own experiences involved one-night stands, or perhaps two. If a sex partner began to develop amorous intentions, and not just to relieve horniness, Tom would cut it off. "Sorry, but I'm not interested in matrimony," Tom repeated often. He did join a group that met perhaps once a month at a friend's house. There were six or eight guys who joined in a massive orgy, in which individuals would switch in an amazing pattern of activities. Tom learned all sorts of new techniques that had never occurred to him when he was with Tony. Now his repertoire grew exponentially, although he drew the line on several perversions that he regarded went beyond the pale. He discovered, however, that his body could give him intense pleasure, and in turn, he could give pleasure to others. The mutuality of it heartened him.

Yet this sexual life remained tightly closeted. Most of the men in the group did not want their identities revealed to the outside world. This was particularly true for the two married men who were able to join them from time to time. Tom was certainly thankful that he was not in their position. But closeted he remained to everyone else, except Toby, who enjoyed Tom's sexual adventures vicariously. Tom felt a rush of pride himself when he watched the gay pride parades in New York or other big cities, although he never considered joining the modest gathering at the band shell in Eola Park the last Saturday in June each year. How a bunch of drag queens at a small bar in New York had changed his world!

Tom, his sights now on a new teaching position once he had completed his sixth graduate course, tended now to be shorter with his new crop of students. Fred warned him that some students had moaned about grouchy Mr. O'Mally. "You might want to ease up some."

Tom had not realized that he had become Mr. Grumpy and explained that he was just trying to encourage his students to focus on their work. Nevertheless, he decided to ease up on them so that the headmaster did not possess yet another issue to raise with him.

After his first week of teaching, he drove over to see his parents. "I thought it might be a good time since I don't have grading yet and no major assignments of my class. The deluge begins soon enough." After dinner on Friday, Tom's father drove to Publix to get food for breakfast, which they had forgotten. While he and his mother sat in the living room—it was still much too hot to sit on the screened patio, even in the evening—she looked at him rather uncomfortably. Tom feared what was to come, thinking that one of them was seriously ill.

"Tom, you're never going to get married, are you?"

The question almost caused Tom to gasp, but he tried to maintain his cool. "What do you mean, Mother? I just haven't found the right girl."

"That's not what I mean. You're not the marrying kind. Oh, how can I put it? You just aren't interested in girls." Tom began to stammer denials, but his mother interceded. "You can be honest with me."

At this point, Tom's eyes began to fill with tears. He saw no way out; she expressed her assumption confidently. "How long have you known?" served as his confession.

"Oh, since you were little really. I always knew you were different. A mother always sees these things."

"Does Dad know?"

"No. I've never mentioned it to anyone. Now you might decide to tell him, but I'd advise against it. He just won't understand." Then out of the blue, she asked, "Do you have a boyfriend?"

"Mother!"

"Well, I just want you to be happy. I have known other homosexual men"—Tom could not believe that she had uttered that word—"and they often seem very lonely. But there was this lovely couple at church in Boston, don't you remember those nice gentlemen, Tim and Warren, who always sat together in church? In the winter, they used to hold hands under their topcoats."

"Mother, how do you know all this?"

"Well, I had an aunt Harriet. She was a lesbian. She lived for years with this other woman, who everyone in the family called her roommate, but we all know there was more to it than that."

"I always thought I was a normal boy growing up. Guess not. I was that obvious?"

"Well, you were always neat. That alone is a dead giveaway,'" she laughed. "No, you were always sensitive and considerate."

"I thought I was a brat."

"I've seen bratty children. You were far from it. You could be moody, but that's about it. Oh, and you loved to read and listen to music. Classical music."

"That's what you always had on the radio. I learned to love it."

"A normal—no, that's not the correct term, a *regular* boy would have listened to WBCN. That's what the other kids listened to. And am I glad you didn't. Would have driven me crazy."

He had never heard his mother talk this way before. She seemed an entirely different person.

"For the longest time, I was in denial. You'd grow out of it. A nice girl would change you. All a pipe dream. For a while, I had hoped you'd get married just to stop me from nagging and give me grandchildren. Also a pipe dream. But maybe you could find a nice man and adopt. I'd accept that as well." She was laughing and crying at the same time.

"Listen, Mother, it took me a very long time to come to terms with who I am. You remember I did date in high school and even took that nice girl Emily to the senior prom. But when I got to Kenyon, I met a few others like me. It didn't take me long to understand that this is who I am. And I'm happy with that. I love being gay. By the way, Mother, that is really the accepted term, not *homo*sexual." He drew out the *homo* to make it sound ridiculous.

"Oh, here comes your father. If you want, we can talk further at a later time." This time had been excruciating enough for Tom. He did not relish another chat. Unfortunately, he knew his mother wanted more information and would recognize if he tried to avoid being alone with her.

When his father sat down, she continued a conversation they had been having over dinner: should they move to a place that had better medical care. "I love the winters here but hate the summers."

"And we hate the winters in Boston and the summers here. Perhaps we should be snowbirds and move back and forth," his father added.

"That sounds too exhausting," Tom observed. "Perhaps you could move to Orlando"—he could not believe he had just said that, although there was less to hide now, at least from his mother—"or Tampa," he added quickly.

"We have some friends who moved to Sarasota, and they love it. And they have a very good doctor there. We're going to take a drive over there to look. It is a more expensive area though."

"Actually, I understand the west coast of Florida is quite beautiful," Tom noted. "You might find a wider group of friends there who are not only concerned about their latest medication."

"Yes, and insist on showing you their hernia scares."

"You've got to be kidding," Tom said in disbelief.

"That's not the worst of it. Then they need to explain in great detail the pain and suffering they endured because of their knees."

"And most are Republicans. And think Nixon can do no wrong." Their list had gotten to the point that Tom thought they might call a moving company immediately.

The remainder of the weekend went pleasantly. They drove over to climb the Citrus Tower, although Mike could only make it halfway up. That really worried Tom.

"Well, if you do move, I should take you to Disney World. I haven't been there myself, but I'd like to see it."

"I remember you loved roller coasters. Does Disney have one?"

"Yes, I think it's called Space Mountain."

"Good, you can go on it. We'll watch." They all laughed.

Leaving that weekend was a little harder than normal. He really had a much deeper understanding of his mother. She knew the whole person and not just a partial performance. More importantly, she did not reject him, as so many other parents did when they learned that one of their children was gay. He also worried about his father's health. Need he begin exploring options for her? He thought about Whispering Widows but decided it would be too expensive. Despite it all, he was still glad he had only a one-bedroom apartment.

He made a concerted effort to treat his students better than he had the first week. He praised them even if they gave a really stupid answer to a question and corrected them so gently they did not realize they were being corrected. He actually had a student thank him at the end of class. Perhaps his anger about having to work at Catholic had had an impact on his teaching.

After school, he stopped Toby in the parking lot. "I wanted to tell you that my mother knew I was gay for quite a while. Perhaps since I was a kid."

"Oh, mothers always are the first to know. My parents have known for years, and they're cool with it. They think Jeff is too good for me. Actually you're lucky that she has taken it the way she has. It could have been disownment. Or *homo*cide," he laughed. "By the way, a guy you used to know asked for your telephone number."

"Who's that?"

"Josh Simmons."

"You're kidding. That's been over a long while ago."

"Well, don't be so sure. And if you will take my advice, if he calls you, listen."

Tom surged his shoulders and climbed into his car. He had almost totally forgotten about Josh and was rather uneasy about contacting him again. It had been a very strange relationship, if one could even dignify it as such.

Tom forgot all about it until a few days later, his phone rang. "Tom, this is Josh. I wanted to talk with you and apologize for my very weird behavior."

Tom started to say that they really did not have anything to talk about, when Josh interrupted him. "I know you think I'm a real flake, perhaps schizoid. But will it really hurt you to hear me out just for a little?"

He remembered what Toby had said—to listen. "Sure."

"Can we have dinner again, but this time out? We could have dinner at the Beef and Bottle on Park Avenue. It's a steak house, and I'm personally an unapologetic carnivore. But if you're a vegetarian, we can go elsewhere."

"Sounds fine to me. When?"

"How about next Saturday? Say, seven o'clock."

"I'll put on my best frock and see you then." Josh was surprised how cordial Tom sounded. And Tom was surprised how cordially he had ended the conversation.

When Tom arrived at the Beef and Bottle, he found Josh standing outside, obviously watching a young man in shorts walking down Park Avenue. When Josh saw Tom observing him, he looked embarrassed. "Don't worry, I look all the time. Just need to be cautious they don't see you ogling. That's why one should wear dark glasses even at night. It's not just a fashion statement," Tom said, trying to ease Josh's embarrassment.

Still slightly flustered, Josh opened the door for Tom. Once inside, Tom noted how dark the restaurant was. "Good evening, Mr. Simmons, good to see you again," the maître d' greeted them.

"John, I'd like a table in the back room if possible."

"Certainly, sir, it is not a busy night, and the room is empty right now." He guided them through a series of rooms to the back of the restaurant. It was a small room with only three tables.

When they sat down, Josh explained that Beef and Bottle was always very busy during the week but, unlike other restaurants, was very quiet on Saturdays. At that their waiter came to the table and presented them with the menus. Tom was surprised to see that the menus were actually printed on bottles of Lancers Rose. The waiter took their drink order—Tom a gin and tonic, and Josh Scotch on the rocks—and disappeared. "The steaks are really the only thing to get here. There are other items on the menu but are not up to the beef." Tom scanned the menu and decided on the large filet. He had grown up in a household of carnivores.

When the waiter asked how he wanted his filet cooked, he replied, "Pittsburgh."

The waiter gave him a bewildered look. "Very rare, charred on the outside, practically raw inside," Josh translated. They both laughed when the waiter disappeared into the kitchen. "I guess since we're both from the Northeast we can both translate for these Southern rubes." Then he continued, "So you like your meat raw?" Josh said with the obvious double entendre.

"Any way I can get it," he said, but he cautioned himself about going too far down this road.

Josh, however, tried to set him at ease. "I need to apologize again for being so fucked up. I totally screwed up, and I really want to make amends and see if we can start over." Tom just listened since he really did not know what to say.

"First, I want to say that the initial time I saw you at Toby's, I was smitten. You are handsome, educated, charming, sexy. I knew that since you were available—Toby told me—that I needed to make moves on you. But unfortunately, I have a past that keeps getting in my way. That experience with the priest and my parents' complete rejection of my story have really left a deep scar. And I haven't been able to really deal with it."

"Why not?" Tom was rather naïve about these sorts of traumas since he had never experienced anything like that.

"I've been to several therapists and a psychiatrist, and they've all been useless. They all tell me to put it behind me. To get on with my life. Well, I haven't been able to. Then there were two of them that told me I was a queer because I had been molested, and I needed to have sex with women to get over it. One told me my 'lifestyle' disgusted him, but he thought he could help. That was the last time I saw him. So you can see that I've been pretty messed up, which is no excuse for the way I acted. And here I am doing another dump on you."

The drinks came, which caused a pause in the conversation. Tom took a long drink from his glass and thought that he might need to order another. He was not sure if Josh was worth all the drama.

"Well, anyway," Josh continued, after he downed a big swallow of his Scotch, "I wanted to tell you about my issues, which I did when I invited you to dinner. Probably again too much. And I lied when I said I don't fuck on the first date. That has never stopped me in the past. I just didn't want you to think I was only interested in getting into your pants." Another pause, another swallow. "So I invited to go to Playalinda, a nude beach which has a reputation for open sex. I wanted you to rub my ass in the worst way."

"I wanted to rub your ass in the worst way as well. But your body language suggested I keep my hands to myself."

"That was not my intent. And I would have gladly engaged with that guy on the beach. You were looking at him too intently to notice that I was hard. But then I freaked out and demanded that we leave."

Tom just stared at him, although interrupted when their salads appeared.

"I love sex," Josh continued, "I really wanted to fuck you. But I still have so many hang-ups from my past that I really have to be drunk to get up the nerve. Then when I have the nerve, the drink prevents me from getting it up."

*My god, what a mess this guy is*, Tom thought.

"In conclusion," Josh said with a ironic smile, "I'd really like to get to know you better, and have you see that under this mess is a decent guy. And I'd love to get naked with you and explore your body." Josh had not noticed that the waiter had walked up behind him, holding their plates and listening to this true confession. His eyes were wide open.

After he put the plates down and made a hasty retreat, Josh said reassuringly, "Don't worry, all the waiters here are queer. He'll probably come by later to invite us up to his apartment for a three-way." They both laughed and began eating. An awkward silence persisted at the table for a few minutes, until Josh said, "For now I'd just like to spend some time with you, discuss books, cruise good-looking guys. That sort of thing."

"Sounds fine to me." Then Tom quickly changed the subject from Josh's personal hang-ups. "So how did you get to know Toby?"

"We met at a meeting of Central Florida Democrats. I think there was one other person there." He laughed. "Anyhow, we found we had a good deal in common, other than just party politics. He invited me to dinner, and we've been friends ever since. We worked together on the great lost cause, trying to get McGovern elected. Toby and Jeff let me hang out with them. At first I thought they'd be interested in some intimacy, but they have a very closed relationship, which is fine with me. I'm not sure I could do that, having sex exclusively with just one guy." That final remark did not impress Tom, ignoring his own proclivities for multiple partners without a thought of commitment.

They exchanged small talk for the remainder of the meal, and Josh did not bring up any more of his hang-ups. They split the bill—Tom insisted—and walked out onto Park Avenue. "Well, I'd love to have you come over to my apartment. It's just two blocks away."

"Oh, I'd love to, but I'm driving over to see my parents tomorrow. Early start."

"But can we get together again?" Then plaintively, "Soon?"

"Sure. I've really enjoyed this evening, and I look forward to doing it again." Then he added rather forcefully, "soon." And he was not lying. He enjoyed being with Josh as long as he was not wallowing in self-pity. He could understand the hurt that Josh had been through, but he concurred with the multiple therapists: Josh had to move on. He concluded that he would give it another chance, but he probably needed to make it clear that he was not a psychotherapist.

On the following Monday, Toby deliberately followed Tom into the faculty lunchroom. "How did your dinner go with Josh?"

"Fine, other than the fact he's a psycho."

"But a very rich psycho. You could buy lots of valium with that."

Tom laughed sardonically. "Well, I did agree to get together with him again. Culturally and politically we have a lot in common."

"How is he in bed? I've seen him shirtless but not the entire package."

"We haven't had sex. At least not yet."

"Sounds like you're just dating, and you both want to preserve your virginity."

"A little too late for that in my case." They both laughed.

"I really think Josh has some serious issues. He told you about being raped by a priest?"

"Yeah, it was very emotional."

"I think he tells the story as a defensive measure: 'Don't get too close to me because I'm fragile.' I have read about other people who have been sexually molested as children who never really get over it."

"Perhaps I should stop seeing him."

Toby thought a moment. "Well, I probably shouldn't tell you this, but he is really hooked on you. He called me Sunday morning and said he wished he had met you a long time ago. Gushed about how much you two have in common. Sounded almost like puppy love."

Tom felt uncomfortable about what he saw was a burden placed on him. Yet, he still liked Josh—a great deal. They had had a terrific dinner. A lot of the clouds that hung over him had dissipated. All he knew, he would have to take it easy.

In fact, they took it very easy. Tom found that taking graduate courses seemed like a second job. Both his fall and spring semester classes required more work than the ones he had taken previously. The assignments still consisted primarily of busywork, but he still had to complete them. The workload at Catholic had also increased since he had earned the wonderful title of Assistant Department Chair. Why he had been assigned this task eluded him. Both Hank and Barbara had been there longer and understood the inner working of the school better than he did. He concluded that the administration had punished him for giving out too many Cs last year. Finally he needed to see his parents more often. His father had suddenly aged very much for a man who was just turning seventy. Household tasks that he had normally undertaken now passed to Tom. Although his parents hired a lawn service, Tom undertook some basic repairs and general maintenance to save his parents money.

Josh also seemed to have more responsibilities. He spent a good deal of time in Jacksonville and twice had to fly to New Hampshire: "God, I don't want to go!" After his return from the second trip, he remained in a rancid mood for days, although he would not explain what had happened.

Yet Tom and Josh did manage to talk over the phone for extended conversations. Tom felt like he was back in high school, lying on his parents' bed talking in whispers on the phone. (Although he requested many times, his parents refused to get him his own extension in his bedroom.) They talked about their lives, but more often they discussed books. They both loved Victorian literature and exchanged theories about what motivated Little Father Time to kill off his siblings in *Jude the Obscure*. They had theological discussions about the nature of God, Josh vehemently disagreeing with Hardy. Tom was not so sure about what he thought, since he did not possess the certainty that a good Catholic should. Exposure to the Catholic administration where he worked, on top of Josh's experience, had certainly damped his convictions, which were fairly weak to begin with.

Josh had begun reading William James's *The Varieties of Religious Experiences* and recommended it to Tom. "My past experience with God at times leaves me with a Little Father Time view. But then I realize that is the Catholic version that I have imbibed. The god that wags his fingers at every transgression. And there are loads of them."

Tom agreed but said he was more neutral than hostile to the divine.

"For quite a while I was a solid atheist, but oh, what does James call it, the ineffable. Feelings that you cannot understand. Something out there bigger than I am."

"One that destroys?"

"Not always. Mondays, Wednesdays, and Fridays mostly. The rest of the week rather different."

"And?"

"As I said, I used to see God through my Catholic filter, and it wasn't pretty. But I've come more and more to see that as a distortion. It is the institution that is evil, not God. I think I told you before, I have a sense of something outside of me, something that is benevolent, caring. Not at all what I experienced within the Catholic fold. But I have not quite been able to grasp it. And I wonder if it is a real presence or something I just hope does."

"You think about this a lot, don't you?"

"Guess I do. I have a love-hate relationship with religion. I really want to believe that there is a force of good out there, but unfortunately, I haven't seen it in the institution that pretends to represent Him. But I'll keep searching. Perhaps He'll find me." On that note, they changed the subject.

About once a month, they would have dinner together, trying different restaurants in the Orlando area. Tom always complained that the food in Central Florida could not match what he had grown up with in Boston. They both bemoaned the fact that they could not get Maine lobster. Josh had once tried Florida lobster and claimed it was almost inedible. What they did not have was sex.

After every meal, Josh this time made some excuse that as much as he wanted, he needed to go away early the next morning and needed to pack or go to sleep early. The excuse was always different, but there was always an excuse. Each evening as they parted, however, Josh would always find a way to give Tom a big kiss, not just a peck but inserting his tongue in Tom's mouth. Afterward, most evenings, Tom would go home and masturbate.

Tom was not, however, totally chaste. During the week, he would often take time to go to the Silver Hammer and pick up a guy to take back to his apartment. In particular, there were three men, all somewhat older, who were regulars at the stayovers. For Tom, these occasions were strictly to deal with his sexual tensions. He felt no attachment to any one of them, although each had hinted that they would have loved a more permanent arrangement. For some strange reason, Tom always felt his ties to Josh were the most important ones, emotional ones that compensated for the lack of a physical engagement. It baffled him, but there it was. He discussed it briefly with Toby, who only shrugged his shoulders in bewilderment. "Whatever floats your boat," was the only insight Tom could get from Toby.

By April, Tom had almost completed his sixth graduate course and decided the time had arrived for him to begin looking for a job. He knew through the teacher grapevine that a number of vacancies had occurred. So he applied in the Seminole and Orange County system. He told them that he would be eligible for a teaching certificate at the end of May. The Orange County office sent him to a high school in the western part of the county, farther away than he would really wanted to go, but he would take it if hired.

He interviewed with the principal whom he found to be sensible, professional, and competent, who seemed really interested in the education of young people. He also talked to a few of the teachers in the English department and took a liking to them. He now had only to wait.

The telephone call came three days later. He accepted the offer immediately. While the pay might be considerably higher than at Catholic, he knew that his drive would be longer, his classes would be much larger, and he would confront a lot more grading. Nevertheless, it would be worth turning his back on Catholic High and Father Humphrey.

His first telephone call went to his parents. They were somewhat surprised that he wanted to change jobs since he had always taught at a Catholic school. He explained where he was currently did not hold a candle to the Boston Catholic schools and the money was better. That seemed to satisfy his father. The second call was to Josh, who instantly invited Tom to a celebratory dinner at the Beef and Bottle. Tom then poured himself a large gin and tonic, deciding tonight was not the one to grade papers.

On Saturday night, Tom met Josh again at the Beef and Bottle; and as usual, they sat in the back room. For some reason, Josh seemed a little bit subdued, but Tom kept up the energy, telling all his plans for the new school year, that he intended to take two more courses toward his master's, and other plans for some travel over the summer. He hoped that Josh would want to go with him to the Florida Keys. Tom had never been there, although he had lived in Florida almost two years. Josh said he would love to go with him. Tom hoped that did not mean separate motel rooms.

After dinner, as they walked out, Tom again noticed that Josh seemed nervous or agitated. Instead of the usual excuse about having to get up early the next day, though, Josh asked, "Would you like to come over to my place? I got a bottle of champagne to celebrate."

"Happy to." Tom left his car in the lot behind the restaurant and walked with Josh to his apartment, which was only a few blocks away. The closer they got to the "Whispering Widows," the more nervous Josh got. Finally when they climbed into the elevator, Tom took hold of Josh's hand, which seemed to calm him. Obviously Josh intended to have sex with him, but a man with that much experience, Tom thought, should not be that nervous.

As soon as they entered Josh's apartment, he grabbed him and began to kiss him. He began to rub his body up against Tom's. Tom could only give a sigh of relief, finally.

Josh then pulled away and began removing his clothes. Tom then did the same. Soon they were both naked. Tom marveled at Josh's body. He had seen him naked before on the beach at Playalinda; he had studied the beautiful muscles and his glorious rear end. But now he was fully erect, and the vision was astounding. Tom walked over to Josh and embraced him. He began to run his hands over Josh's rear end, and Josh began to tremble. Tom thought it was out of desire. Then he slowly reached around and took Josh's erection in his hands. At this point, he heard what seemed to be a sob. He looked at Josh's face and saw he was crying almost uncontrollably.

"What's the matter? Did I hurt you?" Tom's voice trembled.

"I can't do it. I can't go through with it. I thought I could, but I can't." He was almost bawling by this point.

"What's the matter? You seemed so anxious."

"I was, but not in the way you think."

Tom pulled him over to the sofa and made him sit down. "Do you want to put your clothes on?"

"Thanks." With that, he pulled his shorts on. Reluctantly, Tom did too. "I've been misleading you. I have never had sex with a man before. All that bravado was fake. I don't fuck on the first date, or the second, or the tenth. I have never been able to do it. Every time I get close, I think about that pervert who raped me in junior high. When you touched me, I knew it was you, but all I could see was his face leering at me. Your smell became his smell. You have been kind and patient, particularly patient, while I played the cocktease all these months. I wanted you to penetrate me so that your sensations would replace his." Josh continued this way, crying, shaking. To Tom, it was a surreal scene. Here was a tall, handsome, muscular man practically in hysterics. All he could think to do was to hold him.

"I never had those experiences, but I can only imagine how they have messed you up. But you really are a terrific guy."

Josh took a deep breath. "I know I can't expect you to hang around a freak like me. I just want you to know that I have fallen in love with you. You are the most decent guy I have ever known. You stuck with me even though I was totally frigid to you. I won't blame you if you had gone out and got fucked somewhere else." Tom said nothing. But the announcement of Josh's feelings startled him. He had never really thought about him in that way, until now.

"Do you want me to leave or stay awhile?"

"If you just will hold me for a while, I'd really appreciate it."

"I'm more than happy to." And for about a half hour, Tom just cradled Josh in his arms. Eventually, they both got dressed, and Tom began to leave. "Listen, I do not want this to be the end of our relationship. Perhaps we can work something out. Maybe you can get some help."

"Tried that. I think I told you it was a colossal failure."

"Don't give up hope. You are a terrific guy. I don't want to lose you. If we only have dinner once in a while, discuss novels, and hang out naked on the beach, that would suffice." Tom pulled Josh close to him again, overcoming a slight resistance, and kissed him. He walked back to his car and drove home. For the longest time, he sat in his car outside his apartment building and thought about what had just happened. He realized he was in a slight state of shock.

The next day, Tom decided he needed to do something. He thought of calling Josh but decided he needed to do some more thinking first. He considering contacting Toby, but something told him that was a bad idea. Finally, he settled on is cousin Eddie; why—he did not really know. Fortunately Eddie was home and invited him over.

"You've certainly been a stranger. I talk to your parents more than I see you, and you're just a few miles away. Are you in trouble with the law?"

"Oh, nothing like that. It's a personal problem, and I thought you could help."

"How long has she been pregnant?"

"Ha, ha. No, this is serious. I've been dating this girl for a while." Eddie was stridently heterosexual, and Tom did not see any reason to distract him with the truth. "We've been getting very serious, but we haven't gone to bed yet."

"How long?"

"Over a year. Well, finally we got very close to it, and she broke down into hysterics. It turns out she had been raped by a priest when she was fourteen. She has been carrying that around all these years. She's terrified about sex. I asked her about getting psychological counseling, but she says she's tried, and that hasn't helped. I thought as a lawyer, you would know some good counselors who might be able to help her." He almost slipped and said *him*.

"You've come to the right person. I actually have had a number of rape victims whom I have represented in legal actions against the perpetrators. Women often have trouble opening up to men counselors, so I normally send my clients to a woman. Her name is Beverly Abbot, and she has had great success in this area. She told me these women have gone through something very much akin to what men experience on the battlefield. Shell shock. Sounds crazy, but she certainly is successful. She's not inexpensive, so I hope your girlfriend . . ."

"Barbara." Tom laughed internally to think that Barbara was a serious girlfriend.

"Barbara has some financial wherewithal?"

"Oh, I don't think money is an issue with her."

"Marrying her for her money, eh?" Eddie gave Tom the full name, address, and telephone number of Beverly Abbot. Before Tom drove away, he made a copy of the information just in case Josh purposely lost it. Then without calling, he drove to Josh's apartment and rang the bell.

Josh answered with a surprised look on his face. "I never thought I'd see you again."

"Oh, you're going to see a great deal of me. I talked to my cousin who's an attorney."

"What would he know about me?" Josh sounded a little angry and violated.

"Eddie thinks it's my girlfriend, Barbara. Anyhow, he has dealt with cases like yours." Josh gave him a look of disbelief. "Just stay with me. He gave me the name of a counselor who deals with rape victims. Now granted they are generally women, but she has been very successful in helping people in these circumstances. Now I know you are a very proud person who would like to punch me in the nose right now. But, and this is a big *but*, I will pester you to distraction until you make an appointment with this woman. You are going to get cured, you are going to love sex, and you are going to fuck my brains out, soon."

"You expect me to go to some woman and spill out all my secrets. You have to be joking."

"Damn right I do."

# Chapter 3

Apopka High was a long way from Cardinal Cushing. The deferred maintenance list must have been so extensive, Tom thought, that the county had just given up on it. Although the school district had provided air-conditioning for more affluent sections of the county, that benefit had not yet reached Apopka. Orlando Catholic was not air-conditioned either, but the smaller classes made the heat somewhat more tolerable. The classes of Apopka held generally thirty or more students stuffed into small classrooms. The body odor often became overwhelming, with or without the windows open. Moreover, in many instances, the windows in Tom's classroom would not open at all. He took to wearing a lot of aftershave to help cover the smell. He now appreciated the stories of ladies and gentlemen in the eighteenth century carrying heavily perfumed handkerchiefs to cover the nose to avoid the stench.

The school drew from a particularly poor section of the county. It sat in the midst of the farm country, where much of the winter produce for the United Sates is produced. There are also large fern farms, which supply local florists. Most of the workers are migrants who came in for the two growing seasons, in between which they migrated north. They lived in deplorable conditions and were poorly paid and often robbed of their earnings. By law, however, their children must enroll in the local schools; for the older children, that meant Apopka High. These children attended school during the winter and early spring while their parents worked in the fields and then were transported off to other harvests. Most teachers became so frustrated with the disruption of the migrant children's education that they generally paid little attention to them. Perhaps because he was a newcomer, he tried to give them special attention. He obtained help from a group of nuns who worked with the families, although they too felt somewhat abandoned since the bishop paid lip service to their service but gave them almost no resources.

The other burden for Apopka High was that it had just recently been integrated. Until 1970, the black children had all gone to Phyllis Wheatley down the road. A federal judge, however, declared this contrary to Supreme Court decisions and required a blending of the schools. Now some children from Apopka were bussed to other high schools to make room for the black children. Teachers were also shuffled around, causing tremendous resentment on the part of those white faculty forced to teach at the former all-black schools and the black teachers who came to Apopka but received treatment as outsiders, not much different from the migrant workers' children.

The hostility of the original white teachers toward the newly integrated black ones amazed Tom. While he fully acknowledged that racism was rampant in New England, at least they generally expressed their feelings privately. Here at Apopka High, the bigotry was openly and often loudly expressed. Tom's family was probably no different from others in Boston, but he never once heard either of his parents express such bigotry directly. Once when he visited a friend, Mike, from high school, he overheard Mike's father talking about Chinks and Yids and asked his parents what those words meant. His parents refused to tell him, and they forbade him to go to Mike's house again. Now some of the teachers at Apopka High used such terms openly. One man, Owen Roberts in the English department, in particular used degrading terms to describe anyone who was not Anglo-Saxon. Tom very quickly gravitated to those who did not, and his closest compatriot became a black science teacher named James. Yet despite all these drawbacks, Tom rejoiced in his new position. The pay was certainly better, but even more so, he now did not feel the penetrating eyes of Father Humphrey and Sister Alice slicing into him. And while not all students seemed eager to delve into the joys of British literature, Tom encountered a number of students eager to learn and, he suspected, escape Apopka.

Tom soon discovered that a huge gap existed between Apopka and that part of the county and Winter Park, where he lived. It was as if integration had not even taken place, since clearly people in Apopka still lived a segregated existence. He even learned that the Episcopal Church in Apopka had the Grand Dragon of the KKK in one of the stained glass windows. He decided to check it out, and it was true. It spoiled what otherwise was a tiny gem. Why, he wondered, could not the Catholic churches in Florida look less industrial, although he was glad Margaret Mary lacked windows dedicated to the Klan.

The day he had visited Holy Spirit, he called Josh to report his findings. In fact he called Josh every day to catch up. He asked how his day had been and if he had any news. He was really interested to find out if Josh had had a session with Dr. Abbot. Josh had been seeing her since July, having agreed to make an appointment following a titanic struggle with Tom.

Josh finally called Dr. Abbot and arranged an appointment. He appeared at her office as scheduled and filled out the reams of paperwork before the receptionist ushered him into Dr. Abbot's office. The doctor looked up in surprise, obviously shocked. "Is something the matter?" Josh asked, somewhat irritated.

"Oh, I'm so sorry. I usually work with women, and that's who I thought you were. Your chart only reads J. Simmons, so I expected you would be a woman."

"Well, actually, it's Joshua Simmons, and last time I checked, I'm a male," he said somewhat sarcastically.

Again she apologized profusely. "I assume you know that I work with people"—she stopped herself from saying *women*—"who have been sexually molested. While less common, it does happen to men. Often the scars are very deep and take some time to heal, but with perseverance, they can be healed." She put a great deal of emphasis on the word *can*.

Josh was still skeptical.

"Just remember everything is confidential here, and anything you tell me will not go outside this room unless you want me to talk with anyone." She paused to let this sink in. "Now, tell me your story."

At first haltingly, then with growing confidence, Josh told his tale about being molested by Father Benson over several years when Josh was a teenager and then finally forcibly raping him when Josh would not consent to be penetrated. He then continued with the account of his angry parents refusing to believe him and in fact ridiculing him for telling such false tales. By the end of the recitation, Josh was in tears.

"I'm sure it is difficult for a devout parent to believe that a clergyman could do such things. But I know it to be true since I worked with a young man about a year ago who had exactly the same experiences you did, and he had the same problem at first with his parents. They at least came around. Moreover, I've talked to other therapists, and they report other cases of Catholic priests molesting young boys in their care. It's disgusting. Taking advantage of the power differential for their own sexual gratification. Now the important question, what impact has this experience had on you? Obviously since you're seeing me, it has something to do with your sex life."

"Well, in the first place, it made me become a homosexual."

"I doubt very much if that is the case. Homosexuals seem to be born that way. I know there is a good deal of controversy about its origins, but every male I've dealt with clearly state they never knew a time when they weren't attracted to men. Did you ever have attractions before Benson molested you?" She never used the title *Father* in any of her references to him.

"Well, actually, I remember being attracted to the guy who lived next door to me. One time he was taking a shower, and I was intrigued with his body." He was too embarrassed to tell Dr. Abbot that he got an erection looking at the boy. Dr. Abbot had already surmised that.

"And I bet there were others. Benson did not cause you to become gay. But he did cause you a great deal of trouble otherwise. There's absolutely nothing wrong with being homosexual. There is of an older man taking advantage of a young boy. And there is definitely something wrong with parents who ridicule their son. Have you experienced any other problems?"

"Well, I've never been able to have sex with anyone. I get very aroused but then have a panic attack and can't do it. I break down practically—actually, I break into tears."

"What you have developed is what professionals call 'gross stress reaction.' Soldiers exhibit this syndrome as a result of battle shocks. It leaves the soldier devastated. It was called shell shock in World War I."

"But I've never been a soldier."

"You don't need to be to have the same reaction to an intense shock. And you've had that, not only because that priest raped you but also the hostile reaction of your parents. Let me ask you something. Are you involved with anyone at this time?"

Josh told her about Tom and their relationship. "I'm surprised he still has anything to do with me after I freaked out when we tried to have sex."

"What are your feelings for him?"

"Well, I've told him I love him, and it's true."

"And Tom?"

"He told me that he had fallen in love with me, and I believe him."

The doctor thought a moment. "If you're willing, I'd like to work with you for a month or so and then bring Tom in to help us. I'll explain as we get into it. But I promise you that if you stick with it, you can have a very satisfying sex life."

Joshua himself took a minute and then agreed.

That evening, he invited Tom over for dinner, although not quite as fancy as the first one, when he was showing off. When they had finished, he told Tom that he had seen Dr. Abbot. He then explained what they had discussed.

"Well, that's good. I don't plan to be a virgin the rest of my life."

"If you're a virgin now, that's another miracle God must have performed recently."

After school let out for the summer, Tom spent much of his time reading books he had planned to use in the fall, and he was enrolled in two more education courses, which also gave him a good deal of homework. He devoted as much time as he had left to watch the Watergate hearings. Fortunately, he could skim his textbook assignments while watching the hearings. He became a big fan of Senator Sam Ervin and now understood why the senator from Florida was so unimpressive. Each evening he would call Josh, and they would chat for about an hour, Tom reporting the Watergate hearings and Josh about his work. Tom did not know when Josh saw Abbot or what transpired. And he never asked.

Finally, he got a call from Dr. Abbot. "Joshua is aware that I'm calling. If you don't mind, could you come in to see me? You could be a real help to Joshua. But at this point, please don't discuss it with Joshua. That will come later."

Tom immediately agreed and set up an appointment. When he met with her, she explained what Josh's problems were. "Well, he had told me the bit about the priest and his parents."

"You probably don't know how long it went on and how traumatizing it was. The molestation actually went on for years. He started literally indoctrinating him to his advances, very slowing winning over his trust and progressing also at a snail's speed to make Joshua comfortable. But as Joshua matured, he came to realize that this was not good. When the priest tried to put his penis in Joshua's anus, he rebelled. The priest got mad and raped him. So this was not with consent but forced. Joshua has come to see sex in a very negative light. He thinks of it as being forced. So even though he really wanted to make love to you, the vision of the priest intervenes. So we've slowly dealt with these issues. What he needs to learn is that the events he associates with the priest he now needs to associate with someone he truly loves. You."

"But how does that happen? How can I be of any help?" he asked rather anxiously. Instantly he worried that Abbot would think he was only interested in sex.

"When he's ready, you will do something intimate with him," she said, showing no signs that she regarded his eagerness as untoward. "Then we'll move on to the next step. But there will be strict limits of what you can do with each other. It has to be very gradual and carefully planned. We anticipate you will eventually be able to have intercourse with him. Of course, you will have to decide who plays the female and the male role," she laughed.

Tom did not think that remark was particularly funny, but he let it pass.

The next day, Josh called and asked how his session with Dr. Abbot went.

"So you knew about it."

"Oh, yes. In fact, I hope we can take the first step. I know you plan to go to your parents' house this weekend, but I would like to meet you at your place and spend the night. We need to take it very gradually. If you don't mind, I just want to sleep with you. This time with our underwear on. And if that works, naked."

It sounded very bizarre to Tom, but he agreed to it. He had to accept that Dr. Abbot really did know what she was doing.

He drove to his parents' house on Friday. They spent a good deal of time discussing Watergate. His father was very pessimistic that Nixon would get off scot-free. "They don't call him Tricky Dick for nothing. And I can't believe all of our stupid neighbors who think he did nothing wrong and that those senators are only trying to persecute him. Ignorant fools."

"It looks, Dad, as if you don't have an opinion."

The next afternoon, when his father had gone to Publix, his mother asked, "So do you have a boyfriend yet?"

The question embarrassed Tom, and he turned slightly red, which his mother noticed. Yet he decided he must be honest. "Well, as a matter of fact, I do."

"Oh, that's wonderful! What's his name?"

"Josh."

"Does he have a last name? Don't worry, I won't hunt him down."

"Simmons."

"Josh Simmons. Joshua Simmons. Nice name. How old is he?"

"I've never asked. But I think he's around thirty."

Then came the question he did not expect. "Well, when can I meet him?" The look on her son's face caused her to smile. "Well, of course, we want to meet him!"

"We! Dad too? When did he know?"

"Certainly. We're both happy that you've settled down," seemingly ignoring his last question.

"But when did Dad know?" he asked again. This conversation seemed surreal to Tom. He thought his parents' reaction would be the opposite from what he was hearing. "Obviously you've spilled the beans to your husband."

"I haven't told him explicitly, but he'll have to know eventually, and I think it best come from me. You'd get all tongue-tied, so I dropped some subtle hints. And I think he's pretty much figured it out already."

"How?" Knowing his mother, Tom assumed the hints were not quite so subtle.

"Said something about the way you threw a ball."

"Obviously Father's not into stereotypes," Tom said with a bit of sarcasm.

"Oh, come now. We both love you very much, and I'm glad I know all of you. And frankly you were terrible at baseball."

"You're probably right," he said with a sigh.

"So when are we going to meet Josh?" she persisted.

"Well, I guess we could come over for a day . . . if you'd like."

"Why not come for the weekend?"

That clearly was too much to ask. He would not be sleeping with Josh in the same room in his parents' house. He mumbled something about seeing what he could do, but he told his mother that Josh was very shy. "And not out."

"Out of what, dear?"

He realized his mother did not understand the slang. "Out of the closet. Gay men who aren't public about their sexuality, such as to their parents who don't know."

"Well, as I've said, I've suspected for a long time. Probably Josh's parents do too."

"I highly doubt that. You don't know his parents."

"Sounds like I don't want to meet them either."

"Very perceptive, Mother." He had an entirely new understanding of his mother—the dutiful housewife, the devout Catholic, the loving mother. Now he discovered she had hidden sophistication. "I'll talk to Josh and see what we can work out. But you'll really like him." He was relieved when his mother did not ask what they did in bed. He would have to admit they did nothing.

As he drove home Sunday afternoon, he began to worry what to expect with his sleepover with Josh. He had been very carefully instructed by Dr. Abbot to allow Josh to take the direction. "I have worked with my abused and molested women who have shut down sexually, and my technique works almost all the time. I'm sure it would be just as effective with a male." *What if this is one of the instances when it does not work?* worried Tom. *What if it works for women but not men?*

When he drove into the apartment complex, he found Josh in his BMW with the top up, the engine running for the air conditioner, and reading a book. The daily afternoon thunder shower had just passed; and while the temperature had dipped down below ninety, the humidity made it unbearable outside. He rapped on Josh's window to get his attention. Josh put his book down and smiled broadly. He reached into the back seat and pulled out a pizza box and a small case.

"I didn't know what you would have ready, so I brought a pizza. Hope you like pepperoni and mushrooms. All you'll need to do is heat it up."

Tom could not get over how organized Josh always was, thinking about what was needed in every circumstance. He was sure that among other things, Josh had a pair of underwear in that bag. Tom dragged his own bag up the stairs to the apartment, opened the door, and bowed to Josh to enter. *"Apres vous."*

Josh put the pizza in the oven and his bag in Tom's bedroom. *Yes, he is going to spend the night,* Tom thought. When he came back to the kitchen, Tom poured each a drink. By now Tom knew exactly what Josh liked and always had some Scotch on hand.

"So how was your weekend?"

"Very different." He explained his mother's invitation.

Josh looked not in the least surprised. "Anyone as nice as you must have thoughtful parents."

"Well, what do you think? I suggested just a visit for the day, although Mother wanted us to stay the weekend."

"I think we should do it. But you're right, just a day trip." Tom did not need to explain his support for the short visit: the sleeping arrangements. They therefore decided that they would go over just before Tom had to be back in school. After finishing their drinks and eating dinner, they discussed the Watergate hearings—Josh had not been particularly interested in politics, but his relation with Tom persuaded him that he should pay some attention. When he told Tom he had not voted in the 1972 presidential election, he received a long lecture from Tom.

Then came the moment Tom dreaded. "Well, some of us have to go to work tomorrow, so we'd better get to bed." Josh seemed so nonchalant about it; Tom felt terrified.

They walked into the bedroom, and as Tom pulled down the covers, Josh began removing his clothes. Tom did not dare look at Josh as he removed his shirt and shorts. Normally he slept naked, but now he kept his Calvin Kleins securely on. Finally he turned around and saw Josh in paisley boxer shorts climbing into bed. *How typical of him,* Tom thought.

Tom also got in bed and quickly turned out the light. Then he heard Josh say very quietly, "Aren't you going to kiss me?"

Tom did not know if this was an invitation to something further. A kiss in bed generally was. Or he thought more likely one of the steps that Dr. Abbot had mentioned. "Sure," he said and turned toward Josh. They fumbled around a bit but then found each other's lips and kissed. It was not a deep passionate kiss, tongues fully engaged, but it was not just a peck either. Some sincerity stood behind it.

They pulled apart, and Josh rolled over. But not before he said, "Tom, I love you."

"And I love you, Josh." And again, he meant it. Tom lay on his back until he finally fell asleep. He thought that this was the first time he had slept with another man in probably a year. He had abandoned his trips to Playalinda, and he did not stop at the Silver Hammer anymore. Two or perhaps three times, Josh and he had gone to the Parliament House and hung out with Toby and Jeff. His life now centered on Josh, and that was not a bad thing.

He woke up the next morning with a start. He realized that Josh had essentially wrapped himself around him, his erection pressing on Tom's rear end. He really did not want to move but savored the sensations. Then he looked at the clock and saw that it was after eight. He gently nudged Josh. "I forgot to set the alarm. It's after eight."

"Oh god. They'll fire me. Oh, they can't. I own a third of the company." But he did jump out of bed and walked toward the bathroom, his erection clearly visible inside his boxers. Tom figured that was a good sign that another sleepover could not be far behind.

The next day, Tom had one of his graduate courses in the afternoon, a course on teaching specific subject matter in secondary schools. The students were now grouped with their respective peers, so that Tom joined with three other English teachers. They met with a specialist from the county office. Tom was very leery of "specialists" since the few with whom he had dealt quoted profusely from teaching guides that had little practical application in the classroom. The adage had been, "Those who cannot write novels, teach literature, and those who cannot teach become administrators." But Anna Stevens was truly the exception to the rule. She had taught high school English literature for many years before going into administration.

She began, "How many of you have a number of black students in your class?" It was obviously a post-integration question. All four students raised their hands. "How many of you use *Huckleberry Finn* as one of your novels?" Now three of the students raised their hands, including Tom.

"I don't teach American literature, but I guess if I did, I'd use the book. It's a classic," the one abstainer excused himself.

"Do you think the book might be offensive to your African American students?" Stevens asked. All four shook their heads.

One student piped up, "Why, Twain humanizes Huck. He's a sympathetic character."

"True, but isn't there a fairly significant role reversal in the story? Doesn't Huck Finn act more like the adult and Jim the child? Isn't there still a minstrel show quality to Jim's character? And do you think your African American students would appreciate the fact that the word *nigger* is used constantly?" No one in the class responded. Most studied their shoes.

"Now I'm not for banning the book, but if you use it, how careful are you to put it in its historical context?" Again, shoe inspection, including Tom, who saw himself as a paragon of non-racist virtue. "You might explain that when Twain wrote the book, the term was in constant use, but it has only more recently become recognized as an offensive term that should not be used."

"Well, you hear the word used all the time in Ocoee," observed a male teacher from rural Orange County.

"It's still offensive," Tom observed. He almost used the term *red-necked bigot* but stifled it.

Dr. Stevens continued, trying to avoid any tension. Have any of you used a novel written by an African American?" No one raised their hand. "Do you think that if you did, your African American students would feel more included? Otherwise, all they read are books by white men." Tom knew at once that her use of *men* was very deliberate.

"But I don't know any."

"That was my next point. Have any of you read or even heard about *Native Son* by Richard Wright? Or Ralph Ellison's *Invisible Man*? And I have listed some others on this handout which would be appropriate for high school students." There was a pause. "How many women do you have in your classes? How many of you assign books by female writers?" The process repeated itself.

When Tom left the class, he had two long lists of possible new reading assignments, including a book by Maya Angelou, which he somewhat cynically thought would cover both bases.

That evening he had a long telephone discussion with Josh about what he had done in class. Josh was immediately supportive of expanding the horizons of his students, especially the white males. At the opening faculty meeting at the end of August, Tom mentioned his graduate class to Owen, whom he thought was more open-minded than others, that he planned to introduce *Huckleberry Finn* with a good deal of historical context and was using *Native Son* in his reading list.

Owen had never heard of the book and asked who Richard Wright was. When Tom explained, Owen's only comment was "You're having your students read a book by a nigger?" Tom went home despondent.

The next sleepover came two weeks after the first one. The routine was exactly the same, but both Tom and Josh seemed much more relaxed. They both climbed into bed, sporting their respective choice of underwear, kissed, and retreated to opposite sides of the bed. The next morning, Tom found Josh entwining him again, his erection warming Tom's back. Tom fought the urge to put his hand on it. He hoped that would come soon enough.

At breakfast, Tom asked Josh when he knew he was different. "It was in high school. My parents packed me off to boarding school after my 'lies' about Father Benson. My roommate had a stash of *Playboy* magazines which he would jerk off to when he thought I was asleep. When he was out of the room, I looked at some of them hidden under his bed. I realized that those naked women did nothing for me. I could not get turned on by them at all. It was quite clear to me that I had an attraction for my roommate and not his magazines. You?"

"Actually pretty similar. A friend in junior high had gotten a copy of *Peyton Place* and had dog-eared all the salacious parts. He would show them to me, and frankly I could not get at all excited about the description of Betty Anderson showing off her breasts. Actually it sounded pretty revolting." They both laughed.

The next day, Tom sat watching a report about the Supreme Court decision on the Watergate July 24, 1774, tapes, when the phone rang. Irritated because he knew it was some salesperson trying to sell him new windows and interrupting his civic duty to keep abreast with the Watergate drama, he found that Dr. Abbot was on the other end of the line.

"I wanted to let you know that Joshua is making excellent progress. I know it seems slow to you, but in essence, we are rewiring him. We are taking the bad sexual experiences with Benson and turning them into good sexual experiences with you. Joshua told me how much he enjoyed sleeping with you."

"I might add a bit of additional information. Each morning, I woke up with Josh wrapped around me. And he had quite an erection."

"Very good. He didn't tell me that part of it. So he's made more progress than I even thought. Well, the next step is sleeping together naked. Again, there should be no physical contact unless he initiates it. I know this must be hard for you"—Tom wondered if she meant that as a pun—"but it is very important that he determines the next steps. But I'm very confident that Joshua will be able to put the past behind him and have normal sexual relations."

Tom was gratified to hear her say *normal* because all he ever heard all his life was that his sexual activities were dirty and perverted, anything but *normal*. It was heartwarming to hear it called what he considered it to be.

Tom's mother had called several times asking when she was going to meet Josh. He had tried to put her off, but she was very insistent. "But what does Dad know?"

"Well, we haven't really talked about it fully yet. I really haven't found the opportune time, but I certainly will before you two get here. And anyhow, I know that he knows. I told you that. He's said some things over the years that he knows you're different, same way I did. You remember, the baseball thing." Tom thought his mother seemed perhaps too sanguine about her upcoming conversation with his father. It sounded more like a wish and a prayer. "But he loves you and wants you to be happy, no matter what that involves." *Like having sex with men*, Tom wondered. "And I told him you had a special friend and did he want to meet him. And immediately he said yes."

Tom saw no way out of what he expected to be a very uncomfortable visit. But Josh did not seem to have any qualms. "They're not going to ask us what we do in bed," he quipped.

*Not much to tell there*, Tom thought. "That's what every straight person immediately thinks about when introduced to a gay person, what he does in bed. Is he the husband or the wife?"

"And that's pretty much the same for a gay guy who meets another," Josh quipped.

"Well, it's only for a day visit. That, at least, is a consolation. We can always escape if things go south," Tom observed.

They decided to combine the visit to Clermont with the next sleepover. The last Saturday in July, they drove to Tom's parents' house. Tom was somewhat self-conscious because he knew that his parents' house would look pretty insignificant to Josh, coming from his background. Yet Josh was the picture of graciousness. He complimented Tom's mother several times on things she had, the vase she treasured and a nondescript painting that his mother regarded as a lost masterpiece. For some reason, Josh just had an instinct, a second sense, of how to please her without being maudlin. He was kindness personified.

Over lunch, his father discussed the insurance business with Josh while Tom's mother asked about hobbies. They finally got to the core questions: did Josh think Nixon would get impeached. "No, I hope he resigns and saves the nation some heartache." They all approved his answer.

Before they left to drive home, Tom's mother pulled him aside. "You have quite a catch there. Don't let him get away." She smiled broadly. "Your father won't say that, but he told me how much he liked Josh. And he took the news . . . you know . . . very well, don't you think?"

"Thanks, Mom. You've been a real trooper." Tom was almost in tears.

As they drove back to Orlando, Josh said, "You have great parents and, obviously, very accepting. I only wish they were my parents." Tom began to tear up again.

When they got home, they went to a Chinese restaurant that Josh recommended for dinner. They returned to Tom's apartment and sat on the sofa together until Josh indicated he wanted to head for bed. "Do you mind if I take a shower first?"

"Not at all. I think I'll take one after you." Tom actually wished Josh would invite him to join him, but no such luck. After he had showered—with the bathroom door closed—Josh came out in his boxers. Tom then went in and dutifully closed the door and removed his clothes. He had left a fresh pair of shorts in the bathroom. He showered, put the shorts on, and returned to the bedroom. He found Josh sitting up in bed reading one of Tom's books from the nightstand.

"Richard Wright. I haven't heard of him. Any good?"

"He's one of the African American authors I learned about in class. I've decided to use his book in my senior class in the fall."

Josh put down the book, turned his back to Tom, and pulled down his boxers. Tom quickly turned around himself so that it did not appear he was staring, which, of course, he was. They both climbed into bed, and Tom turned out the lights. Josh moved over to him, and they hugged. Tom was in ecstasy. At last he felt Josh's naked body next to him. And there was no sobbing. Instead, he thought he heard Josh laughing. "Anything wrong?"

"You're very wet."

"What?"

"You're leaking. Like a fountain," he laughed.

"Oh god, I'm sorry," realizing what Josh meant.

"No, I take it as a compliment. It's really hot. Now give me a kiss and go to sleep."

They kissed, and Tom immediately rolled on his stomach to conceal the telltale wetness.

The next morning, Tom awoke with Josh, as usual, wrapped around him. The difference was that the warmth of his erection was not through his boxers. Tom got wet all over again.

On Thursday, August 8, Toby called Tom and Josh and invited them to an "Impeachment Party. Bring plenty of champagne."

Tom knew that the occasion was Nixon's announcement of his resignation from the presidency before he actually was impeached. Josh tried to make excuses—not that he was a Nixon supporter, he assured Toby—but in the end relented. Toby had piles of snacks on the table in front of the television. Four champagne flutes sat next to a cooler with four bottles on ice. "I'll never be able to drive home," Tom observed.

"Oh, you're such a wuss, O'Mally. This is not a time for restraint. This is a time for celebration. *Ding-dong*, the witch is dead."

"Oh, how queer!" Jeff said, "Quoting *The Wizard of Oz*."

They watched as Nixon humbled himself, claiming he was doing it for the best interest of the country. The jeers and laughter from the gathering almost drowned out Nixon's voice. Toby turned up the sound, but the noise still drowned him out. At the end of the speech, Toby went into his balcony with two potlids and banged them together, making loud cheering noises. Finally, a neighbor came out and told him to shut up.

"Bet we'll hear from the leasing agent tomorrow," Jeff observed.

As they finished the champagne, Toby talked about the latest outrages from Catholic High. "Now they want to guarantee that all the faculty attend Mass each week."

"How would they do that?" Josh wondered.

"We have to get a monthly letter from the priest, testifying that we have been faithful. Next, if I miss a Sunday, I suppose I'll need a doctor's note."

"How can they do that legally?" Tom asked.

"It's a private school. They have no restrictions on how absurd they can be."

"Well, thank God I teach at a public school. Even if half of my students are juvenile delinquents, at least I don't have to go to church."

"Well, I thought you did go to church," Josh asked.

"Yes, but I'm not forced to go, and sometimes I don't, which is fine."

"I really loved going to Mass," Josh said rather wistfully.

"Well, why don't you?" Jeff asked.

"It's complicated," was all Josh would say.

When Tom and Josh got outside, Tom asked him, "I'm surprised you said anything about church. And especially that you missed it."

"Oh, I don't miss the Catholic Church. I could never go inside one of their churches ever again. But I do miss the religious experience. But I haven't been able to duplicate it. I once tried First Baptist and ran out halfway through the service."

"After what happened to you, you still believe in God?"

"God had nothing to do with it. It was a bunch of sick perverts who take advantage of kids."

"I don't know if I even believe there is a god."

"Oh, I know there is. I once came upon a nineteenth-century English theologian, William Paley, who said that if some ignorant person came upon a watch lying on the ground, even though he did not know what it was, he would understand that someone had made it. Then Paley argued that considering the human eye, one would have to come to the same conclusion, someone made it. Therefore, God. I know that sounds pretty simplistic and hooky, but it resonates with me. I can't imagine our bodies, the natural world, this universe without concluding that it came into being not by accident but was created."

"Then why would he allow something like what happened to you?"

"He didn't. We aren't puppets. We have free will. So some people are just evil, but not because God made them that way." Josh's arguments did not totally convince Tom. "Remember, our founding fathers were not traditional Christians. Most were Deists, but they all believed in a Creator. I cannot accept that this universe, our human bodies, came about by accident."

"Do you believe that priest will spend eternity in hell?"

"I don't think hell exists, but it's late, and that's a discussion for another time." Josh laughed. "Give me a proper kiss good night." Josh wrapped his arms around Tom and gave him a deep, passionate kiss. He clearly pushed his groin against Tom's.

"Hey, you faggots get the fuck out of here." A man stood on the balcony above them. "I'm going to call the police and have you arrested." He ran inside his apartment.

"We'd better hustle. He probably will write down our license plates. See you soon."

Two weeks later, Tom had his first faculty meeting of the new school year. Not fondly, he remembered of the opening sessions at Catholic High. His impression from last year that it was primarily administrative details, which could be stultifying boring, but not offensive. They were not told to make sure every student received As to keep the tuition payers happy. On the other hand, there was always the concern that if grades were too low, it would reflect badly on the faculty and, by extension, the administration. Some things never change. If all the students get low grades, it must be your fault as the teacher, even though the students don't pay attention in class or complete their assignments or pass even the easiest exams.

This year, however, he was spared the sermon. Instead, the principal introduced a woman dressed in a nun's habit. "This is Sister Mary, who works with the Holy Community of Apopka. The sisters there work with the migrant workers who pass through this area twice a year to work on the harvest. Because of the recent court-ordered desegregation, Apopka High will now begin admitting the children of migrants who had originally gone to Phyllis Wheatley. Sister Mary wants to say something about working with these children."

Owen, sitting next to Tom, said, "Goddamn spics."

"Owen, shut up!"

"First it's the jigs and now the spics." At that, Tom got up and moved several rows away.

Sister Mary then explained the difficulties those migrant children faced, since they are moved around and do not stay in one school for more than a few months, if that. She described their cramped living conditions and the grueling poverty they experienced. Most spoke only rudimentary English. She explained that the nuns' ministry would do everything they could to support the teachers. They would be holding English classes after school and assist the children with their homework. "But don't worry, we won't be doing it for them."

For the most part, the teachers listened politely, although a few, especially Owen, expressed their discomfort with their body language or by making huffing sounds. Apparently Sister Mary had grown accustomed to such a response since she continued on totally unfazed. Before returning to his classes to complete preparations for the opening of school the following Monday, Tom stopped by the principal's office to complain about Owen's rudeness. "If he acts that way in front of the students, he will undermine everything those nuns are trying to accomplish."

Instead of addressing Tom's concerns, the principal essentially began attacking Tom. "It seems you Northerners come down here to teach us how to act. Well, we've been dealing with the Nigras and Mexicans for a long time, and we know what problems they bring. Things have not been the same here since integration." Tom had heard black people called a variety of insulting names, but *Nigras* was new to him. Perhaps it was better than the alternatives.

"Thank you, Mr. Johnson. I'll keep that in mind."

After he completed his preparations, he drove home in a fury. When he knew Josh would be home from work, he called and, through his rage, tried to explain what had happened.

"Oh, dear boy, you haven't lived here long enough. When I moved to Miami five years ago, I too was appalled at the amount of open racism. But you get inured to it eventually. It's part of the culture of the South."

"But when I moved here and expressed some worry about Southern attitudes, my friends convinced me that Florida was just a misplaced state. It had more Latin American or Northern influences than Southern."

"That might be partially correct for the urban areas. But once you get outside city limits, say, Apopka, it's almost still the antebellum South. Did you know the previous Orange County sheriff was a member of the Klan? So don't be surprised by what your principal said today."

"I should never have agreed to move here," Tom said exasperated.

"Well, then you would never have met me. That would have made me sad. By the way, up for another sleepover this weekend? How about my place this time?"

# Chapter 4

Tom received the telephone call from Dr. Abbot and, at her request, went to her office after school let out. He was grateful that Thanksgiving had passed, and the remainder of a few weeks before Christmas break looked attainable. Dr. Abbot understood it would take some time to reach her office, and she said she would gladly wait.

Her receptionist had gone for the weekend, so Dr. Abbot opened the door for him. "May I give you a hug?"

"Sure, but why,?" Tom said, rather flabbergasted.

"This is totally unprofessional, and I could have my license revoked, but I needed to show you how much I appreciate your cooperation with Joshua's cure." She never referred to him by his nickname.

"I didn't know I did anything. Josh did all the work."

"Yes, but you were infinitely patient with him. You didn't dump him because he wouldn't have sex with you. Most other men would have." Not much confidence in the male gender there. "And you put up with his highs and lows."

"Well, I guess it's because I love him." Tom thought to himself that he knew eventually he would get in Josh's pants.

"That's obvious. And he's head over heaels in love with you. Joshua is fully able to have normal sexual relations with you. There is nothing you have to avoid that might set him off. The Benson scars are fully covered. But there is always a possibility that something might set it off again. I seriously doubt it, but you need to be aware of that possibility."

"What should I be on the lookout for?"

"Any reversion to his terrors, then give me a call, and I'll do an intervention."

These assurances did not put Tom totally at ease. He still tended to be on pins and needles when he was in bed with Josh. In fact, at one point, Josh scolded him for being too timid. "I'm fine. Now do that again. It feels great."

They had agreed that during the Christmas break, Tom would move his stuff over to Josh's apartment. He would continue to rent his old apartment at least for a time to make certain everything was working smoothly. The Saturday after meeting with Dr. Abbot, Tom brought the first box of his books to Josh's apartment. "Please stop calling it my apartment. It is *our* apartment."

"Well, I'm not helping with the rent."

"You will be once you've finished with the lease on your old place. And now let me see what books you've brought me. I'm just about done with my pile. I just finished *Catch Twenty-Two*. So I only have one left."

"What did you think of it?"

"I definitely identify with Yossarian. A lost soul with lost balls."

"From what I've seen coming out of your cock, your balls are in great shape."

"Well, perhaps we'll see tonight."

As they ate dinner, Tom brought up what he thought would be another sensitive subject. "My parents want us to go over to their house for Christmas. They want us to stay. In the spare bedroom. Mother was explicit about that. No one is to be on the sofa in the living room."

"You have some incredible mother there. What about your father?"

"Mother claimed it was at his insistence. I'm not sure if I believe it. She does have a way of getting what she wants."

"No, that's fine with me. I really like your parents. In many ways, they are more my parents than what I'm stuck with. We just have to make certain the springs don't squeak."

"Wait a minute. If you think we're going to fuck with my parents in the next room, you've got to be kidding."

"Yeah, I guess I can see your point." He then began to talk in a high-pitched tone. "Oh, son, sounds like you were having a great time. Does he have a big—"

"Stop it, you louse." But they both laughed hysterically.

After dinner, they sat on his patio overlooking the lake and then retired to their bedroom. Tom had discovered that having sex with Josh was not a frantic, "let's get it over with so I can climax," but a slow, loving experience that lasted much longer than he had experienced with other men who seemed only concerned about how soon they could achieve an orgasm. Finally they had reached a peak, when Josh whispered, "I want you to penetrate me."

"Are you sure?" asked Tom, remembering the horror that Josh recalled about being anally raped by the priest.

"I couldn't be any more certain." He then handed Tom a bottle of lube and rolled over. *Obviously,* Tom thought, *he has been cured.*

The day before Christmas, Tom and Josh drove over to Clermont. Tom's father helped them carry their bags to the spare room, while Tom delivered some food that Josh had prepared. "You're not going to believe what a phenomenal cook he is."

"I'm eager to see," his mother said, smiling. "He's such a nice and polite boy."

"And I'm not?"

"Well, sometimes," she smiled.

Tom had warned Josh that his parents would insist they attend Midnight Mass together, and they plotted out a way of excusing themselves. "Well, you should go," Josh insisted. "Tell them I'm allergic to incense."

It did not go that way, however. That afternoon, just before dinner, Tom's mother said, "We need to tell you something about this evening. Tom probably told you, Josh, that we normally go to Midnight Mass at our Catholic Church. Well, we won't be going this year."

"The heavens will fall!" Tom exclaimed in mock horror.

"We now attend the local Episcopal Church, Saint Matthias. And their service begins at nine, which for us old folks is a much better hour."

"What brought that on?" Tom could never imagine his parents ever attending another church expect Catholic. They were Irish after all, and the Episcopal Church was allied with the Church of England—the nation that had persecuted the Irish for generations.

"You did, dear."

"Me!"

"Yes, when you told us about how those sisters were working with the migrants, we decided that we would see what the local parish church was doing. When we mentioned it to the monsignor, he said that the diocese was not very supportive of their work. He said we need to focus our attention on stopping the scourge of abortion and prevent homosexuals—and I despised the way he said that word— from polluting our society. Well that did it. I told him my son was homosexual, and he had a wonderful partner. I thought about saying what you did in bed but refrained."

"Oh, thank God, Mother." He wondered if she actually did know what they did in bed.

"So we looked around and found Saint Matthias. And I asked them directly what sort of ministries did they have. Well, the priest knew about what the nuns were doing in Apopka, and he said that they were beginning a group to help young migrant children how to read. Well, your father and I signed right up."

"Well, I'd love to go with you this evening," Josh said. Tom gave him a quizzical look, but Josh gave him a reassuring glance.

They ate dinner at six; the main course was the beef en croute, which Josh had prepared. Clara demanded that Josh give her the recipe, but Tom argued, "Mother, if you knew how long it took Josh to make it, you'd never want to undertake it."

"Well, I never," she cried in false resentment.

"Oh, I can remember when I was quite young, you discovered the joys of TV dinners."

"Please don't reminded me, especially in front of Josh."

As they dressed for church, Tom explained that his parents had been very active in church affairs, primarily efforts to end the war in Vietnam and supporting the civil rights movement. Their church in Boston had been very supportive. They also were great fans of the Berrigan brothers.

Saint Matthias was not very impressive. The choir could not sing, and the organist made quite a few fluffs; the sermon lacked any real spark, and passing of the peace was inordinately drawn out. Tom was exceedingly thankful that there was no guitar music, no condemnations of others, and no sense that the clergy stood several steps closer to heaven.

"Good evening, and a Merry Christmas to you, Mr. and Mrs. O'Mally."

"Merry Christmas to you, Father Thompson."

"And this must be your son," he paused, "Tom?"

"Yes, sir, and this is my friend Josh Simmons."

"Pleasure to meet you both. Your mother brags about you all the time, and she said you had a very nice friend."

*No sign of judgment there,* thought Tom.

"May I introduce my wife, Ann." They chattered for a while until the line behind them grew embarrassingly long. "I hope you two will come again when you're in town."

"We'd be delighted to," said Josh.

When they got home, they drank a glass of Mike's eggnog, which was strong enough to down a horse. "The recipe quotes Mark Twain," his father boasted, "that too much of anything is bad for you except too much bourbon, which is just enough."

"Well, this eggnog certainly lives up to his motto," Tom urged.

As they prepared for bed, Josh commented, "Hmm, a church that lets you eat the bread and drink the wine. A church that seems to welcome everyone. A church were the priests can get married and not have to rape little boys for their sexual jollies. Not bad." They embraced and fell asleep in each other's arms.

The next morning, they finished breakfast before exchanging gifts. "Mom, I'm curious why you never said anything about Father Sullivan's offensive sermons against homosexuals."

"Well, at that time, I wasn't sure I had a gay son. And, Tom, I think the accepted term is *gay* rather than *homosexual.*"

"Of course, Mother." They all laughed. The pile of presents under the tree shrank slowly. But the gift Tom appreciated the most was his parents' acceptance of him and of Josh. The O'Mallys had even given Josh a lightweight sweater in a rather garish shade of red. Josh promised he would wear it whenever it got cold enough. Tom hoped it would not happen very often. Josh saved his present for Tom until they had gotten home: a gold bracelet in a Tiffany's blue box. Tom was so touched that he actually began to cry. He could not believe how wonderful this Christmas had been.

As they snuggled into bed, Josh muttered almost to himself, "It'd be interesting to see if any of the Episcopal churches around here are as welcoming. I really like the fact that it was close to the Catholic Church without the offensive parts. Perhaps I can find God there."

Tom considered Margaret Mary welcoming and only rarely did the sermon dwell on the type of offensive sermons he had heard in Boston. He wondered though if decorum and a desire to avoid controversy dictated the choice of topics in very proper Winter Park. He certainly did not have a strong attachment to the Catholic Church. His parents' decision absolutely surprised him, but they undoubtedly were unrepentant liberals, which clearly was more important to them than their religious ties. When he first heard about the nuns working with the migrants, he took some personal pride that they were part of his church. Apparently though, they were an anomaly, not representative of the church in the South. Like in other things, he was discovering that Catholic Church in the South was quite different from the version in the North. A slight sense of cultural superiority began to creep into him, which he recognized as totally inappropriate. He could think of many things in which Northerners could not take pride. Still . . .

Tom and Josh celebrated New Year's Eve with Toby and Jeff. Josh outdid himself in the culinary department, and Toby in astonishment asked, "Do you eat like this every night?"

"Oh no, this is a very simple meal in comparison to our normal fare," Tom lied. "It's like having Julia Child in the kitchen every night. In fact I believe Josh could teach her a thing or two." Toby and Jeff began humming the theme to *The French Chef.*

"Pass the sauce béarnaise sauce, s'il vous plait," Toby said in a fake snobbish tone. "Oh, listen, before I forget. I just heard about a scholarship program offered by a local group that promotes good feelings between English-speaking nations. They pay for a local teacher to attend a seminar at Oxford University for the summer. Tom, you should apply."

"Why me? Aren't you interested?"

"Actually I thought about it, but I asked the head if I would get anything extra if I completed the program. Of course, the answer was an abrupt no. But I think the public schools do. So you should try. A summer at Oxford University. All that luscious English cuisine. Would get you away with all this tiresome French food."

"You really should look into it. Would be a great experience," Josh urged him.

"Josh, are you trying to get rid of me? Besides, I had planned to finish my last graduate class during the summer. The one class I need was not offered this fall."

"At least give it a shot. I might have to be in New Hampshire this summer anyhow. And I'm still not ready to introduce you to my open-minded family."

"I'll look into it."

On the Monday following, schools reopened, and Tom made the journey to Apopka. Driving up the Semoran Boulevard, he passed an amazing array of strip malls and car dealerships that had sprung up like mushrooms in the dark, all in response to the opening of Disney World. It was sprawl at its worst.

By now, James and Tom had become fast friends. James was often the recipient of snide comments and behind-the-back jibes, especially from Owen. The older faculty deeply resented these newcomers and reported horror stories about former colleagues now forced to teach in "those schools." Then they heard rumors that Phyllis Wheatley might be closed and consolidated with Apopka. "That means all those Nigras will be here along with those spics," Owen said rather loudly in the teachers' lounge. He wanted to make certain James heard him.

"I would love to return to Boston. At least the bigots pretty much kept it to themselves. I wish my parents had never decided to retire in Florida."

"Perhaps you could persuade them to move back."

"No, actually, they're pretty happy here. They've recently joined an Episcopal Church in Clermont and have a new group of friends. Apparently they are generally more liberal than most in the area."

"It must be a very small church then," quipped James.

"It is." They both laughed.

Both Tom and James had begun volunteering at the Migrant Center after school let out. They now taught young children how to begin reading. In reality, more important was getting them to speak fluent English. Sister Mary told them that they encourage the parents to use English at home rather than Spanish so their children would be able to succeed in school. Josh began volunteering there on Saturday mornings.

One Saturday afternoon, Josh returned late from his tutoring chores. "I had an interesting conversation with Sister Mary. She now knows you are a practicing homosexual and sleeping with me."

"How did she take that? Will she let us volunteer there anymore."

"No, she said she was delighted to hear it. And then I told her about my experience with Father Benson and my refusal to return to the

Catholic Church. Again she said she could not blame me but asked if I
had found a substitute spiritual home. I told her no but that I enjoyed
going to the Episcopal church with your parents."

"And?"

"Well, first she was very impressed that your parents were so
supportive. And she suggested that I give the Episcopal Church another
chance. She said they are very close to the Catholic ritual and, warning
me not to repeat this, that at least in Central Florida they had more of
a social presence than her church."

"Social as in the country club set?"

"Well, I guess that too. They do have a reputation. Apparently, they
always use the correct fork at dinner. But she said the previous bishop
was very much involved in supporting the civil rights movement, and
the current one has greatly increased social ministries. So I think we
should give them a try."

"Well, there's the one right down the street from where we live."

"From what I understand, that's the Republican Party at prayer.
Let's do some exploring if that's fine with you."

"I've gone to church all my life. I have no problem, just as long as
it's not some church where they speak in strange languages and roll
around on the floor."

That Sunday, they walked into the Episcopal cathedral in downtown
Orlando, ironically across the street from the Catholic cathedral. It was
faux Gothic with beautiful stained glass windows and an exceptional
choir, all those features that Tom missed. At first Josh seemed somewhat
nervous but quickly calmed. The dean had a strong Southern twang that
Tom found a little grating. He could never quite get over his Northern
prejudices.

The congregation was quite large, and Tom spotted quite a few
male couples. Obviously the church welcomed gay couples. (Tom had
taken his mother's injunction seriously.) The preacher was a younger
man whose message touched on the gospel as it related to some issues
of racial discrimination. Another positive in Tom's mind. At the end,
the preacher was obviously trying to suppress a smile. Since Josh and
Tom sat in the rear of the church, they could see what had amused him.
On the back pew sat four men, each holding up signs: 9.8, 7.2, 10, 2.3.
Tom doubted that this was a normal occurrence at the end of every
homily. The congregation then sang a final hymn, "Come Down, O

Love Divine," a hymn tune by Ralph Vaughn Williams. Tom wondered why the Catholic church could not have such beautiful music. If he heard another Palestrina Mass, he thought he'd choke. Since Vatican II, the Catholic Mass had begun to include hymns, but most were either borrowed from the Protestants or composed by those who knew nothing about music that could be sung.

At the end of the service, they were greeted by quite a few parishioners, especially a number of male couples who obviously shared a great deal with Tom and Josh. The welcome could not have been warmer.

"I say we return next week," Josh suggested.

"Agreed."

Easter came early that year, March 30. On the evening before, in what was called the Easter Vigil, both Tom and Josh were received into the Episcopal Church. They had gone through a crash course on how to be proper Anglicans. Both had been so enamored by their welcome, and Josh was so anxious to find a spiritual home, that they asked when could they be properly become Episcopalians. The dean worked with them so that they could be received, the term used to welcome former Roman Catholics into the church. Tom's parents drove over Sunday morning, and after the Easter service—Tom marveled at the fact that he had attended church twice that weekend—they all went to a local restaurant for a proper Sunday brunch. Tom had entirely too many Bloody Marys, and he received a scowl from his mother. He assured her that Josh would drive them home.

Two days later, Tom received word that he had been named the winner of the scholarship to the Oxford University summer program. Now he had to carry on with his regular job, finish his penultimate graduate course, and begin tackling the lengthy reading list he received from Oxford. On the one hand, overwhelmed; on the other, however, elated that he was about to spend three months at Oxford among the Dreaming Spires. Yet he also feared he was abandoning Josh, although Josh had already warned him that he needed to spend most of the summer in New Hampshire dealing with family business. His mother had become infirmed with Parkinson's disease; and he and his brother, despite the fact that they despised each other, had to carry the burden of the family business. Josh at times thought of just chucking the whole thing and give it all to his brother. But Josh realized that was exactly what his brother wanted, and he therefore refused to help him accomplish that. "In many ways this works out for the best. You'll be busy in the Bodleian, and I'll be dealing with dysfunction in Portsmouth. We'll both have glorious summers." Then he added, "My hope is that my brother and I can agree to split the company. I'd take the offices in the South, and sonny boy could have the North, which is the larger portion." Tom could not actually remember if he ever heard Josh's brother's real name. He had always been "sonny boy."

Tom also told Toby about his good luck. "You know I said I thought about applying for that scholarship, but once you told me you were interested, I decided not to compete with you," Toby claimed. "I didn't want to see you crushed."

"You're such a sport. But I thought you weren't interested because it would not get you any more money."

"Actually they would have made me headmaster, but I decided I didn't want the job."

The weeks that followed were hectic to say the least. Tom completed his graduate course; fortunately, the professor was not particularly demanding. At school he had to confront a set of angry parents who objected to the fact that their darling children had to read a book by a black man. Actually, the description of the author was often more insulting than that. Tom tried to explain to the parents that their children should be exposed to the broad variety of American literature. Apparently they believed the variety should stop with Caucasians, preferably males. The principal was not supportive at all and seemed to enjoy the heat Tom faced. The only solace he received came in the form of a black father who came in to thank him for including *Native Son* in the assigned readings. He said that he had read it himself. "I cried when that lawyer defended Bigger in court. I just pray my son can get a sense of pride out of that book." Tom almost cried himself and did take the time to write a note to Herr Higgins, the principal, about his meeting with the black father. Tom had had such high hopes when Higgins brought Sister Mary to discuss the migrant workers, but apparently Higgins was merely concerned about having their assistance with problem children. That was about as far as his liberality went.

Tom knew next year he would be able to teach one course on British literature since that was his first love. The teacher who had monopolized all those courses had decided to retire, and Tom was given the opportunity to teach a survey. He hoped the he might find some appropriate books by other than dead white men at the Oxford seminar.

James paid him a visit after school one day and thanked him for including the Wright book in his curriculum. "It meant a great deal to the black students here. It is really the first time they seemed to have been noticed."

"I also plan to use some of Phyllis Wheatley's poetry next year, if the conformity police allow it."

"That would be great because a number of our students used to attend that school. You're a real ally."

The glow of that support quickly wore off, when Owen accosted him in the faculty lounge and said loud enough for all the other teachers to hear, "So you got all our students upset because you had them read that nigger stuff. Next you'll require them to read something by a queer faggot." And then there were the papers and final examinations to grade.

At home, Tom already had begun to feel homesick. Josh had made a few trips to New Hampshire and stayed away a few nights. The bed seemed very cold, lonely, and big without him. They also made a few weekend trips to Tom's parents. Tom worried a lot that something might happen to them while he was gone. To add to their burdens, as new members of the cathedral, they had been persuaded to volunteer. Josh became an usher—Toby said they picked him because he was so handsome he'd attract all the queers into church. Tom found himself being trained to be a lector. "Typical of new converts; they fall into the miasma of church affairs. Pretty soon one of you will be off to seminary." Yet Toby and Jeff did accompany them a few times and seemed to like it. Toby pointed to the music as the chief attraction, "but a little too much incense for my taste."

On the other hand, Tom's parents thought the amount of incense was just fine. They had paid a visit a week before Tom was to leave for England. For the first time, they stayed in the extra bedroom; Clara complimented Josh on its décor. "Would she expect any less in a gay household?" Josh observed.

On Sunday, they all attended the cathedral and had lunch out. Tom's father picked up the check.

"My, a good deal more pageantry than at Saint Matthias. I loved the use of incense," Tom's mother observed.

"It is the cathedral, after all," explained Tom. "Somewhere in the Bible, it requires cathedrals to put on a big show. Although I understand that last Christmas, a woman wore a gas mask because the incense would be so thick."

"You're joking," his father said.

"Would I kid about something like that?"

"Well, we might be attending more often. Your mother and I are seriously thinking of moving to Orlando."

"Not anywhere near you two," Tom's mother hastily interjected.

"We really do like the folks at Saint Matthias, but in general, we find Clermont too small."

"Not Brookline, Massachusetts?" Tom asked.

"No, indeed. And we're concerned about medical care there. I won't want to have to depend on the hospital, for instance. So we're going to do some exploring here and, if we find what we want, move—"

"Well, you better wait until I get back from Oxford," Tom said, pinching himself mentally about where he was headed.

"Sure. I guess we really would need your help."

After the O'Mallys left, Josh seemed especially content. "Everything is falling into place. Most importantly, we found each other. And we have a close relationship with your parents, which should get even closer. I was thinking of asking them to adopt me."

Tom was not quite sure if Josh was joking or serious. "Well, that would mean we would be committing incest."

"Vice is nice, but incest is best, they always say. No, what I mean is that your parents have been more parenting to me than mine ever were. I don't think I have ever been in a better place as a result. And that starts with you. You made my life whole again. While the memory of what happened is still there, it ceased to have power over me. I no longer have that vision in my mind whenever we get naked together. And I've found a spiritual home. My faith means a great deal to me. Whatever happened back in that sacristy did not destroy that faith. God is more real to me than He ever was. I don't think you are as deeply religious as I am. And that's fine. But at least you share those experiences with me just like we share each other in bed. It will seem strange to say, but to me, they are an extension of each other."

"I think I understand," Tom inserted, "but I'm not quite there with you. But I'm happy to journey with you."

They sat together on the sofa and looked out over the lake. A full moon lit the entire scene.

Two days later, Josh left for Portsmouth. They vowed to keep in constant communication.

"I wish you could come over some time."

"I doubt if I can get away. I'm trying to make some major changes in the way things get done. I foresee some spectacular fights. When you get back, I know that things will be a lot different in my work life. I've dealt with a great many issues that needed correcting. This is the last frontier."

"You've been watching too many episodes of *Star Trek*."

The weekend before he would fly to London, he made a visit to his parents. They primarily wanted to talk about Josh and when he would return. "You seem more interested in him than your own dear son."

"We just don't want you to do something stupid and lose him. He's a real catch," his mother opined. "Someone that nice and handsome doesn't come around every day."

"Thanks for the vote of confidence," Tom said as he made an exaggerated frown.

His mother gave him a big huge. "You know you deserve someone that sweet."

He attended Saint Matthias with his parents and was greeted as if he was a longtime member of the congregation. The organist still played several wrong notes and the congregation sang on several different pitches. But the enthusiasm with which they sang the final hymn—"Praise, My Soul, the King of Heaven,"—made Tom feel that the angels in heaven could not do any better. His father looked at him, and they both raised their eyebrows, not a look of condemnation but one of appreciation for the spiritual gusto behind the dissonance.

Tom flew to London and spent a few days there before going to Oxford. He had not been outside the United States since he had traveled to Ireland with his parents or his college trip to Paris where he focused on the social scene rather than the cultural. He now acted like a kid in a candy store. He stayed in a B&B on Ebury Street, eating his dinners at the Ebury Wine Bar across the street until he discovered Poule au Pot. It was a bit more pricey, but all the waiters were from France and absolutely gorgeous. He knew that lusting in his heart was adultery, but he suspected that Josh was not above that either.

115

He also indulged in some London theatre. He saw *Much Ado about Nothing* at the Barbican, but also stooped to see *The Mousetrap* and *No Sex Please, We're British*. He regretted his decisions and vowed to see more Shakespeare.

Finally he took the Oxford Express to Oxford, getting off at the High Street stop as instructed, and made his way past Saint Mary the Virgin and the Radcliffe Camera, to the entrance of Exeter College. He registered and was shown his room, which he was told had previously been occupied by Tolkien. He wondered if Frodo Baggins had been invented there.

He loved the school at once. Most of his fellow students where either high school teachers or college professors. The conversation over dinner was always stimulating even though the food left much to be desired. Later, some of them discovered Brown's on Woodstock Road, where they would go from time to time for a real American-style hamburger. He attended lectures each morning and had a tutorial in the afternoon with an Oxford don. The topic was the twentieth-century English novel. He picked as his research project Kingsley Amis, whom he had only a passing knowledge of his writings. He was in absolute heaven.

The major drawback was that he missed Josh incredibly. They had a phone conversation every other evening, Josh complaining about dealing with his mother and brother, and Tom gushing over his love affair with Oxford. Tom was almost embarrassed by what a wonderful experience he was having.

"I wish you could take some time and come over. I could show you around Oxford, and we could rent a car and see some of the sights around here. Blenheim Palace is just a few miles away. And you get to drive on the wrong side of the road!"

"I wish I could, but there's no way I can get away right now. But you may have some visitors. Toby and Jeff said they might come see you at the end of your stay."

"That would be nice, but it won't be the same if you're not here too."

"We'll be back together soon enough in September. But that's the earliest I can get back to Orlando. Just in time for the lovebugs."

"The constantly-in-coitus. Boy, do I wish we were."

"Well, I'll have some exciting news for you at that time."

"Don't keep me in suspense. Tell me now."

"Can't. Not everything is fixed yet. But I think you'll like it. I still have a lot of thinking to do."

"That sounds mighty serious."

"It is. That's all I'll say for now."

"Okay, be that way. I love you anyhow."

In fact, during the last week of the program, Toby and Jeff did show up. They stayed at a B&B on the Iffley Road and enjoyed guided tours from the by-now expert on Oxford. Although the summer experience had been beyond his wildest imaginings, he could not wait to get back into Josh's arms again. Only a few more weeks.

"I have a suggestion, let's go to Brown's for dinner," Tom proposed to the weary travelers. "That's where a bunch of us go about once a week to escape the dreary Exeter cuisine. Then we can go out and get a drink at my favorite pub. Would you believe it, Oxford has its own bona fide gay pub."

"Ah, a break from bangers and mash or fish and chips. Sounds good to me," Toby observed. "And a pint or two of English ale would also hit the spot." He asked Tom the name of the pub and then remembered he had promised to call his parents. "They're worried that I'll get mugged by some husky English bloke. But no such luck so far. But there's still hope at that pub of yours," he quipped.

"Slut," was Jeff's rejoinder.

# Book Three

## ADAGIO LAMENTOSO

# Chapter 1

Tom looked at the clock; it was 5:30. The dry cleaner closed early on Fridays, and so he decided to listen to the voice message later. He was certain it was not his parents and that it was not an emergency. If it were urgent, there would have been three or four messages.

He drove to the cleaners, found it closed, and decided to stop at the Silver Hammer for a libation to the weekend. He discovered that on a Friday evening, the bar was much more crowded and livelier. Although he had often stopped there in the late afternoon after school, he had not been there normally in the evenings. If he went out at night, it was always to the Parliament House. Although he did not recognize any of the younger men, he was glad to see that now they outnumbered the old-timers who now tended to cluster in the corners, seemingly pushed out by the glamor of the younger men.

Tom purchased his normal glass of chardonnay and looked around at the prospects. He obviously felt the eyes of the potential contenders on him as well. Soon he engaged in conversation with an attractive man, perhaps a little older than Tom, but certainly a good candidate. Stuart suggested they have dinner together, and they withdrew to a nearby restaurant to share a meal. Afterward, they retired to Stuart's apartment and shared other things. Although invited to spend the night, Tom decided that he really needed to get a good night's sleep and begged off, promising to keep in touch.

When he got home, he noticed that the answering machine showed two messages waiting for him. He listened to the first, which was from Toby inviting him over to meet some friends. The second, also from

Toby, suggested that if he hurried, he could still meet a very interesting guy. Tom dialed Toby's number, but Jeff answered and told Tom he had missed out. "There was this guy whom you would have really liked. But they left. Perhaps you can meet him again some other time."

One Monday, Toby accosted Tom in the hallway. "Don't you ever pick up your messages? I called twice. I wanted you to meet this really neat friend of mine who had just moved back to Orlando from Jacksonville. A really cutie, and he's unattached." Toby emphasized the *and*.

"Well, sorry. But I was having an assignation with a cute guy who I met at the Silver Hammer. We had some good recreational activity at his place."

"Well, obviously it wasn't a sleepover because Jeff told me you called around eleven. Must have been a real quickie."

"Quiet. Barbara's coming down the hall." Tom had sighted her bright-red hair bobbing toward them.

"You two better start moving toward your classrooms. The final bell is about to ring." She pranced off down the corridor.

"You know she's really mad at you," Toby postulated, "because you haven't taken the bait."

"Toby, you're crazy. She has no interest in me whatsoever."

"That's because you're a faggot," he said in a whisper, "and you won't know a female flirtation if it bit you on the neck."

"Oooh, a hickey."

They both laughed as they each entered their respective classrooms across the hall from each other. Tom's students thought it was very strange to see their teacher in such a good mood. Mondays he normally stormed into the room with a pile of papers that almost glowed with red marks.

At lunch, Tom asked Toby about what he had missed on Saturday. "His name is Josh Simmons. He had been living in Orlando, but then I guess he got transferred to Jacksonville. How he lasted a year, I have no idea. Anyway, he just moved back and seems very lonely. He's handsome, he's rich, and he has a nice bulge in his trousers."

"Sounds promising. When can I meet him?"

"I think you missed your chance. A guy we met at the Parliament House was there. Syd, nice guy. They left together, and if I'm not mistaken, Syd followed Josh out of our parking lot and up Orange

Avenue. And I know for a fact that Syd lives in the opposite direction. I think Syd found out what that bulge was."

"Well, keep your eye out for another handsome, rich, bulgy kind of guy. I'd certainly be interested."

On Monday, the next week, Sister Alice called a department meeting to discuss the upcoming final examinations. As usual, the talk concerned grading, making certain that the little darlings are discouraged by low grades. "Most of you have been careful to encourage our students by recognizing their abilities. A few, however, are still entirely too harsh. For instance, Mr. O'Mally, you gave about a third of your students C or below. That is not acceptable."

"But, Sister," he said with a little too much politeness to be sincere, "C is an average grade. Thus, I gave two-thirds of my students above-average grades. On a normal curve, that would be entirely too high."

"Our students are not normal." *You can say that again, Sister,* he thought. "We have demanding entrance requirements so that our students are much better prepared than students in the public schools. Thus, they should expect much higher grades." Again, Tom thought, *No, our students are much wealthier, so they can afford our tuition.* He almost said this aloud but refrained. "So you need to keep that in mind when you do your grading. I've also noted that your examinations are entirely too difficult. Have you actually covered all that material?"

"Of course, Sister."

"They read all those novels?"

"Well, I can't guarantee that, but we certainly discussed all of them extensively in class. I'm fairly certain that those students who actually did read the books will do very well on the test."

"Are you accusing a third of your students of not reading the book?"

"I have no way of knowing. I don't install cameras in every student's house to check up on them."

Sister Alice scowled, "Don't get fresh with me." Tom felt as if he was back in Saint Timothy's elementary school for a moment.

At lunch, he told Toby about the exchange. "You'd better be careful with her. She holds a great deal of power. You know she always has one eye on you. That's because she has only one eye," he chuckled.

"All I know is that I have to get out of here. I am not certified to teach in the public schools. But I'm going to finish my graduate work. I plan to take two courses this summer."

"Have fun. I got mine, and I almost died of boredom."

"Why are you still here then?"

"Lethargy," Toby laughed.

Just then Barbara walked up to the table. She looked very stern. "Tom, you just should not talk to Sister in that tone. It's disrespectful and, frankly, could get you fired."

"Oh, they could never replace such a brilliant teacher as Tom. Oh, I forgot, they aren't looking for brilliance."

"Was that aimed at me?" snorted Barbara.

"Of course not, sweetie. Just a general observation." At that, Barbara marched away from them. "Good fashion sense," Toby observed. "Red dress of a shade that clashes with her red hair." Tom could not help but laugh. "Does she still want to get into your pants?"

"Oh, that ended a long time ago. In fact, I'm surprised she came over to the table. She's been avoiding me ever since the great debacle."

"Probably for the best," Toby suggested.

Tom did not feel like going straight home that evening, so he headed to the Parliament House. The place was almost as quiet as the Silver Hammer during the week. There was no show, and only a few men were on the dance floor. Most sat around the bar outside the theatre and chatted, obviously old-timers. A few younger men stood around the periphery of the bar, obviously looking for action. As Tom ordered his drink, he caught the eye of one of them, a particularly good-looking young man, probably a few years younger than Tom.

Tom walked over and stood next to him. "So are you from around here?" Tom asked, using one of the banal pickup lines, a clear signal of sexual interest.

"No, I'm from Baltimore. Down here for a conference. You?"

"I live here. What's the conference?"

The conversation continued in the vein as each downed several more drinks. Finally, the invitation was proffered to visit the man's room upstairs. By this time they had exchanged names. Tom agreed, "just as long as you keep the curtains drawn." His new friend asked what Tom meant, and he explained the shows that were often put on upstairs. Henry, that was his name, said he was no exhibitionist. They got drinks to go in paper cups and walked up to the second floor.

Tom woke up as light began streaming through the crack in the curtains. He rolled over and saw that there was a young man sleeping next to him. He tried desperately to remember the guy's name. With effort, he could remember talking to him in the bar and vaguely recalled coming up to his room. They must have had sex, but Tom could not recall it. He snuggled up to what's-his-name, but then began to worry about how light it seemed to be outside. He checked his watch and sat bolt upright. "Oh fuck! I'll be late."

The man next to him stirred and looked as confused as Tom felt. "I have to be at school at eight fifteen, and it's after seven now." He thought for a moment, deciding on a course of action. He had to go back to his apartment to change, which would mean he would get to school no earlier than nine. The best alternative was to call in sick. "Could you be very quiet? I need to make a phone call."

"Sure. What's wrong?"

"Got to make an excuse for missing school." He picked up the room phone, dialed nine for an outside line, then dialed the school.

"Good morning. Catholic High School. How may I direct your call?"

"Hi, Fran. This is Tom O'Mally. I've come down with a terrible stomach bug. I can't possibly make it in today. Could you please tell Sister Alice when she gets in please."

"Certainly, Mr. O'Mally. Hope you get well soon."

Tom hung up and saw that what's-his-name was walking toward the bathroom. "Gee, I got to get going also. The conference begins at nine." Tom admired the rear end as it moved away.

As the man started the shower, Tom poked his head into the bathroom. "Listen, I've got to go also. Had a great time last night. Glad we could hook up." He put on his clothes and walked out the door. *If only I could remember what that great time entailed*, he thought. As he drove toward his apartment, he passed a car going the other way. He saw Sister Alice driving, a look of recognition on her face.

The next morning as he walked to his classroom, he ran into Toby. "What happened to you yesterday?"

"Bad stomach bug."

"Yah, it's going around," as he walked off.

When Tom got to his own room, he saw Sister Alice standing outside waiting for him. "Why were you absent yesterday?" she asked in her best accusatory tone.

"I had a bad stomach bug. Couldn't keep anything down."

"Well, then what were you doing driving down Aloma yesterday morning if you were so sick?"

He panicked just for a second, just long enough to confirm Sister Alice's suspicions. "I had to go to the drugstore to pick up some medication my doctor prescribed."

"Well, I'm glad it worked," she said as she walked away, a cloud of suspicion trailing after her.

On Wednesday evening, Tom stayed home and watched a rerun of *Bonanza*. He always had a crush on Michael Landon. On Thursday, Tom decided to head for the Silver Hammer to see if he could get lucky. He downed several drinks in hopes of snaring something, but the only really attractive man there had other interests. After having stayed too long, Tom headed home.

The next day, he ran into Toby in the hall. "You look terrible. Have you been burning the candle at both ends?"

"No, still getting over the bug."

He had decided to visit his parents that weekend because the next week were finals, and he would have to spend the next weekend grading. He drove to Clermont taking nothing with him so that he could devote his attention to his parents. When he entered their house, the first words out of his mother's mouth were "You look terrible. Are you getting enough sleep?" Again Tom blamed his stomach problems. "Did you see a doctor?"

"No, it was just one of those twenty-four-hour versions. I'm much better now."

"Well, you don't look it."

That weekend, Tom helped his father fix a stubborn sliding door onto the patio and volunteered to come over during the summer to do some painting. His parents peppered him with questions about his job, what he did for entertainment, but most frequently about whom he had dated. His mother seemed particularly concerned about the last item. Tom had learned long ago how to be extremely vague, revealing no substance, while appearing to be very forthcoming. "Mom, I'm so busy with work that I only get a chance to date occasionally. And there aren't many single women around that interest me, frankly. Orlando's not Boston, where there are lots of well-educated women." He was really just making this up since he had not really looked much into the quality of single women in Orlando.

"What about at your school? They can't all be married."

"Well, there is this one teacher in my school that I took out once. Her name's Barbara."

"Oh, yes, you mentioned her once before."

"We didn't really hit it off. And besides, the school discourages romantic attachments among the faculty."

"What do the priests expect, that all the faculty be as sexually frustrated as they are?" his father asked snidely.

"Now, Mike."

This reference to clerical celibacy got his father off on one of his tirades about the Catholic Church. He had a pet theory that all the priests and nuns had sex together. He was not nearly as religious as his wife; the fact of the matter was that although the family went through all the appropriate Catholic hoops, they were not nearly as inwardly devout as some families. Thus, on Sunday, Tom accompanied his parents to Mass, but it was clear to him that they had not developed any close friends there. Afterward, they went to Denny's for the breakfast buffet, and his mother mentioned how uninspiring the church was in comparison to their previous church in Brookline. Tom wondered just how happy his parents were and if they thought they had made the right decision to move to Florida.

The next week, final examinations tethered Tom to his desk. He carefully graded each exam without looking at the student's identity, which they recorded on the exam with their student identification number. He did not want to be accused of favoritism, and in fact, the temptation to downgrade certain students might be too great if he knew their names. In general, he could guess the students' identities anyhow because of the quality of their essays. One student in particular, Brad, had been hard tackled too often to have more than mush for brains, Tom concluded. He could always guess that Brad had written one particular exam because of the number of non sequiturs. Brad clearly had not read one assignment or listened to one class discussion. He clearly deserved to fail the class, but because he was a hero on the football squad, that was not an acceptable outcome. So Tom assigned him a D for the exam and the course. Later, after he had turned in his final grades, the headmaster called him in to explain that Brad could not get a D, since that would make him ineligible to play football next season. "So I have changed his grade to a C."

"But, sir, that is certainly not fair to the other students who actually read the books and did the assignments. Brad did absolutely no work at all."

"For your future information, football takes precedence over academics. You should know that by now. It's what brings the alumni back and the donations flowing." Rarely had he heard the headmaster so honestly frank. Thoroughly demoralized, Tom decided to swallow his troubles in the Silver Hammer.

Thus further encouraged to seek a change in his career path, Tom signed up for two graduate courses, which meant he had two three-hour classes for each course. Although the course assignments did not overwhelm him, he found the readings numbingly boring. Most of the "principles of excellence," anyone with the least bit of common sense could figure out without paying high tuition costs. Yet it seemed a means of escape worth the drudgery.

On weekends, he often met Toby and Jeff at the Parliament House. They would enjoy the drag show, but when it began to get late, Tom would excuse himself to begin the prowl. Occasionally he hooked up with someone he had bedded previously, although whenever anyone said that he loved him, the affair would come to a quick halt. He really enjoyed picking up someone new. *Variety is the spice of life*, he thought. He generally did not like bringing them back to his apartment, preferring to go to their place instead. He often hinted broadly that he had someone at home, and he was out for a quick one. When the shoe was on the other foot, however, he would relent about going to his apartment if the gentleman in question, who was presumably partnered, was hot enough. Monogamy did not seem to be a major value among the men who hung out at the Parliament House.

On the occasions he did not meet up with Toby and Jeff, Tom would go to the Silver Hammer; and as he became more confident, he also went to Southern Nights, despite the patrol car sitting prominently outside. One Saturday evening, after several glasses of white wine, Tom pulled out of the parking lot; and within a block, a revolving blue light pulled him over. "Your driving was rather erratic. I'll need to see license."

Tom normally tried to pace himself, but that night, he had become involved with a veteran about the merits of the war in Vietnam and apparently had more than usual for him.

"Mr. O'Mally, I suspect that you are over the limit for safe driving and need to give you a sobriety test." He continued to explain what would happen if he refused to take the test and the consequences of flunking it. He started to order Tom out of his car but then paused. "O'Mally. Are you the guy who teaches at Catholic High School?"

"Yes, sir, I am."

"Oh." He paused. "So you taught Nancy Miller this semester?"

"Yes, sir, I did."

"She just loved your class. Said you were the finest teacher at Catholic by far. She told me you were a real hard -ass, and she got one of the few As you handed out."

"She's an exceptionally bright young woman. She earned that grade."

"Well, thank you. Actually, she got her mother's brains." He again paused. "Listen, Mr. O'Mally. I'm going to forget our stop here. You don't seem that impaired not to be able to get home. Just make certain in future you limit your intake of alcohol or arrange for someone to drive you home. Good night, sir."

Tom could not believe his luck. He had been too intoxicated to drive. What's more, he had pulled over outside a gay bar. What were the chances he would have driven away rather spending some time in jail? Now if Brad's father had been the cop, Tom knew he would have ended up in the state penitentiary at Raiford.

He found he had some difficulty focusing on his schoolwork. Lacking sufficient sleep to concentrate in class, he had even more trouble getting his assignments completed. His first paper for Philosophy of Education class received a C. He determined to stay in at nights and to get more sleep, but it was easier said than done. That next weekend, he ran into Toby and Jeff at the Parliament House.

"Tom, you look terrible."

"That's the greeting you give me every time you see me."

"That's because you always look terrible. You need to stop burning your candle at both ends. And stop drinking so much." He noticed how quickly Tom downed his gin and tonic.

"What, do you think I have an alcohol problem?"

"Not sure, but the signs aren't encouraging." Tom was about to walk away, when Toby changed the subject. "Look, there's Syd over there. You never did meet him, did you, Tom?"

"No, didn't you have a party a few months ago that I missed?"

"Yes, we met Syd here and took him in. He had just moved to Orlando from up north. He met another friend of ours, Josh Andrew. They dated for a while, but Syd broke it off. Said that Josh was a psycho and dumped him. Actually I had thought of getting you together with Josh, but it's a good thing I didn't."

The three of them went to the show. Afterward, Tom excused himself. "I have a paper due next week that I have to work on." For the first time that week, he got a good night's sleep.

The next morning, he skipped church and got to work on the paper, "The use of evaluation means other than testing." He had checked out a pile of books from the school library the previous Friday and worked on it all morning. As a gift for his hard work, he sat out by the community pool that afternoon reading a Robert Ludlum novel, *The Matlock Paper*. He hoped that none of his colleagues from school would see him, since they all thought he read nothing but Victorian novels. He did not want to disabuse that myth.

For the next two weeks, he limited his excursions to the Silver Hammer to once a week. He got more sleep, and the next two papers in Philosophy of Education received As.

He did make a trip to Playalinda, thinking he might have some beach fun. The temperature was unbearable. He made the mistake of taking off his scandals when he entered the beach, and he almost scorched his feet. There were very few people on the beach; and taking a dive into the ocean, he found the water temperature to be more suited to a bathtub. After a half hour, he gave up, drove home, and completed more of his assignments.

He stayed fairly focused on his schoolwork and his Ludlum novel, only venturing out once a week. He had promised to visit his parents in August before the beginning of school. Since neither of his graduate classes had a written final examination, instead requiring a term paper, he planned his work around his parental visit. The prior Thursday night, however, he took a break and went to his favorite haunt, the Silver Hammer. There he met a nice young man, invited him home, and bedded him. The next morning, he awoke with cotton in his mouth and a raging hangover. That still did not prevent him from coupling with the young man who awoke next to him, although he mistakenly called him Bill when his real name was Otis.

That evening, he drove to Clermont, greeted at the door by his mother. "Tom, you look terrible. Are you getting any sleep?"

"Mom, I'm taking two graduate courses, and so sleep is at a premium."

"Well, a master's degree is not worth dying over. I guess you don't have any time to date now."

That was the last time that his mother brought up the subject of matrimony during this visit. She had not, however, given up. Otherwise, the weekend was very restful. They discussed various relatives, reminisced about life back in Boston, and recollected trips they had enjoyed together, especially the two-week trip they took to Ireland when Tom was fifteen. "Remember your father trying to kiss the Blarney Stone and almost fell?"

"He never really needed any help with the gift of gab in the first place."

"Now don't get cheeky, son," his father scolded with a fake Irish accent.

"I guess I should admit this," his mother remarked, "but I truly loved seeing the English Cathedrals, especially Wells and Salisbury, when I was there as a girl. I thought the new Catholic cathedrals like Westminster were ugly in comparison. And they're never going to finish it."

"Which reminds me, son. Your mother and I have been attending the local Episcopal church here of late."

"But you're lifelong Catholics. What brought this on?"

"Well, it's complicated. First, we don't much like the priest here. If you thought Father Sullivan was a problem, this one's far worse."

"The few times I went with you, I certainly agree. I didn't find him particularly scintillating."

"Then there is the issue of the Migrant Laborers Ministry. We read about a group of nuns in Apopka who have begun a ministry to the migrant workers and their families. We read about the terrible conditions they live under and wondered how we could help out. Remember we volunteered at the food pantry and the soup kitchen in Boston? Well, we talked to Father O'Brien, and he discouraged us. Told us that the bishop didn't approve of their ministry. He said they should be focusing on anti-abortion efforts and, as he called it, the scourge of homosexuality. I told him the scourge of poverty and discrimination was far worse."

131

Tom perked up immediately when he heard that. "Well, that did it for your mother. She hadn't made any real friends there and actually had met some people from the Episcopal church. So we tried it out and liked it very much. So we've stayed."

"And I just love to sing their hymns," his father added. "Much better than ours by a long shot." Both his mother and his father had lovely singing voices, which Tom had to admit was lost in singing the normal Catholic hymns. Congregational singing had only recently been introduced in the Catholic service, and his mother always commented how bad they sounded. "And some of their members are involved in the immigrant workers ministry, working alongside those Catholic nuns."

"But you're Irish Catholic. You're supposed to hate everything English because of the way they treated Ireland."

"Well I've been doing some research at the library," his mother chimed in. "It wasn't the Anglicans who massacred the Irish. It was the Calvinists! If you remember your European history," she lectured, "it was Oliver Cromwell and then William of Orange who invaded Ireland, and they were both Calvinists." Tom shook his head in agreement, knowing full well that his mother was just rationalizing and ignoring much of the historical antagonisms between Ireland and England.

So Tom accompanied his parents to the Episcopal Church. They were quite right about the friendliness of the small congregation, especially the elderly priest who conducted the service. Although the service followed the same pattern as the Catholic Mass, he had some difficulty following along in what was called *The Book of Common Prayer*. He always found the Catholic Missal somewhat confusing, but he felt that authors of the Episcopal service book had gone to considerable lengths at obfuscation. His mother, however, was quite used to the book, which seemed remarkable since they had only recently become Episcopalian. "No, it's here," she would command, leafing quickly through the pages to the correct spot. "It's quite logical." Tom, however, did not quite agree.

He did appreciate the sermon on the section in Matthew where Jesus calms the waters for the disciples. The rector talked about the current political turmoil revolving around the Watergate hearings. He talked about the importance of calm in these troubled times, and he compared the calm deliberations in Congress with the agitation coming out of the White House. It surprised Tom that such a sermon would be preached in the midst of the Bible Belt in what normally would be Nixon Territory. Afterward, his mother explained, "Oh, they're remarkably liberal here, considering we're in Central Florida." He then remembered that many in the congregation had become involved in the ministry for migrant workers, the effort that originally attracted his parents to the church in the first place. "It's a little liberal oasis in a desert of conservatives," she continued. Although Tom had heard no diatribes against abortion or gays at his church in Winter Park, he certainly had not heard any clarion calls for liberal activism either.

What impressed Tom the most was the singing. While the choir left a great deal to be desired and the organist did commit a few errors, at least the small congregation sung with gusto. He immediately recognized the opening hymn as based on a tune by Bach, the fugue in $E^b$ major, commonly known as the St. Anne fugue. In fact, at the bottom of the music score was the designation St. Anne tune with words by Isaac Watts. "Oh God our help in ages past, our hope for years to come." Tom's mother afterward remarked with what gusto her son had begun to sing halfway through the hymn. For the first time in quite a while, Tom had enjoyed going to church.

The following week, Tom completed the two papers due for his graduate courses. He was quite confident that they both were excellent papers, which would mean he would retain his 4.0 grade point average. To celebrate on Friday, he went off to Parliament House, ending the evening by accompanying two other men back to one of their apartments. Tom did not normally engage in group sex. Someone always got shunt to the sidelines. But as he recalled, this engagement was particularly satisfying, although with the amount he had to drink, some of it remained in a haze. He drove home Saturday around noon and slept it off.

On Monday, he returned to Catholic to get his room in order for the beginning of the school year. He worked on some lesson plans, which he had to rework after Sister Alice said he could not do a unit on black authors. "Too controversial. Parents won't approve."

*And they would remove their precious children along with their tuition money*, Tom thought.

Again, the following weekend, Tom frequented the bars. Friday night, he spent at the Hammer; and Saturday, he returned to the Parliament House, in hopes of reuniting with his friends from the previous Saturday. He did not see either, instead spending his time with Toby and Jeff.

"I haven't seen you around school yet. Letting everything go to the last minute?" Tom asked.

"Well, I have something to tell you. You know I've been thinking about getting out of Catholic."

"So have I. That's why I doubled up on my courses this summer."

"Well, actually I have found a new position. I'm starting at Winter Park High. One of their history teachers died suddenly, and I had my application in already, so they called me."

"Oh, crap. I thought you said you were too lazy to look for another job. Who am I going to eat lunch with?"

"Barbara, of course."

"Bitch."

"And I had enough of this place after I got reamed out by the headmaster, or really the master of the toilet, about turning in a student on the baseball team for plagiarism. Father Shit-for-Brains said I had no proof even though I showed him the book Andy copied several paragraphs from. The head insisted it was just a coincidence and dropped the charge. That was the final straw."

Toby's departure cast a pall over Tom's work at Catholic. The school year began with the usual lecture from the headmaster, although at least Tom was not singled out for reprimand. He did have another run-in with Sister Alice about some of his recommended readings for his students. "I think seniors can handle *Sister Carrie*." Apparently, however, Catholic schools cannot teach about fallen women, and she disqualified his choice. Ironically, Barbara, who had overhead the conversation, whispered to him, "Sister probably would think Nancy Drew or the Hardy Boys would be too controversial." Although Barbara seemed to be sympathetic, he did not trust her to keep confidentialities the way he used to trust Toby.

The next week, Tom noticed some redness on his penis. At first he thought it was a wayward pimple—he still would get one occasionally—but it became bigger and seemed to be turning into a rash. Worried, he called Toby, the only one he knew he could trust if it was what he suspected. Toby gave him the name of a doctor that many gay men used, especially if certain problems existed.

Dr. Anderson, an obviously effeminate man, tut-tutted the entire visit. He said that he had to report the incident to the health department and asked the name of his partner. "I don't remember either of their names." Anderson's eyebrows shot up over his forehead. "Actually I don't think we even introduced ourselves before we climbed into bed." At this point, Tom was just trying to goad Anderson. He had succeeded. Anderson gave him a lecture about the use of condoms and avoiding promiscuity. Tom figured that Dr. Anderson had in his practice quite a few promiscuous men who did not use condoms but needed treatment. Probably they provided a large portion of his income. Anderson himself, Tom thought unkindly, did not attract enough men to contract a venereal disease.

Shortly thereafter, Tom received a strange telephone call from Toby, asking to see him. Tom suggested the Parliament House, but Toby asked if he could come over to see him at his apartment. When he arrived, he had a rather somber look on his face. Tom wanted to ask Toby how he liked his new job but was never given the opportunity.

"Tom, I'm really worried about you. I don't want to seem like I'm lecturing you, but I need to get some things off my chest." Tom knew he was in for a lecture. "You have not looked well for some time, and I suspect you got some unwelcome news at the doctor's."

"You are right there."

"You seem to go out to the bars almost every night."

"That's an exaggeration," Tom interjected, although he had to admit to himself it was somewhat close to the truth.

"Well, the number of times you came to school during the week last year with an obvious hangover seems to belie that remark." Toby now seemed somewhat angry. "You've got to pull your life together."

"Is this an intervention?"

"If you like, yes. Tom, I'm your friend. I admire you and like you very much. I hate to see what you are doing to yourself. You should know that there was talk last spring that some in the administration thought you should be fired. You are on a tether. Not only do they suspect that you drink too much, but Sister Alice is convinced you are a homosexual. And she hates faggots, as she calls them. Us."

Tom did not realize such talk existed. He was the hail fellow well met, a man who always had a smile and a joke.

"I know this is going to sound weird, even insulting, but have you ever thought about going to a counselor? Perhaps you could get some help straightening yourself out. Oh, I don't mean it that way. You know what I mean," he said in exasperation.

"Perhaps you're correct. That rash was a wake-up call, to say the least. And I'm getting tired of waking up in the morning next to a man or two that I really don't know and have trouble recollecting the wonderful time we had the night before. When I can't even remember if I came or not . . ." He trailed off.

"Listen, Tom," Toby jumped in. "You're a terrific guy. You just need to get a grip on yourself. That's why I suggest you go talk to someone."

"Well, who do you suggest?"

"I can't be of any help there, I'm afraid. I suppose you will have to let your fingers do the walking through the Yellow Pages."

That in fact was what Tom did. He looked through the phone book. He knew he wanted a male therapist, preferably someone closer to his age. He actually hoped to find a gay one, although that description never appeared in the advertisements. Finally he found a man who seemed to fit the description and, from his photograph, certainly could bat on his team. So he called Doug Rogers to get an appointment.

Rogers had his practice in a small office building on Michigan Avenue. Tom had to fill out some paperwork before being admitted into what could pass for a Hollywood set for a psychiatrist's office, complete with lounge chair and boxes of Kleenex scattered around the room. Rogers asked some questions about Tom's background and then allowed Tom to launch into his story. Tom started slowly, not filling in all the details, and continued to get more detailed as he received encouragement from the counselor. Finally, everything flowed out: gayness, orgies, venereal disease, the works.

After Tom had completed his saga, Rogers smiled benevolently at him. "Although your lifestyle disgusts me, I believe I can help you." At that point, Tom discovered that Doug Rogers was a Christian therapist of the evangelical type. He assured Tom that if he prayed to Jesus, he would be converted into a solid heterosexual with the praises of Jesus on his lips. At the end of the session, Doug asked if Tom wanted to set up the next appointment. Tom said his schedule was very full right now with the beginning of school, but he would call to set something up.

On the way out the door, Doug handed Tom the King James Version of the Bible and told him to read certain verses in Leviticus.

He told Toby about the whole sorted mess, but Toby only urged him to try again, perhaps asking some questions over the phone before making a firm appointment.

The next appointment was with a woman, Helen Smith, which turned out to be a better experience although with an unexpected punch line. After Tom had gone through his litany of horrors, which took an entire hour, Helen asked to see him the following week. Dutifully, immediately after school, he drove to Altamonte to discover his fate. "Tom, I know that all your life you have been attracted to men, that you regard yourself as gay. My sense, however, is that you are what some call bisexual. That is, you can function sexually with men and women."

"But I did go to bed once with a woman, and I could do nothing."

"I'm sure that you had anticipated that you could not, so you couldn't. Frankly, if you found a good match, you would be able to function sexually without any problem at all. All you need to do is find the right woman."

Tom was quite skeptical about her theories. Yet the idea of marriage began to worm its way into his thoughts. If for no other reason, he could prove he was "heterosexual." And perhaps if he was careful, he could slip away from time to time to satisfy that other part of his sex drive, which he was convinced no amount of female companionship could alter.

# Chapter 2

Tom refused to hang out in straight bars in a quest to meet women. He had gone to one of the bars attached to the ABC liquor stores but found that most of the women there he would not take home to his mother. That had become his only real criterion. He also looked at the unattached women at church. Actually there were very few of them that would do. Either they were too young, too old, or too married with children. He did attend a few of the young people events sponsored by the church but had been frightened off by an extremely anxious young woman whom he found neither intellectually nor physically attractive.

He held strong reservations about whether this plan would lead to a transformation. Toby could not help laughing when Tom told him the counselor's advice. Nevertheless, Tom thought it worth a try. If what Toby said was true about the rumors at Catholic, he could not take chances. He had heard about a young teacher in the English department who was seen being very affectionate with another man. The school dismissed him unceremoniously without ascertaining if anything illicit had actually happened. Tom had taken chances being out in public places identified with known homosexuals. He had not worried too much because even students whom he taught last year would not be old enough to go to the Parliament House or the Hammer. Even if Tom ran into a former student, that student would unlikely claim to have seen him in the bar because he too would be labeled as queer.

The one good outcome to Tom: he spent a great deal less time in the bars than he had previously. Perhaps once a week he would go either to the Parliament House or the Silver Hammer for a libation and, with any luck, some action. He had found his teaching load had increased because he had been given two advanced literature courses, and to his surprise, the students seemed eager to learn. On top of that, the professor in his next education course dealing with legal issues really did expect his students to do some serious work. As a result, Tom reduced his bar time significantly.

Since Toby had bailed to a public school, Tom did find himself spending more time around Barbara. She had avoided them mainly because of Toby's rather caustic attitude toward her. She had apparently pretty much forgotten the debacle of their one and only date. She had resigned herself that she and Tom would just remain friends.

As a result, they often had lunch together. He discovered that she was not as much the sycophant to the school's powers as he thought. She expressed open criticism of some members of the English department and their antiquated notions about literature. Tom told her that Sister Alice had forbidden him to use some black poets and *Sister Carrie*.

"She did not want me to teach *The Scarlet Letter* because a clergyman was involved," Barbara exclaimed.

"I knew it! I thought to myself she won't approve. She must think that sex does not exist."

"That's because she's never tried it." Tom could not believe these words were coming out of Barbara's mouth.

"Now, Barbara, she did take a vow of celibacy."

"With men. I'm sure she'd stay clear of those nasty creatures. But I'm not so sure about women."

"Barbara, I'm shocked," Tom said in mock horror.

"I won't be if I were you. No telling what goes on in the convent." They both laughed.

"And I bet most of the priests are perverts as well," she continued. Tom winched at that comment but kept his own counsel. He wanted to ask her what she thought about gay people but decided against it.

On Thursday evening, Tom called his parents to see if they wanted to have him visit. "Oh, I'm sorry, son, this is not a good weekend." That really puzzled Tom since normally they pestered him to visit and then complain they have nothing to do. "Your father has been doing some carpentry work for the nuns and wants to complete the job this weekend."

"Do they know you're lapsed Catholics who attend a heathen church?"

"Oh, they know and don't care. Sister says she'll get help anywhere she can find it, even from Episcopalians."

"Well, we could just have a visit. Gossip about relatives."

"Sorry. This Saturday I'm committed to work with young children on their reading. And . . . next week's pretty busy as well. Let's make it for two weekends from now." Tom agreed and concluded that his parents were not that unhappy after all.

Instead, on Saturday evening, he went to the Parliament House and met up with Toby and Jeff. He bought one gin and tonic and nursed it all evening. Toby wanted to say something but decided it was best to leave it. Miss P was in fine shape, if increasingly inebriated as customers passed her free drinks. After the show, the trio ran into Syd, who obviously had been stalking the patios. Tom decided that the temptation to order another drink was building, so he decided to leave. As he walked out, Syd ran up to him and suggested that they go home together. Although Tom was not particularly attracted to him, he agreed, and they went back to Tom's apartment.

When he awoke the next morning, he thought that this was perhaps the first time in quite a while he recalled the name of the man sleeping next to him, remembered the sex they had shared, and did not have a splitting headache. There was something to be said for abstinence.

After breakfast at Denny's, Syd explained what a wonderful time he had had and hoped that they could get together again soon. Tom always had a bad time telling someone that he really was not interested, so he said, "Sure. Can't the next two weekends, but perhaps we can work out something later." Clearly Syd was not boyfriend material. When Tom asked him what books he had read recently, a standard question he asked anyone as a sorting technique, Syd said he never had time to read because he enjoyed too many television shows. Tom did not ask him to enumerate them, since he was sure Syd would list *Hawaii Five-O*, which he detested, and not mention *Bonanza* in reruns.

Tom had the next weekend open, and he began thinking about where he should go. He certainly did not want to run into Syd at the Parliament House. The decision took care of itself. On Monday, Barbara approached him in the teachers' lounge. "If you don't have any plans for this weekend, I was wondering if you'd like to see a play with me. I have two tickets for *Mame* at the Municipal Auditorium, but my sister can't come, so I thought you might enjoy seeing it."

In fact, Tom had seen the original production with Angela Lansbury on a trip to New York. But he was so flattered by the invitation, he accepted. It turned out, however, to be a huge disappointment. Tom figured that the cast was not the first or even the second touring troupe but third at best. Tom never heard of the actress who played Mame, although Barbara assured him that she was well-known on daytime television. The stage was not raked, and the auditorium floor was flat so that it could also serve as a basketball court. To make matters worse, a woman with a blond Southern Baptist bouffant wearing a towering feathered hat sat right in front of him, essentially blocking his view of the stage. He politely asked her if she could remove her hat, explaining that he could not see the stage. She merely huffed and said that he would just have to look around her. He almost asked her what her natural hair color was forty years ago, but Barbara rapped him in the ribs, foreseeing a scene.

In reality he did not miss much. The voices of the actors were not up to Broadway standards, and the acoustics were so bad it was impossible to hear them anyhow. There was no live orchestra, just music piped over the loudspeakers. But the audience gave them a long standing ovation. *Obviously they've never seen a real play on Broadway*, Tom thought haughtily.

"Oh, wasn't that terrific! Although I'm really sorry you had trouble seeing."

*And hearing, and staying awake*, he thought.

"The touring companies that come to Orlando are always terrific. This show was probably the best. But I've always wanted to go to a show on Broadway. Have you ever been?"

"Well, actually, yes. Every year for my birthday, my parents took me to New York to see the sights. We went to the Metropolitan Museum of Art, saw the show at the Radio City Music Hall, had lunch at the Automat, but the biggest treat was always the matinee of a Broadway show."

"Oh, tell me what you saw."

Tom did not dare mention *Mame*. "Well, we saw my favorite of all, *My Fair Lady*, with the original cast. My father said he had to mortgage our house to get those tickets. We also saw *The King and I* and *High*

*Society*. We did it for about ten years, so there were others. I guess my other favorite was *West Side Story*."

"You said you ate at the Automat. What's that?"

*Clearly civilization has not reached the South*, Tom thought. "Horn & Hardart. You go in, get a table, and there are small boxes, like mailboxes, with windows so you can see the food. Then you put some change in, the door unlocks, and you take out your apple pie. We jokingly called it Horn and Heartburn."

Barbara looked very puzzled. "Well, we usually go to Morrison's Cafeteria."

"Probably the same type of food. Generally bad."

"Oh, no, it's quite good."

Tom knew that the general quality of restaurants in Orlando were usually quite poor. "Who do you go with?"

"My parents. I'm originally from Orlando. A Florida cracker. They have a house in Altamonte."

"How nice. Well, I want to thank you again for a nice evening. Guess I'll see you at the pleasure palace."

"We should do this again sometime."

"Yes, Barbara. Again, thank you." They walked to their respective cars and drove home alone. Tom considered stopping at the Hammer but thought better of it.

The next weekend, he made his long postponed trip to Clermont. His parents excitedly told him about their various projects for the migrant workers, and his father insisted on driving him over to the center to show him his handiwork. His father had always been handy with tools and buzz saws, and obviously those skills had not diminished with age. In fact, Tom thought his father actually looked healthier than he had when he first moved to Florida. His mother lamented the fact that she had to give up her normal tutoring with the migrant children in order to visit with her son. Tom could not quite tell if she was serious. After complaining about the lack of support from the diocese for the migrant ministry, she then switched subjects.

"Are you still going to school on top of everything else?"

"Oh, yes, Mom. I can't wait to get a job in the public schools. Catholic is not interested in educated students, just collecting tuition money."

"Well, I suppose school interferes with your social life."

"And the production of grandchildren," Tom added.

"Now don't get cheeky. I'm just thinking of your happiness. You need companionship. As it says in the Bible, man should not live alone, although where it says it, I'm not sure."

"Is that even in the Bible? Well, you'll be happy to learn that I was on a date last weekend."

"First time? What's her name? Is it serious?"

"Calm down, Mother. Her name is Barbara, and we've been out twice. I mentioned her before." He did not go into any details about the first debacle. "We went to a play at the Municipal Auditorium."

"Was it dreadful?"

"Pretty much." He told her about the blonde with the hat. "It was not quite the Shubert or even Radio City Music Hall."

"Well, tomorrow will be interesting. At coffee hour, we are going to hear one of the assistant priests from the cathedral."

"The Catholic Cathedral in Orlando?"

"Of course not, dear, the Episcopal one. He's a retired military man who is going to talk to us about why the Vietnam War is immoral."

"Here in Clermont? He'll be lynched."

"Well, not in our church. We are a liberal oasis surrounded by Southern Baptists, Pentecostals, and Nixonites." She repeated her litany of horrors. "Most of our members are there because they don't agree with most of our neighbors on just about anything."

"You can take the woman out of Boston, but you can't take the Boston out of her," Tom observed.

"That's for sure," commented his father, who had been largely silent during this exchange.

The next morning, they went off for church, listened to strong argument against the war at the coffee hour, heard an equally rousing sermon about the importance of racial justice, and sung joyfully and with gusto, although seriously discordant hymn at the end. The organist then played the Bach fugue in G minor on the electronic organ, missed rather more notes than was decent. The sour notes, however, could not obliterate the sheer *joie de vivre* exhibited by that congregation. He had rarely seen such fervor in any Catholic service he had attended. Tom and his parents retired home, where his mother had prepared a roast leg of lamb, Tom's favorite.

"Now if you want to bring Barbara over to meet us, that's fine. You can both stay in the guest room, or if you're shy, you could sleep on the sofa."

"Mother."

"Oh, don't be silly. You are twenty-six and, I'm sure, no longer a virgin."

"Mother!"

"Son, you're also too old to blush." It was as if she was trying to torture him, and it was clearly working.

Monday brought more misery. After school, he met with the mother of one of his problem students. Carl had sat in the back of the class absolutely refusing to participate. He claimed that "these dumb novels" had no practical purpose. He claimed to be going into his father's business once he left school and did not care about Stephen Crane. Actually Tom did not care much for Crane either, but those gods who determined the canon required the assignment of *The Red Badge of Courage.*

His mother, outfitted with a towering bouffant, which seemed to be the compulsory dress code, expressed her distress that her son received a D for his test on Crane. "I'm sorry to tell you, but your son clearly did not read the book. He was fortunate that I did not give him a failing grade."

"That is pure nonsense. I saw him reading the book every night myself. If you don't change his grade, I'll go to the headmaster."

"Go right ahead. I'm sure he'll back me up."

Of course, he did not. He told Tom to raise the grade to a least a B. Tom showed him the paper, and the principal relented and allowed Tom to change it to a C+. Tom became more determined than ever to get a public school job.

He told Barbara about his confrontation with the parent and the headmaster. "I know how frustrating this can be," she reassured him, "but I know for a fact that the school is concerned about staying afloat and wants to hold on to every tuition-paying student. The bishop has been less than generous."

"Oh, I know. We got a big plea two Sundays again at Margaret Mary's to pitch into a special collection to build a new and improved residence for his eminence."

"We did as well."

Tom also remembered what his mother said about support for the migrant workers. "And also my mother said the diocese is not providing any support for the migrant workers ministry. I never heard that mention at Mass either. Must all be going to the manse."

"Well, I'm glad no money is going to those sisters. I understand they are a bunch of socialists."

Tom decided not to pursue that line of discussion, fearful he would become a go-between for Barbara and his mother. Then Barbara added, "Why don't we go out for dinner this weekend. You've never been to Morrison's, have you?" Tom admitted that he had not and agreed to give it a chance. He later regretted that he had. This time, he insisted he would pay.

Morrison's was every bit as bad as he feared. Afterward, he suggested that at some time it might be fun to go to Disney World before the winter crowds arrived. "It's been open a year now, and I've read they've gotten most of the bugs out. I love roller coasters and want to ride Space Mountain. And the Haunted Mansion looks neat." Tom allowed his enthusiasm to display.

"Are you serious? That's for kids, not grown adults."

"Well, perhaps I haven't grown up yet, or at least refuse to admit it."

"Instead, do you want to go to the movies? I understand *When Harry Met Sally* is a good one."

But Tom had had enough of Barbara for a while. "Oh, I can't this weekend. I promised my father I would help him with some carpentry work at the migrant workers center." Barbara sniffed slightly in indignation but accepted his excuse. He only hoped she would not see him as he drove to the Parliament House.

"I don't know why I hang around her so much," he commented to Toby when he saw him the next Saturday. "Since you're not there any longer, I guess I've been thrown together with her."

"Unless you have the hots for Sister Alice," quipped Toby, "there's not many others there our age to talk to. And she is not always blindly loyal to ole Catholic High."

"Admittedly she does understand some of its weaknesses—oh Christ, here comes Al. Can we depart for the theatre?" Al had been stalking him for weeks now, perhaps thinking they could make another go at it. Once they found seats for just the three of them together, Tom continued, "Well, I did find out that Barbara doesn't have much of a social conscience." He told them about her comment about the migrant workers.

"Oh, it gets worse. She's a big Nixon supporter and thinks the war in Vietnam is nifty. Beat back those dirty Commies," Toby reported.

"Yes, and she did say something derogatory about the nuns who run the migrant center. Called them socialists. I'm going to avoid her as much as possible."

Try as he might, however, he kept being thrown together with her. She sat with him at department meetings, she positioned herself next to him when he took a break in the teachers' lounge since their breaks overlapped, and she pulled up her tray at lunch. He did not want to be rude to her, but he did not have any way of gently getting rid of her. And Toby was correct: there really were no other teachers he was close to. So they continued to be "friends." They again had dinner at Morrison's. Near Christmas, she produced two tickets to *The Nutcracker*. "Do you like ballet?"

"Yes, a great deal, although I haven't been to anything since moving here. I understand the Orlando ballet company is pretty weak."

"Well, I guess Mr. Super Sophisticate knows it all."

"Not exactly, although my parents took me several times to see the ballet in Boston, and once, we saw the American Ballet Theatre perform Prokofiev's *Romeo and Juliet* in New York. That was unbelievably beautiful."

Barbara gave him a strange look. "I didn't think men liked ballet. Think it's for sissies."

"Not when you are a super-sophisticate like me," Tom said, trying not to bristle. "We saw John Kriza as Romeo. What an athlete he was. He did these incredible leaps." He did not mention how beautiful his rear end looked in his tights that hugged every crease. Nor did he tell her that he became aroused watching Kriza dance. Reluctantly, Tom agreed to attend *The Nutcracker*.

The performance was even worse than he had anticipated. The music was piped in, the sets and costumes embarrassing, and the dancing showcased children in the ballet school in roles designed for adult dancers. One of the principals was quite good, but the men dressed in saggy tights that did not do justice to their anatomy. Nevertheless, he praised the performance as brilliant, equivalent to one by the ABT.

"Why do you hang out with her?" Toby again demanded.

"It keeps me out of the bars."

"You're in one now."

"And I don't drink nearly as much."

"Well, that's a fact. We were seriously worried that you were becoming an alcoholic. And you forgot to mention it also prevents a reoccurrence of the pox."

"That too." Tom did have two drinks and one pickup. He found it rather enlightening again to remember what had transpired the evening before. He also had insisted on the use of condoms.

He spent most of Christmas week with his parents. His mother went out of her way to prepare him all of his favorite recipes plus a few new ones, which verged on the spectacular. "I've been watching Julia Child on public television. One problem is getting the ingredients here at Publix. I cannot find shallots anywhere."

"Mom, it was terrific even if you shortchanged me."

"Well, she said you could substitute green onions instead."

"The chocolate, what did you call it?"

"Mousse, dear."

"Obviously without the antlers."

"Very funny. Are you still seeing Barbara?" Tom knew he was in for the third degree.

"Occasionally, nothing serious." He wanted to make sure his mother knew he was dating but not to anticipate anything serious transpiring.

"Well, I'd like to meet her anyhow. Please bring her over next time."

They attended the midnight service the Episcopal Church. The music was again dreadful, but members of the congregation greeted him as if he had been a member for years, even though he had only been there once before. Barbara had suggested they go out for dinner on New Year's Eve—"not to Morrison's but somewhere nicer"—but Tom explained he was staying with his parents until just before school began again. Actually he came home before New Year's Eve and celebrated with Toby and Jeff at the Parliament House. He awoke the next morning with a crushing headache, the result of "falling off the wagon," as he complained to Toby, essentially trying to pass the blame to him. Also he grudgingly discovered his bed was cold and empty when he awoke on New Year's Day.

Immediately after he returned to school, he enrolled in another graduate course, his sixth. The new job seemed closer than ever. The state would allow him to start a job with eight graduate courses so that conceivably if he doubled up again this coming summer, he could thumb his nose at Sister Alice and Catholic High School. He did not mention his plans to Barbara because he knew she would vigorously object. She showed obvious disdain when he told her he could not meet her on Tuesday after school because of his class. "You aren't still thinking of teaching at a public school. Those children are undisciplined and not nearly the caliber of students we have."

Barbara clearly had ulterior motives to keep Tom at Catholic. Subtlety was certainly not her strong suit. They did go to dinner a few more times because Tom wanted to keep Barbara as an ally at school. He did become nervous, however, when she invited him to have dinner with her parents. She ascertained that he had nothing planned for that weekend before she sprung the invitation on him.

Mr. Stevens was a mousy sort of man, overwhelmed by his wife's brassy voice, which matched her red hair. They were clearly mother/daughter. Their ample bosoms served practically as bookends. Tom scrupulously avoided anything controversial; and when Mrs. Stevens tried to bait him, he attempted to evade confrontation.

"I'm sure you are a strong supporter of our president. I don't know how he withstands those demonstrators. We need to stop those Commies before they invade our country. Although they probably have already taken over California."

That was too much for Tom. "Well, I guess we got dragged into that war under false pretenses. I thought Nixon promised to get us out."

"Yes, it was Kennedy and Johnson who got us into it." She ignored his comment about Nixon. "I'm ashamed of some Catholics who demonstrate against the war. The Berringer brothers!"

"Berrigan," he corrected her. He almost told her that his parents are strong supporters of the Berrigans and that his mother had actually marched in an antiwar demonstration in Boston. Generally speaking, the meal did not go well. As a result, Tom had a terrible case of indigestion. He was not sure if it stemmed from the conversation or the rather indigestible barbeque.

Barbara pestered Tom about setting up a visit with his parents. Out of exasperation, he agreed, not only to get Barbara off him but also to satisfy his mother that Barbara actually did exist and was not some sort of phantom. Tom insisted, however, that they only drive over for the day, instead of overnight as Barbara had wanted. The day went pleasantly enough. Tom's mother insisted on driving over to the migrant center to admire his father's carpentry and to see where she gave reading lessons to the children. Barbara remained unimpressed. They had dinner—another Julia Child special, which Barbara did not fully appreciate.

"Why was the steak wrapped in pie dough with that weird paste spread on it?"

"Mother said it was called Beef Wellington, which is stuffed with foie gras. She said she couldn't get it around here, but she saw an advertisement in a food magazine and ordered it."

"She shouldn't have bothered," Barbara commented later. Tom almost told her it was made from goose livers but decided the information would be wasted on her.

Tom's parents also had a discussion after the dinner. "What could he be thinking of?" his mother asked. "She is so crass. Entirely not suited for him."

"He must be desperately lonely or something. Perhaps he's attracted to big boobs?" returned his father.

"Mike! No, I suspect she is trying to trap him. I certainly hope he's not foolish enough to fall for it."

# Chapter 3

Tom arranged his summer so that he had as little free time to devote to Barbara as possible. In addition to the two graduate courses he undertook, he also added a part-time job at Jordan Marsh in the men's shoe department. Apparently the department had lost some employees, and they were desperate enough to hire him. Weekends were filled with regular visits to his parents. He explained that his mother had taken ill, and his father needed assistance. One time he slipped and reversed the caretaker and the invalid. Barbara, after accepting the absences, finally asked if he was trying to avoid her. He did not want to alienate her, so he took one weekend off and took her to dinner.

In reality, his mother was in perfect health; and although he did make two trips to Clermont, most weekends he could be found at the Parliament House, generally in the company of Toby and Jeff. Some thought they were a threesome because they appeared together there so often. Tom also ran into some of his old tricks; either he looked the other way or they refused to acknowledge him. He did, however, limit his drinking, which Toby approvingly noted.

One Friday night, Tom had gone to the Silver Hammer and saw a man he seemed to remember. The man walked up to him and said, "Hi, Tom. Long time no see." When Tom seemed rather confused, he added, "I'm Stuart. We had, I guess you'd say, almost a one-night stand. It was probably two years ago."

"Oh, I'm sorry. Now I remember. We had a very nice time as I recall," he said, smiling. They chatted a bit, discovered that neither had any serious relationship, and drove toward Tom's apartment.

Stuart worked for Disney. It seemed like every young person worked for Disney. He was not, however, a character actor, scheming for a part on Broadway, but an accountant in one of the back offices. They hit it off sexually, spending a number of nights together. Yet Tom did not find Stuart intellectually stimulating. *How can an accountant be scintillating?* he wondered. One of his great disappointments was that he never found anyone who shared his interests, not since Tony, that is. They talked especially about music but also recommended books to each other. And discussed them. They also had good sex together. That is what Tom really sought, and so far, he had not found that in Orlando. Nevertheless, Stuart was a good substitute, at least for physical gratification.

They alternated between their apartments practically every weekend during the summer when Tom was not visiting his parents. When he was not away, he was very careful about where he went so that Barbara did not see him. He felt fairly confident she would not run into him at the Parliament House. He enjoyed spending time with Toby, Jeff, and Stuart and then go back to his apartment with Stuart to spend the night. He appreciated being with Stuart when he did not have to have a conversation with him. Dancing at the Parliament House, watching a show, clowning around with Toby, or having sex, Tom found he liked Stuart's company. He had a great body, loved all the things in bed that Tom did, but possessed a rather dull wit. Tom hated to generalize about accountants, but it did seem that anyone caught up so completely with numbers could not have much interests outside a spreadsheet. Tom had decided that he was going to break it off just before school started again.

On the second Sunday morning of August, they climbed out of bed around ten and drank coffee and ate sticky buns from Publix, their normal Sunday routine. "Listen, Tom, I really think we need to call it quits. I've really enjoyed being with you; but unfortunately, I don't see much of a future in it. I really don't think we have much in common other than the Parliament House and fucking. I'd really like a long-term relationship with some guy, but I don't think it's in the cards for us. I'm sorry."

Tom did not quite know what to say. He had been rehearsing those very lines for his own departure speech, and now they had been taken away from him. At first he felt relief that he did not have to be the villain, but then he felt hurt. The very thing he had planned to do had been done to him, and it wounded deeply. Only later did he see the irony in this exchange, but at this moment, he did not know how to reply. He thought about telling Stuart the feeling was mutual, then saying he was deeply disappointed, even though he was not, despite his injured feelings. Finally he said nothing. They kissed as they normally did when Stuart left. Tom showered and curled up with one of his textbooks—he always read his assignments early so that he would not fall asleep—and later polished his term paper. He called his parents after dinner, knowing that they were involved with some volunteer work every Sunday afternoon.

The next weekend, he visited his parents, telling them that once school started, his visits would be more infrequent. His mother wondered how they could be more infrequent than they were already. For some perverse reason, he enjoyed accompanying his parents at Saint Matthias, joining in the cacophony of the congregational singing. They intoned "Praise, My Soul, the King of Heaven" with gusto. The sermon again touched on some social issues to which the congregation shook their heads in agreement. In some ineffable way, Tom felt some divine spirit there.

The next day, Tom returned to his classroom. He first met with Sister Alice before the usual meeting with the headmaster. He sat, his arms folded defiantly across his chest, looking around his surrounding with obvious anger. Barbara saw him and slipped in next to him. "Okay, what happened this time?"

"She's had my booklist for Honors English since last May. Just now she tells me I can't use one of the books."

"Which one was it?"

"Heller's *Catch Twenty-Two*."

"I warned you that she won't accept it."

"Well, why then did she wait until now? I could have easily changed it. Now I have to rework the themes I had built around it. I told her it fit in with what the history honors class is doing with war. She merely told me to find another book. I should pick *Portnoy's Complaint* or *Catcher in the Rye* to see how they fly."

"You'll just get yourself fired if you did that."

"Not a chance," Tom said smugly. "Half the department is half dead already. A puff of wind, and we'd be down to just you and me."

"And Eddie."

"That's true. He only looks half dead."

"You've noticed. I'm so sick of this place I have half a mind to quit right now."

"And where would you go? Orange County has a hiring freeze, and the other counties around here are in bad shape as well. Apparently tax revenues are down. Or something."

They sat through the usual oration about how to treat the students nicely, not expect too much from them, and grade their papers accordingly. Tom felt by this point he could give the talk himself. Afterward, he walked with Barbara to the "banquet," which traditionally concluded the opening day festivities.

"Are you still working at Jordan Marsh?"

"No, I left last week. It was hard enough taking two graduate classes and working there. I just couldn't handle it now."

"Perhaps we can now spend some time together. I really missed you this summer."

"Oh, I did also. But I should be freer now."

"How's your mom?"

Tom hesitated for a moment wondering why she asked until he remembered. "Oh, she's doing much better. I'm glad I spent so much time with her." He practically gagged on his lie.

"So you won't be going over there this weekend? Perhaps we could have dinner. I know you've missed Morrison's."

"I've thought about the Salisbury Steak all summer." They both laughed.

He had dinner with Barbara, which was actually enjoyable. They both complained bitterly about school, which to Tom seemed out of place for Barbara since she normally defended the school whenever he had criticized it in the past. He wondered if she was just trying to get on his good side. She invited to come to her apartment for a drink, but he pleaded exhaustion. He promised her next time.

When he left her off, he drove directly to the Parliament House, where he had to endure the same lecture from Toby. "Why are you hanging around Barbara so much? You know the only thing she has on her mind is matrimony." At least Toby did not nag him about his drinking anymore.

"I know that. But she's company. My efforts of finding a long-term relationship have not been good." He had already told Toby the Stuart saga. "And I certainly could not have a live-in partner, not with my parents or the school for that matter. So I hang around her at school since you deserted us. And we have dinner once in a while."

"You're playing with fire," Toby warned.

But Tom paid no attention, later picked up a visiting tourist, and took him home.

Tom did try to avoid Barbara the next week, but she was quite insistent. He invented another visit with his parents. Barbara looked crestfallen, so Tom promised to get together the following weekend.

Tom decided to make the best of it. He made reservations at an Italian restaurant, Villanova, and ordered an expensive bottle of wine. They finished that and had another. The dinner was one of the best he had eaten since moving to Florida. To make it nicer, they did not talk about school the entire time. By the end of the evening, both seemed very relaxed.

Afterward, when she asked him if he wanted to come up to her apartment, he agreed. She offered him a nightcap, which he accepted, although he had second thoughts before he did. She sat close to him on her sofa and put her arms around him. He resisted at first but then relaxed. She then led him by the hand into the bedroom, turned down the lights, and began to kiss him.

"Do you love me?" she asked.

"Of course I do," Tom answered without really thinking. He was not quite drunk enough that he could not perform but sufficiently under the influence that he had little resistance. He did have the presence of mind to ask her if she had any condoms, but she assured him it was the wrong time of the month. Tom really had no real knowledge about the fertility cycles of a woman and so took her word for it.

After he had climaxed, he rolled over and fell asleep. Barbara awoke him the next morning with a cup of coffee and a big smile. "Wasn't that lovely?"

"Yes, I had a good time," Tom lied, since he could barely remember it, other than recalling how strange she smelled. Not the intense musky smell of a man. Before he left, he promised to stay over next weekend, a promise he lamented afterward.

Much as he tried to evade her at school the next week, she seemed to be persistently with him. He tried to avoid her without seeming rude. It was almost an impossible task. She followed him into the teachers' lounge and sat with him at lunch. She looked at him adoringly at the most inappropriate times. On Thursday, she reminded him of his promise to spend the weekend with her, but he knew the effort would be too much for him. Finally on Friday he stopped her in the hall, apologizing that he could not keep their date. "My mother had taken a turn for the worse, and I need to go over there this weekend to help out."

"Oh, I'm so sorry to hear that," she replied, a tone of skepticism in her voice.

"And I may have to go over next weekend as well."

Barbara said she understood, but clearly she did not.

He tried not to appear to be totally ignoring her although he seemed busier than usual. Two weeks passed of avoidance, until one morning Barbara approached Tom with an anxious look on her face. "We need to talk." And before he could interrupt her, "It's urgent. Meet me after school."

Tom worried the entire day. At three thirty, he walked out to the parking lot and saw Barbara standing next to his car. "Get in," she commanded.

"What's wrong?"

"We have a big problem." She hesitated, and all sorts of wild things crossed Tom's mind, but he tried to block out the obvious one. "I'm late."

He almost asked for what, but thought better of it. He knew this was no time to joke. "What do you mean?"

"I missed my period." He looked at her as if puzzled. "Don't you understand, I'm pregnant."

"Oh fuck!" He thought quickly, "Well, you'll have to get an abortion. I don't want a child."

"Tom, that's out of the question," she also screamed. "We're Catholics. We can't have an abortion. It's a sin."

"But, Barbara, I can't be a father. I'd make a lousy father." He kept trying to find reasons why this nightmare had to go away.

"Well, if you did the decent thing, you'd marry me."

"I'm not ready for marriage." He almost snapped his response.

"But you said you loved me, didn't you? Did you mean it?"

"Of course I did." He did not want to admit he had lied.

"Well, you need to take responsibility for what you did." Tom could feel the trap snap shut. He soon realized he had no other way out. She

155

could do all sorts of things to hurt him: tell members of the faculty, call his parents.

The following Friday, they both took a personal leave day and headed for the courthouse, got their marriage license, and scheduled an appointment with a county clerk. They arranged for the marriage to take place on Monday afternoon after school let out. Some of the teachers asked Tom why he was so dressed up. After the ceremony, they had dinner at an Italian restaurant in downtown Orlando. Barbara was in high spirits; Tom felt claustrophobic as the trapdoor slammed shut. They talked for the first time about where they were going to live. "I have two bedrooms, so you should probably move your things there. Then we would have a nursery." To Tom, it all seemed so surreal. He could only hope that he would wake up and find it was all a bad dream. When he brought over some boxes of his belongings to her apartment, he accepted it was not.

The dread overwhelmed Tom again, when Barbara said that she had arranged to have dinner with her parents that weekend. "They need to see their new son-in-law." Tom thought they had already met him once; wasn't that enough? He wondered why she had not pestered him about more meetings with her parents. Perhaps they did not like him because of his political views. For all Barbara's talk of her devotion to her parents in the past, he thought she would want to involve them more frequently in their budding relationship. After all, he had taken her to see his parents in Clermont, and her parents lived in Altamonte, maybe five miles away. Clearly they had not been particularly impressed when they met Tom before, and perhaps even tried to persuade Barbara to dump him. Barbara's pregnancy would therefore have the effect of forcing both Tom and her parents to accept her determination to possess Tom.

When they arrived at her parents' house, he clearly understood by the hostile greeting he received. The first sight of Barbara's mother glowering at him had an astringent effect on him. When Barbara went into the kitchen to help her father prepare dinner, her mother pulled her chair closer to Tom. "So you knocked up my daughter? Good thing you married her, or I'd have come after you with a shotgun." That concluded the pleasantries. "You robbed us of a wonderful church wedding. Of course, we could not have a proper wedding mass with her in her condition. She cried how you had forced her to have sex!"

That he had compelled her to have sex was news to him. Later he asked Barbara about what her mother had said. "Well, I didn't want them to think I was loose, and Mother thinks all men are sex crazed. Hope you don't mind." He also asked Barbara if her father always made the dinner. "Mother has severe back problems, so that standing in the kitchen is out of the question." Her mother's girth seemed to be the primary source of her problem.

During dinner, Mrs. Stevens again pontificated about the rotten treatment President Nixon was getting. "Probably the best president we've ever have." She then explained how she would deal with the war protestors with the family gun that she had previously mentioned to Tom. He knew Barbara was also a strong Nixon supporter and sidestepped any discussion of politics, for she invariably disagreed with him. He knew he could never bring his parents together with hers; Mrs. Stevens would probably shoot his parents if they disagreed with her views, which they most certainly would. Yet throughout all this, Mr. Stevens sat quietly by, nodding his head in approval when it seemed necessary.

One pleasant occurrence was the surprise party some of the faculty threw for them. Of course, a few refused to attend; Sister Alice said it was not a true marriage because it had not been conducted by a Catholic priest. But those who joined the festivities brought some nice presents and warm wishes, although Chris the chemistry teacher, said quietly to Tom, "She got quite catch in you." Tom did not know quite how to take that comment.

What Tom dreaded most was the confrontation with his parents. He had told them nothing at all about his marriage, and the longer he waited, the more nervous he got. When he called them, he did not even tell them he had a surprise or that he was bringing Barbara. Nor did he tell Barbara that his parents were unaware of the "good news."

The look on his parents' faces when they entered the house told Barbara all that she needed to know. "We're so glad you brought Barbara with you, but we actually hadn't prepared enough for dinner."

"Oh, we wanted to take you out for dinner to celebrate. You see, Barbara and I got married two weeks ago."

"There's no decent place to dine out here in Clermont," was his mother's only response to the news, obviously in a state of shock.

His father filled in the breach. "Why didn't you tell us sooner? We would have loved to drive over and attend." Tom's mother looked like she was going to begin to cry.

He decided to get it all over at once. "And guess what? You're going to be grandparents."

"Isn't that wonderful?" Barbara chimed in.

His parents sat dumbfounded—for what Tom thought seemed like hours.

The weekend was also endlessly long and stilted. They did find a place to eat that Friday, and his mother ran to Publix before they awoke to get enough for breakfast and dinner. Tom lay awake for a long time listening to the mumbled voices of his parents talking long into the night.

The next day was less awkward. Obviously they tried to make the best of a difficult situation. Tom's father insisted on driving over to the migrant center to show them what new carpentry feat he had completed. Barbara wondered why those people did not get better jobs. "Why do they have to take charity? They should work harder."

It was all Tom's father could do to maintain his temper. "Most of them are treated miserably by the farmers. They often cheat them out of their pay. The good sisters here will often confront the employers and shame them into paying them their wages. They really need the support we provide here." For a moment, Tom envisioned his father in a nun's habit.

Saturday dinner was again awkward, with everyone trying to make small talk. Clara asked about babies' names, and Barbara suggested that it would be *Michael* if a boy and *Clara* if a girl. They all knew she was lying. Tom's father asked if she planned to return to work after the baby was born, and Barbara announced that she would be a stay-at-home mother. Tom wondered where the money would come from to support a family of three on his salary.

Tom's mother told them that they planned to attend church tomorrow morning and would they like to attend. "Tom told me you no longer go to a Catholic church. Well, I could never go to anything other. And I don't want Tom to go either. It would be a bad influence on our child."

Tom and Barbara left early so that his parents could attend church.

"She trapped him. She got pregnant so that he had no choice. She's a bitch in my estimation."

"Clara. I've never heard you use language like that."

"I never had reason to."

Tom asked Barbara that question about finances on the way home. "Well, first, you'll have to quit graduate school. We obviously cannot afford that, and there's no need to get a master's degree anyhow. Catholic does not pay any extra for advanced degrees."

"But what if I want to teach in public school?"

"Oh, don't talk nonsense." That ended the conversation. She later broached her idea that his parents would be able to provide a little extra each month so that the child could have proper parenting. Tom tried to explain that his parents lived on a limited income, but Barbara brushed that off claiming they were totally self-centered if they refused to make sacrifices for their grandchild.

Gloom descended as Tom now felt totally ensnared. He was a prisoner with a red-headed warden. No more stops at the Silver Hammer, no evenings with Miss P at the Parliament House, no trading banter with Toby and Jeff. And worst of all, no more sex with a man. He had no idea how he could arrange for that. Barbara insisted on taking only one car to work, so that he could not even stop by the Hammer on the way home from school. Barbara was always bubbly and happy, never noticing how Tom was slowly slipping into a funk. He needed to have sex, and now the only alternative was Barbara. A few days after returning from his parents, he began to fondle Barbara. "Oh, we can't do that. It might harm the baby."

"Well, when can we have sex?"

"No until after the baby is born."

"Well, could you play with me, please?"

"Oh, don't be disgusting. You just need to control your urges. I can't believe how self-centered you are."

The final blow came two weeks later. Barbara said she was not feeling well and decided to stay home. On his way home, he stopped by Publix and walked into the apartment carrying two bags of groceries. Barbara sat in their living room crying. "What's wrong, dear?" he asked with genuine solicitation since she seemed in quite a state.

"We've lost the baby."

"Oh god. How?"

"I started to have camps this morning and called the gynecologist, and he said to come over. He examined me and said I was having a miscarriage. They took me into like an operating room . . ." She broke down in sobs. Tom could not help but feel compassionate.

"Do you want me to call your parents?"

"I already did. But you might call yours."

"Let me make you supper first." He threw together something that he knew was almost inedible, but he was too upset to produce anything better.

After dinner, he called his parents and told them the bad news. After he got off the phone, his mother turned to her husband. "The bitch faked it. Just to force Tom into marrying her."

"How can you be so sure?"

"I doubted that she was pregnant when she was here."

"How could you tell?" he asked with doubt in his voice. Mike was fairly certain that she was correct; her intuition was normally spot-on. But he did not want her to be too cocky.

"A woman knows, that's all. If she was pregnant, I'm Donald Duck."

Barbara continued to deny her husband his marital privileges, explaining that her uterus had been damaged by the miscarriage and needed to heal. Tom knew that his erection was certainly not long enough to penetrate her uterus and cause any harm. He tried to explain that, but she became furious. "Don't you have any consideration for me after all I've been through. All you think about is your penis." A few nights later, she caught him masturbating in the bathroom. Another even more strident lecture followed about the sins of Onanism.

In desperation he decided he needed to talk to someone. On the Saturday before Christmas, Barbara went to visit her parents. Tom pleaded an upset stomach; Barbara immediately accused him of not wanting to see her parents but left without him. In fact, he could not abide them, but he had an ulterior motive. Once she left, he called Toby and asked him if he would mind coming over. "It's an emergency."

Toby was mystified but agreed. He heard the anguish in Tom's voice. When he got there, Tom explained his predicament. "Since the miscarriage, she refused to have sex. And there is no way I can get out. And," he hesitated, "she even caught me beating off one night."

"I must say I never understood why you married her in the first place. You always made fun of her."

"I guess I never told you, I guess I was pretty drunk, and we had sex once. She got pregnant. She refused to get an abortion, and I was forced to marry her. Otherwise, she essentially threatened to let the entire world know what a rat I am."

"You mean, of course, Sister Alice."

"Precisely." He sighed. "What am I going to do?"

"Well, divorce comes immediately to mind."

"I've thought seriously about that, but I'm sure she would do all she could to ruin my reputation. She's incredibly vindictive. And I bet she'd sue for alimony, which I could not afford." He told Toby about her suggestion that his parents help support them. "On a postal worker's retirement!"

"Well, I could arrange some sort of assignation in our bedroom. I know some men who would be happy to service a hunky guy like you."

"How would I get away when I can't even jerk off in my own bathroom?" They both laughed, but Tom was bitter. "I might be able to get away for a 'doctor's visit,' but it would have to be when she's at school and I'm home sick."

"Let me work on it. I'm sure Jeff would not mind if our sheets had a few pecker tracks."

Just then the door burst open, and Barbara came in. "What are you doing here, Toby?" The tone was accusatory.

"Oh, hi, Barbara." A slight pause, as Toby thought in somewhat of a panic. Tom was even more agitated. None of this passed Barbara's notice even though the pause lasted no more than a second. "I was at Sears and decided to stop by. Had some news about an old friend of ours was getting married."

"Who?" demanded Barbara.

"Oh, you won't know them. Neither teaches at Catholic. He's an engineer at Martin Marietta."

"Since when do either of you know anyone from Martin?"

"We know him from a men's group at Margaret Mary." The lies just kept piling up.

"Tom, you never told me about any men's group."

"I didn't think to mention it." He almost said, "Why should I?" but thought better of it.

"Well, I best be off. Have some more errands to run. Nice seeing you again, Barbara. Take care of yourself, Tom." Barbara did not watch him leave, so Toby was able to wink at Tom as he closed the door.

"I don't want you to see Toby anymore. I don't like him."

"Are you censuring my friends?" Tom replied, anger in his voice.

"Well, for one thing, I'm pretty sure he's a fairy. You shouldn't be associated with him."

"Just how do you know he's gay?" He refused to use her term.

"Just how he prances around. Like a big faggot."

Tom did not say anything more. He walked out of the living room and climbed back into bed. The temptation to tell her the truth about himself was almost more than he could hold back.

A week later, Toby called and told him that he had a friend Steve, "who would love to bed you. He's free on Wednesdays. You just need to tell me when, and I'll set it up. Of course, I just might stay home myself to watch." Tom thought that Toby could in fact be serious.

Two weeks later, Tom again became sick. Barbara offered to stay home, but Tom insisted that all he needed was rest. He also said he had called his doctor and made an appointment.

He drove to Toby's apartment, found the door unlocked, and Steve waiting inside. He had met Steve several times at the Parliament House and found him very attractive. He thought Steve was in a relationship; perhaps it was an open one. He decided not to ask any questions, especially after Steve removed his clothes.

For one hour, Tom experienced total bliss. He felt the passion rise with kissing a man, had the sensation of a cock in his mouth, and his being massaged by another mouth. He felt the joy of being penetrated and hearing the groans of pleasure emanating from Steve and from himself. He felt the ecstasy of an intense orgasm. They showered afterward, and as Steve left, he suggested they do this again sometime soon.

"It might be hard to explain to my wife why I have to go to the doctor's every Wednesday"—Tom laughed—"but I'll work on it." They kissed again, and Steve left. Tom sat on Toby's sofa taking an inventory of his life.

When Barbara got home, she asked him what the doctor had diagnosed. He almost replied, "Blue balls relieved." "He thinks I might be getting ulcers. He wants me to see a gastroenterologist." Another excuse for a Wednesday appointment, he thought.

"Now why would you be getting ulcers?"

"I've been under a lot of stress lately."

"Oh, and you're going to blame me, I suppose. I guess because I don't give in to your filthy desires."

"I didn't say that. But anyhow, sex is not filthy."

"The church teaches that sex is only for procreation. And right now, I cannot get pregnant." Tom did not bother to disagree. He now realized that he had actually married Sister Alice.

Christmas was spent with visits to his parents, which tended to be short, and interminably longer ones with her parents. In reality, they encompassed the same number of days, but the visits to the Stevens home seemed twice as long to Tom. He had to endure long lectures on the supremely good job Nixon was doing in the White House and what a disaster Reubin Askew was as governor. "I bet his actually a communist." Tom had given up arguing.

The first week back at school, Tom called Toby and asked for another rendezvous with Steve. "Your horniness—I mean *wish*—is my command. But remember I might put up cameras and sell the film. Make millions."

The next Wednesday, Tom had his appointment and took another sick day. "Well, you might tell him that your ulcers are not my fault," Barbara insisted.

He drove out of the apartment complex as if he was headed toward Orlando hospital, just in case Barbara was following him. A few blocks away, he changed course and started toward Toby's apartment. Several times he looked in his rearview mirror to make certain he was no being followed. He had become paranoid about the thought of Barbara hiring a private investigator. As soon as he was naked with Steve again, those thoughts fled from his mind. The joy of the physical contact overcame all worry. Afterward, he laughed, thinking that Steve was a perfect cure for ulcers. He knew, however, that the next dose would be a long way off.

# Chapter 4

Tom found that even telephone conversations with Toby seemed therapeutic. It was now March, and he had only been able to see Steve once again. Toby said he would try to think of some other outlet.

"I forget to tell you, I'll be in England this summer. How do you like that?"

"How are you swinging that on a teacher's pay?"

"Well, there's a local organization that provides scholarships for local teachers to attend a summer graduate program at Oxford University. And I won it this year. I'm going over right after school lets out and spend two weeks in London, compliments of my rich husband. Then I'm in Oxford for eight whole weeks. There are lectures on history, politics, and literature. I've signed up for a seminar on twentieth-century Britain."

"Sounds boring to me. And I understand the food is terrible."

"You're just green with jealousy."

"You bet I am." Then he said ruefully, "I can't even go to school here."

"What do you mean?"

"Didn't I tell you? Barbara made me drop out of my master's program. We cannot afford it. Have to save up for the baby, which, unless she has found a sperm donor, is not going to happen any time soon." Toby could hear the sarcasm in Tom's voice.

"Well, I assume Jeff will come over at some point, and you can use our apartment as a private playground. I understand Steve will provide for you any time you want."

"If I can get out of jail. Barbara will be playing guard all summer. No chance I'll get my rocks off at Chez Toby."

"Not even your socks," Toby laughed.

That evening he told Barbara about Toby's good fortune. She just laughed. "What a farce! Somebody's hard-earned money going to waste on that loser."

"Why do you hate Toby so much?"

"Because we all know he's a faggot. He's disgusting, and I wish you won't hang around him."

"Well, I happen to like him. He's my friend, and I don't much care who he fucks."

At that point, Barbara slapped him. "Don't you ever use that word around me again."

"Don't you ever hit me again!" Tom snapped.

"I will when you use words like that. Now I want an apology."

No apology was forthcoming. Instead, Tom went into the "nursery" and sat on a rather uncomfortable chair. He sat there for a while thinking about life and what it had dealt him. He slept in the chair the entire night. The next morning, the two of them hardly spoke at all.

Two days later, a truce had been called, and Barbara even allowed him to have sex with her. But as he mounted her, she lay there inert, never showing any passion or joy in the act. He was merely servicing her in order to produce the required child according to Catholic teaching. Obviously sex was a duty: filthy, unpleasant, but necessary. Tom found no joy in the experience either. *At least I got my rocks off,* he reflected, thinking about his earlier conversation with Toby. His only hope was that she did not get pregnant.

Unfortunately, three weeks later, Barbara announced she had missed her period. Whatever suspicions Tom had about the first one, he had no doubts about this one. And he was rather proud of himself with his outstanding virility. Twice for twice. Unfortunately with the pregnancy, it meant he was in for another dry spell. He called his mother with the good news, but her tepid response surprised him. "Oh, that's nice, dear."

Barbara, always the planner, asked Tom if he had life insurance and a last will and testament. He had neither, so she insisted he take care of both immediately. He called a life insurance salesman who eagerly sold him a $20,000 life policy. Doing a will meant consulting a lawyer. Barbara gave him the name of her attorney; and although he did not necessarily want to follow her recommendation, at this point, he did not want to get into a quarrel. He therefore made an appointment with Don Trelawney for late Friday afternoon. The office was in the Sun Trust building on Orange Avenue. He arrived at the appointed time, but the secretary told him that Mr. Trelawney had been held up at court and would return in an hour. Could Mr. O'Mally wait?

Tom did not want to sit in the rather cramped waiting room, so he decided to take a stroll around Eola Park. He assured the secretary that he would return shortly. He took his walk, marveling at the tackiness of the fountain in the center, which looked like a flying saucer out of an old science fiction film. He wondered if they had used it for the model of the ship in *It Came from Outer* Space. There were restrooms next to the band shell, and Tom decided he needed to stop there before returning to Trelawney's office. When he walked into the men's room, he first noticed how much it smelled. Tom wondered if it had been cleaned in months. Then he saw a young man dressed in casual clothes standing in front of one the urinals. Tom went to a spot two away and tried to be as discreet as possible. But he could not help noticing that the young man had an erection and was stroking it, a clear invitation. Tom looked away and tried to urinate and get out. But the sight of the other man's erection caused Tom to begin to become aroused himself. He started to turn away and zip his pants, when the young man pulled out a badge and informed Tom he was under arrest. "What for?" Tom demanded.

"Solicitation."

"But I did no such thing. I was trying to leave when I saw you."

"You tried to grab my cock."

"I did no such thing," he cried again. At that point, the police officer read Tom his Miranda rights, slipped handcuffs on his wrists, and walked him out the door. A number of strollers watched in amazement when Tom was hustled off to a waiting Orlando Police patrol car.

He was booked on the charge of molestation and solicitation, fingerprinted, and told he could make one phone call. Desperate as to what to do, he knew he could not call Barbara. Only Toby seemed possible. He only hoped he had not gone out.

Toby answered, and in a panicked voice, Tom told him he had been arrested and was at the Orlando Police Department on South Street. Toby asked what happened, and Tom tried to explain, but he was in tears and unable to make himself clear. "Just hang tight. I'll be right there." Toby had the presence of mind to grab Jeff and took him along. "This sounds like the boy might need some legal advice."

The sergeant on duty did not seem very happy about the pair showing up demanding to see Tom, but Jeff announced that he was Tom's attorney, and the sergeant had no choice but to let him see Tom. Toby had to cool his heels in the waiting room, however.

Tom explained what had happened, that the police man was stroking his erection, and Tom had done nothing. "They do that sort of entrapment all the time, especially when it's late in the day and they haven't made any arrests."

"What can I do? I've already been arraigned and have to post bail."

"Don't worry. I'll see to that."

A few minutes later, a guard came to let Tom out and escort him to Toby and Jeff waiting for him outside. Jeff had already explained what had happened to Toby. "God, what am I going to tell Barbara?"

"Nothing," advised Jeff. "All you need to do is explain your lateness, and we can take care of the rest. There is a lawyer colleague of mine who handles these cases all the time. This is a racket carried out by the OPD to make money. You have to pay Townshend his fee and a $500 fine to the court, and everyone goes away happy. The charge disappears from your record, and no one is the wiser. Although the judge, the police, and your new lawyer friend split the taking. Lesson, never take a piss in the public restrooms in Florida."

"I always carry an empty bottle myself," added Toby.

"Where are you parked?" Jeff asked. "We'll walk you there."

Tom found his car and a parking ticket under the wiper blade. "God, I can't have anything to go my way."

When he finally got home, it was nine o'clock. He had driven slowly so that he could get a coherent story together. "You won't believe what I've been through. First, Trelawney was late, and then it took a long time to work out the details of the will."

"Oh, it can't be that hard. Everything would come to me."

"Of course, dear, but there are those contingencies if you predecease me, care of our child, things like that. Then I go to my car, and it won't start. Something with the electrical system. So I had to wait for the tow truck, and it took some time to get it fixed. Luckily it wasn't very serious." He had rehearsed the soliloquy carefully before he entered the apartment.

"Why didn't you call me?"

"I planned to after I called the garage, but the truck came right away."

"I thought you said you had to wait."

"Well, I had rushed back from the phone booth to car in case he did." He started to say that the driver had said he would come right away but didn't. He decided he was digging himself in too deep already. "Listen, I'm hungry. Can we eat first?"

"I didn't wait for you. There's a plate in the oven, and you'll have to clean up. I'm going to bed." With that, she walked into the bedroom and shut the door. It seemed as if she had shut him out once again.

The next day, he made another appointment with Trelawney, apologizing for not coming back. "Oh, don't worry. He would have cancelled you anyhow, he was so late."

He then called Townshend and also made an appointment. He explained to the secretary that his hearing had been set for the following week.

He presumed but did not ask if Townshend was also gay. "I seem to have made a career of dealing with these entrapment issues. I actually discount my normal fees because I think the police have taken advantage of gay people. The restroom had for a long time been a meeting place for guys wanted to get sucked off, but once the police turned their attention to it, the guys they catch now are like you. Just going in to urinate. I bet you didn't even touch him."

"I didn't."

"I know the cop who does it. Real hunk, but straight as an arrow. But he always seems to be in there with a hard-on. So he claimed you touched him."

"Right, but I didn't," Tom insisted again.

"Don't worry, I believe you. But in the courtroom, it would be your word against his. What I recommend to my clients is to plead no contest. You have to pay a five-hundred-dollar-fine immediately. So bring cash. You can pay me in a month or so. Jeff Rosen called me and said you were good for the money."

Tom would have trouble getting the cash since Barbara handled the finances. Apparently she did not trust him. So when she saw a withdrawal from the savings account, she confronted Tom. "Oh, I had to pay the garage and the tow truck owner. I didn't have the cash when it happened, but they were nice and said I could pay them later."

Tom did his best that weekend to be solicitous of Barbara, trying to be empathetic about her morning sickness. He insisted on going to visit her parents with her, and he tried not to contradict her mother too often, although they had quite different views about the Watergate hearings. Instead, he sat with her father, who appeared just as cowed by the women as he was. He learned on Monday that his hearing was Wednesday at ten, so he needed an excuse to miss school. He claimed that Trelawney had called and wanted him to sign some papers, and the only opening he had was Wednesday morning. Barbara complained that these professional people expect mere mortals to adjust their schedules to fit.

Townshend greeted Tom outside the courthouse and showed him the way to the courtroom. The whole process was very perfunctory; the judge asked him his plea, Tom responded no contest, and the judge fined him $500. It all went as planned until Tom started to walk out of the courtroom. At the back sat a young man who jumped up and blocked Tom's exit.

"Hi, I'm Jim Lloyd from the *Sentinel*. Aren't you Thomas O'Mally?" Tom did not answer, and Townshend tried to hustle him from the courtroom. "You're a teacher at Catholic High."

"Just keep walking," Townshend warned.

"So you tried to proposition a cop?" Lloyd continued, practically chasing the two others out into the hall. Tom and the lawyer rushed toward an elevator that was just closing its doors and managed to get in before the doors shut in the reporter's face. They did not manage, however, preventing the reporter from taking their picture.

"What the hell was he doing there? Since when does the *Sentinel* take an interest in these hearings? Must be trying to increase readership. Let's just hope he gets nothing in tomorrow's paper." Tom had turned white. When he got home, he went into the bathroom and vomited. When Barbara arrived home, she knew something was terribly wrong. In desperation, Tom explained that they thought his mother had had a mild stroke. He was at a loss to explain his mood.

He arose early the next morning and opened the door to find the *Sentinel* lying there waiting for him. He turned to the local section and saw his face peering out at him. He did not bother reading the headline, but he knew it said something about a local teacher caught in a restroom trying to solicit a cop. He threw the paper in a trash bin outside the apartment and quickly retreated to the bathroom.

"You got up early," Barbara commented.

"Had to piss like a racehorse."

"Let's not get crude."

What did it matter? He knew that the headline in the paper had sealed his fate. His life would never be the same again. For some strange reason, he accepted his predicament calmly. Instead of taking one car, Tom insisted on driving alone because he had some errands to do. They went to their respective classrooms; and when he entered his, he found Sister Alice waiting for him. She had a smug look on her face.

"Don't take your jacket off. The headmaster wants to see you immediately." As he walked down the hall, he saw one of the regular substitute teachers walking toward him. The interview with the headmaster took but seconds. He was informed that the school did not allow perverts to teach their children, that he was a disgrace to his community and the church. Tom was pleasantly surprised that he had not been told he would burn in hell forever.

He drove home. He sat in a living room chair the entire day, almost totally in a daze. He thought about calling Toby, but he was sure he already had seen the newspaper. He finally heard the dreaded key in the lock. Obviously Barbara was surprised to see him there.

"I thought you'd be gone. You filthy faggot. You don't know the pain I have had to suffer on your account. The humiliation! I always knew there was something wrong with you. Now the whole world knows that you like to have sex in public bathrooms. I won't be able to face my friends again. They will all think I helped you with your perversion." She stopped to catch her breath. "I want you out of here now. I don't ever want to see you again."

She walked into the bedroom and began throwing his belongings into the living room. Tom grabbed a suitcase out of the entrance closet and began stuffing in his clothes. He picked up two of his books and walked out.

He had no idea what he was going to do now. He had no job; he had no place to stay. He figured he would check in to a motel until he could make some decisions about his life. To his amazement, as he walked toward his car, he saw Toby's car parked next to his.

"I figured you would need some help," was all that he said. He got out of his car, took Tom's suitcase, and put it in his trunk. "Just follow me. We faggots have got to stick together."

When he entered Toby's apartment, he found the dinner table set with three places. Fortunately, Toby had not cooked his infamous stew, but Jeff had prepared a wonderful chicken dish with a mystery cream sauce. "I could not let you be tortured on your first night here with Toby's mystery cuisine."

Toby interjected, "Perhaps we can explain. And you are not allowed to speak until perhaps next Tuesday. We have a spare bedroom, nicely furnished, which you may occupy as long as necessary. Once you find some form of gainful employment—and we have some suggestions—"

"I hate to think what they are."

"Quiet! No talking until Tuesday. Once you are gainfully employed, you may contribute to the household expenses. Before then, you can help out with the cooking. Jeff has permanently retired my toque and restricted me to making salads and pouring the water. It's questionable if I can boil an egg. You, on the other hand, are entrusted with other culinary endeavors."

Jeff then continued the monologue. "I talked to Townshend about your fee. He said that he insisted on waiving it since he should have been more aware of his surroundings and asked that your case be heard in private chambers."

"But I have an obligation—"

"Shush!" exclaimed Toby.

"Actually, I paid it for you," Jeff explained. "You can repay me when you get on your feet."

"That's the big problem. I have no job and no prospect for one. I've essentially admitted to molesting a police officer."

"Well, obviously you can't get a teaching job again. Orange County would not hire you after a background check." Jeff was always the more serious of the two. "Toby will have some smart idea that will get you nowhere."

"Now wait a minute, Jeffie, we discussed the solution."

"Ya, Toby here thinks you should become a character actor at Disney. After all, most of the employees at Disney are gay. You could pick up some twink. Fringe benefits."

"And what character would I play? Goofy?"

"Obviously Snow White. You would look fab-u-lous in a white chiffon gown and a fake diamond tiara."

Tom laughed, although his heart was not in it. "Actually, I thought of trying to get my job at Jordan Marsh again. Apparently the department supervisor thought highly of my work. More so than they did at Catholic. I know they were overjoyed to have an excuse to fire me. And if there is no opening there, I'll try Ivey's."

"But for God's sake, protect the sacred name of queer by not taking a job at Sears."

"Listen, I can make some inquires. Some of my clients may be able to help. I may have to tell them something about what happened, but I'm certain that would help your case."

"My picture has been all over the paper. Can't hide it now."

He called his lawyer to ask if an employer can ask about his arrest record. Townshend said, with any luck, Jordan Marsh would hire him without having him fill out a new employment application since he had recently worked there. The employment officer recognized Tom and did in fact waive the formalities to rehire him. "I thought you were going back to teaching."

"Oh, I really just got sick of the paperwork."

"I've heard that a lot from other teachers."

The next confrontation Tom needed to make was to his parents. It took him two days to get up the nerve to call them. His father answered the phone. "Dad, I have something to tell you and Mother."

"We already know."

"How . . . ?"

"Barbara made a special trip over here to tell us. Sobbed the whole time. Best damn act I've seen in years."

"But what she said was true."

"That's not the point. She was doing it as a form of revenge. Why don't you come over Saturday and give us your version."

He told Toby about the conversation and how puzzled he was by his father's attitude. "Well, when I came out to my parents," Toby responded, the voice of experience, "they just shrugged their shoulders. Didn't even say how disappointed they were not to have grandkids."

"Who would want to be related to your kids in the first place?" Jeff interjected.

Tom drove to his parents' house that Saturday; if his butterflies had real wings, he could have flown to Clermont. When he arrived, his mother came out and hugged him, without saying a word.

"Now sit down and tell us what happened." He explained what had happened at the men's restroom in Eola Park. He told them what Townshend had said about entrapment and the police scam behind it. He did not mention the issue of his sexuality. He did not need to since Barbara has provided all the sordid details. "Barbara said you were homosexual, that you didn't like to do your husbandly duties, and lots of other filthy details. We kindly thank her and hustled her out the door. She did not look very happy about our reception."

"That leaves you in a terrible spot," his father added. "You say your lawyer—Townshend?—claimed that the record would be expunged?"

"That's true. There is no criminal record since enough money changed hands to make it go away. The problem is my picture in the *Sentinel*. I have a job at Jordan Marsh selling men's shoes. I can't imagine doing that the rest of my life. Perhaps I could move back to Massachusetts again."

"Unfortunately, there would be a good chance that your story would follow you if the school did a thorough job of researching your background. And with some of the scandals with teachers molesting students, I would imagine they would do a comprehensive search."

"You don't suspect I'd honestly do something like that?" he asked in horror.

"Of course not. But not everyone knows what a decent person you are."

"I have to ask you this," his father turned serious. "Why did you marry her in the first place?"

"Yes," his mother interjected, "we always thought she was just your beard."

"My what?"

"You know. A woman a gay man hangs around with to try to show he's really straight."

"I never heard of that before."

"Aren't you up on your gay lingo?"

"No, but you certainly are."

"Well, we always suspected you were gay . . ." Another gasp of disbelief. "So we started reading about it. Much of it isn't very flattering but clearly false in your case. You did not have a distant, uncaring father and a clinging mother, for instance."

"Let's back up a moment. You *always* suspected I was gay?"

"Well, I always knew you were different. You were sensitive, caring, and neat. That last was something that always surprised me. You rarely dated in high school, and I remember how agitated you got during some of Father Sullivan's sermons, especially when they touched on sex. And you always hung around with that guy, oh what's-his-name?"

"Tony?" said Tom tentatively.

"Yes, that's right. He always seemed a little effeminate to me. Now you aren't at all, so we could not understand why you become such close friends until it dawned on me. Now your father wanted to deny all this." She gave her husband a disapproving look. "But he finally came round."

"Yes, especially after I met that Barbara girl. No son of mine could really be attracted to her." Tom could not help but laugh.

"And we found this group called PFLAG and got lots of good information from them."

"Never heard of them," Tom claimed, still flabbergasted by this conversation.

"Well, you need to take more of an interest in gay issues. They're located in New York: Parents, Families, Friends of Lesbians and Gays. It's for folks like us with a gay child. It just started last year. This is no chapter in Orlando—what a surprise—so we get all our information from the chapter in Washington."

"We still want to know why you married Barbara," Tom's father interrupted.

"We told you, she was pregnant."

"Well, we never really believed it. We thought she was faking it to entrap you. When she 'lost the baby,' we were convinced."

"Well, I had the same thoughts, but I tried to deny them."

"Why didn't she get an abortion?" his father asked.

"She's uber-Catholic and would certainly never have an abortion."

"Or more likely, there was nothing to abort," his mother observed cannily.

"Well, I'm sure she's pregnant now. She threw up for almost a month. And I'll be paying alimony and child support for the rest of my life."

"If she's such a good Catholic, why would she even contemplate divorce?"

"Oh, she wants to get rid of me and to make it as painful as possible. And she obviously can get an annulment through the church because of the circumstances."

"Then she can remarry."

"I bet not. She'll want to bleed me for as long as she can, and alimony would disappear if she remarried. I'll be under that cloud forever."

Tom had learned much that weekend about his parents that he never suspected. They understood far more about him, despite his efforts to conceal his true nature. For the rest of the weekend, the topic did not come up, except when his mother commented on how dreadful Barbara's parents must be. The term she used was "*debris blanc.*" For the most part, they discussed their work with the migrant workers and how lovely the people at Saint Matthias were. He went with them to church on Sunday and noted how enthusiastic his father had become about the singing of the hymns. The church was furnished with the Lenten array, which emphasized the penitential, but even the singing of the hymns showed a joyousness not actually befitting the season. His father's deep baritone swelled as he sang "The Glory of These Forty Days." For some reason, it had none of the gloom that he had found at Margaret Mary the previous week. Perhaps it came more from his discussions with his parents the previous two days; nonetheless, he drove home in much better spirits than when he had arrived on Friday.

The routine settled in quickly. Tom worked four days during the day and had a night shift on Thursdays. He earned considerably less than he had at Catholic, and he had previously regarded his teacher's pay as paltry. Living with Toby and Jeff prevented him from descending into penury. He contributed what he could to the household expenses, while keeping up his car payments. Fortunately he had no college debt. He rarely accompanied Toby and Jeff to the Parliament House because of the cover charge. Once they treated him, but he felt so guilty he turned them down next time they suggested he go with them. He splurged once when he had a drink at the Silver Hammer.

It was on that occasion that he brought someone home with him. He had previously cleared it with Toby that he could have visitors. "Listen, this is your place now. You can bring home any cute trick you want, as long as I can watch. Or perhaps participate," he said with a grin. Yet when the time came, Toby welcomed Tom's new "friend," offered them drinks and smiled when they closed Tom's bedroom door. Of course, the next morning when the overnight guest left, Toby complained because he could not get to sleep because of all the racket in the next room.

Actually, Toby was not the only one who had lost sleep. Both Toby and Jeff moaned quite a bit when they had sex. In fact, often moaning very loudly. They both were very vocal. One Saturday night, after they obviously had not made love in some time when Jeff had had a major court case, they excused themselves early, while Tom continued to watch a really terrible horror movie on television. He heard some faint noises from their bedroom, but he tried to concentrate on the movie instead.

Finally he gave up and went to bed. He could hear the lovemaking more clearly from his bed. He heard the moaning getting louder, the verbal directions more clearly, and the headboard of their bed hitting against the wall separating their rooms. He thought of knocking on the wall, but since it was their apartment, he refrained. The moans and "oh yeses" started to get him aroused. Before long he began to fondle himself. It had been a long time, and it felt very good. Finally he climaxed and quickly fell asleep.

He got up early and began to prepare breakfast for the household. He planned to attend Mass since it was Palm Sunday. Toby and Jeff wandered into the kitchen, clearly not quite awake. Quickly though Toby displayed his playful twinkle in his eyes.

"We were worried about you last night. It sounded as if you were having stomach problems. We heard a lot of groaning. Everything okay?"

"Ya, I had some indigestion. Probably from the lasagna." Toby had prepared it; it had many similarities to some of his other gourmet entrées.

"Well, it finally calmed down. Sounded as if you got a load off your chest."

"More likely, a load on his chest," Jeff interjected.

No mention of the activities in the other bedroom were made. After Tom left for church, Toby congratulated Jeff for his quick wit.

Tom had recovered from his brief contented mood at breakfast. The Mass at Margaret Mary did not uplift him at all. Even singing

"All Glory, Laud, and Honor," that triumphal hymn of Palm Sunday, sounded more like a dirge. The congregation clearly was unfamiliar with the hymn, basically not accustomed to hymn singing at all. Even as tone-deaf as the congregation at Saint Matthias was, their energy had been infectious to Tom. He returned to the apartment in a sour mood.

Toby sat on the patio on probably the last day it would be cool enough to rest there. He heard Tom come in and go to the kitchen. Eventually he joined Toby on the patio.

"I've been meaning to say something to you," Toby began hesitantly. "I know you are going through a rough spell, probably even rougher than it shows on the outside. Ever since the incident at Eola Park, you haven't been the same cheery Tom that I know and love."

"Has it been that obvious?" Tom said sardonically.

"Listen, a friend of mine had some issues, and he went to a psychologist." Tom tried to interrupt him. "Oh yes, I know, you're a macho male who can get by on his own. Only sissies go to therapists."

"I don't see how talking to someone will help. And the last time I tried, I ended up marrying Barbara."

"Well, you won't know for sure unless you try." Again Tom tried to interrupt. "Just shut up and listen. This guy had serious hang-ups which he overcame. Apparently this woman is phenomenal."

"Oh, now I have to spill everything to a woman! Remember it was a woman who claimed I was bisexual and needed to find the right girl."

"Oh, I remember, but this one comes with a solid recommendation and no stupid notions. You're going to have a total collapse if you don't do something about it. I'm serious. You're on the verge of a nervous breakdown. You're totally depressed. I shouldn't tell you this, but I've had conversations with your parents. They're as worried as we are. Now let me give you her name and telephone number."

More than anything, Tom agreed to take her name just to shut up Toby. He made no promises that he would contact her.

"Her name is Dr. Beverly Abbot. Her number is 407-555-9877. I think her office is on Michigan." Tom took the paper and retreated to his room. He had already visited one therapist on Michigan, and that had not worked out at all well.

He had Monday off this week because he had to work the next weekend, which meant that he could not go see his parents on Easter. In fact, he did give Dr. Abbot a call, set up an appointment, and kept that information to himself. He met with her secretly the following week. He met with her on three occasions until she finally recommended that he consult his regular physician about obtaining a prescription for depression. At first he resisted, but he had gained some much confidence in her that he reluctantly agreed. In fact the pills did seem to help his moods, although it had no impact whatsoever on what was the root of his depression. He told Toby that if he saw one more loafer, he would destroy it.

A few weeks after Easter, Toby announced that an old friend of his would be in town for a few weeks and would like to invite him to dinner. "That's clearly an invitation to play chef," Tom volunteered.

"That is unless you want to be poisoned," suggested Jeff.

"I really think you'll really like Josh. He actually was a guy I wanted you to meet several years ago, but somehow you missed out. He lived with another friend of mine, Syd. You remember him."

"Oh, I remember him. Not my first choice."

"Apparently Josh was a real mess, according to Syd, and they broke up. But evidently he's gotten his act together. He's a real neat guy. Oh, and rich!"

"What are you trying to set me up?"

"Well, it won't hurt to flirt a bit."

"But if Syd dumped him? Not a good reference."

"Tom, I think you would be making a big mistake not to meet him." Jeff's seconding of Toby impressed Tom more. Neither one indicated that it was Josh who had mentioned Dr. Abbott to them.

Tom knew in no way was he prepared to take on a relationship. Too much was going on in his life. Barbara had served him with divorce papers, making it very clear that the grounds involved infidelity. He was puzzled that he saw no claim for child support, although she had made a massive claim for alimony. He consulted with Mr. Townshend again. He had to fill out some financial information, which was forwarded to her attorney. Not long afterward, there was a knock on the door. When Toby answered it, he almost screamed. "Well, lookee lookee, here's Barbara. To what do we owe the pleasure?"

"Shut up, Toby. You're still as much of an ass as ever."

"Sure hope so. It is one of my most endearing features. Oh, Tommy, are you in luck." At that point, Tom walked out of his bedroom.

"Let's go out into the hall," she said. "I don't want to be around that creep any longer than I must."

"Feeling's mutual, doll."

When they got out into the hall, Barbara confronted him. "I got your financial statement. It just won't do. You need to get another job on top of what you have now. You've got to supply me with more income."

"Doesn't your attorney normally handle this sort of negotiation?"

"He's not interested in really going after what I need. He claimed I cannot force you to get a better job or take on a second one. He says it's solely based on your income. Well, I'm going to fight that."

"You need it for the baby?" he asked sincerely.

"There is no baby."

"I thought you were pregnant. Did you fake that one as well?"

"What do you mean fake?"

"Well, I know your first 'pregnancy' was designed to get me to marry you."

"That's a lie," she asserted, but Tom could tell there was some nervousness in her voice.

"But what about now?"

"Oh, I took care of that. I had an abortion."

"You! Miss Pious Catholic. That's a mortal sin."

"I wasn't going to carry your filth inside me. I wasn't going to raise any child that came from a queer."

"Well, I guess I'm grateful that once we're done with these formalities, I'll never have to see you again." With that, he walked back into the apartment.

Barbara stood outside, pounding on the door and demanding that Tom come out again. "I'm not finished."

Finally Toby opened the door on a crack. "If you don't go away right now, I'll call the police and have you arrested for disturbing the peace." He slammed the door again, but no longer was anything heard from outside. He then turned to Tom. "I don't suppose you thought this thing could go smoothly?"

"Obviously not," Tom returned.

In some respects, Tom felt a little better. A least that part of his ordeal was practically over. The divorce would be finalized by September.

The dinner guest arrived at six. A tall thin man a little older than Tom, he had a slightly aristocratic heir, as if he came from old money. Toby had warned Tom that he was rich; his carriage confirmed that.

"Tom, so glad to meet you. Toby had told me a great deal about you."

"All lies, I can assure you."

"Not at all. He is very complimentary about you. Isn't that right, Toby?"

"No, I was giving you the flattering portrait."

"I think he's trying to be a matchmaker. Thinks I've been single long enough," Josh claimed.

"Sort of like Emma," Tom said.

"You mean Emma Woodhouse?"

"Yes. You know the book?"

"Of course, I do," said Josh. "Jane Austen is probably my favorite author. I'm very fond of *Emma*, but I especially love *Sense and Sensibility*. I identify with Colonel Brandon."

"So you are familiar with her novels?"

"I've read all of them," Josh asserted.

"Even *Northanger Abbey*?"

"Well, I'm not a particular fan of that one. But the rest I've read several times."

"Ah, a man of my own sentiments. Toby here reads nothing but gay romance novels."

"Yes, I'm reading *Deep Throat* with Jack Wrangler. High-class art."

"I used to be an English teacher, and I would try to fit in an Austen novel whenever I could," said Tom, ignoring Toby, "but I usually had to teach American lit. I'm not nearly as fond of that as I am of British lit. Well, it doesn't matter anymore."

"Yes, Toby told me about your hard luck. As the English say, Keep your pecker up."

"I say that to Jeff all the time," Toby explained, "but it never seems to do any good."

"Bitch!" was Jeff's retort.

"No, seriously, you're too intelligent a guy to be relegate to selling shoes the rest of your life."

"Oh, you know about that as well."

"Yes, Toby has been filling me in on your biography. Hope you don't mind?"

"I even told him what blood type you were."

"Now how would you know that?"

"Easy. Blue."

"Yes, from a working-class family from Boston of Irish descent. Green more like it. Well, Toby said you were in insurance. Once we settle on what we do for a living, we can then turn to sports."

"Yes, I'm an insurance agent. And no, I know nothing about sports. But I'd be happy to sell you a life insurance policy or auto insurance." He went on naming different types of insurance, as the rest began to laugh.

"Is there something like almost ex-wife's insurance?"

"Sorry, I can't help you with that one."

They had a wonderful dinner with the jokes passing back and forth. Josh claimed he was eighty-seven years old but had a portrait of himself in the attic. Only Tom caught the reference. Toby looked dumbfounded.

"You haven't read Oscar Wilde?"

"Listen, I teach history. I wallow in warfare, Nazis, and all sorts of scandals to keep my youngers alert. Don't give me this literary crap."

"Then I'll never explain how I keep my timeless beauty."

This two-tiered conversation continued through the evening. Josh and Tom agreed on their love for the Fred Astaire-Ginger Rogers movies, concurred that *Singing in the Rain* was the best movie last year, and that both wondered about the fuss over *Sleeper*. Toby said he loved *Sleeper* and wished he had an orgasmatron. "But I especially adore the John Holmes oeuvre."

"Never heard of him. What movies did he appear in?" Josh wondered.

"Josh, don't ask. He's a porn star."

"Yes, with the biggest dick in the industry," boasted Jeff.

"These two love watching porn, which suggests the level of their cultural maturity."

"Well, you started the collection."

"Josh, I need to explain," Tom said with a fake tone of exasperation. "A few years back, I dated this guy who brought some of his videos over and left them. Toby asked if he could have them, and so they're now part of what I think is a vast collection of illicit videos."

"There's a mail order house with a large inventory," Toby explained. "I can show you our catalogue."

"Perhaps later," Josh laughed.

"That's not all. While I'm trying to get some sleep, they're out here with a video on and, I think, actually trying to duplicate the action on the screen."

"Often we're better," bragged Toby. "It's life imitating art, so to speak."

As Josh left, while the other two cleaned up the kitchen, he said to Tom, "Listen, I really had fun tonight, even though I did not get to see any of the art films. Would you like to join me for dinner next Saturday?"

"I'd really like to, but I work Saturday until eight."

"Well, let's have a late dinner then."

Josh took Tom to his favorite restaurant, Beef and Bottle. The dark restaurant invited intimacy, and even a same-sex couple did not seem out of place. Josh explained that it was a pickup restaurant, and it had a reputation of catering to a wealthy crowd looking for adventure for either single women or men. Apparently, some of the waiters were available for a nightcap after closing.

That evening, over a leisurely dinner, they discussed books, classical music, and finally religion. "So you used to teach at a Catholic high school. I suppose then that you're a Catholic."

"I guess nominally. O'Mally equals Irish Catholic. I attend Mass once in a while but not 'religiously,'" Tom explained, making the quotation marks with his fingers. "You?"

"Oh, I'm an RC—recovering Catholic."

"Why did you leave?"

"It's a long story. No time to go into it tonight. But the church caused me some problems with my self-esteem. It took me a while to overcome." This really raised Tom's curiosity, but he decided to drop it. Josh had clearly put up signposts: Do not cross. "But I never lost my sense of the divine. I found a spiritual home in the Episcopal Church."

"Funny you should say that. My parents attend an Episcopal church in Clermont. Actually I find it quite nice, although the music is dreadful."

"Well, if you're interested, you could come with me to the cathedral. The music is terrific there. Someone there told me the Episcopal Church has all of the pageantry and none of the guilt."

"Boy, I could do with that." So they agreed that Tom would go with Josh to the Episcopal cathedral the following Sunday. Tom had hoped that Josh would invite him over to his place, but that did not happen. Instead, Tom made his way home alone but knew something special had happened. Toby was very inquisitive about their date and was particularly perplexed that Tom spent the night alone.

"Not even a quickie after dinner."

"I don't think it is that sort of relationship." Of course, he had wished otherwise. "Have you ever heard about friends?"

"Of course, friends with benefits."

The following Sunday morning, the first Sunday in June and Pentecost, Tom walked with Josh into the Episcopal cathedral. He noted that it was Gothic Revival, which appeared not to have been totally completed. It was almost full, and he detected there were quite a few male couples. He quietly asked Josh about that, and Josh explained that in fact a rather sizeable portion of the congregation was gay. He knew a few members of the congregation did not seem happy about this arrangement, but most did not seem to mind. The organist began a Bach prelude, which reverberated beautifully in the high ceiling. Then a grand process began the service, with the choir singing a hymn by Ralph Vaughn Williams that seemed to last interminably, although the thurifer, crosses, candles, choir, banners, and clergy made good use of the time by circumnavigating the interior of the church. The choir was, as Josh had mentioned, terrific. And the congregation clearly enjoyed singing their parts. He was especially struck by the hymn sung before the reading of the gospel: "Spirit of Mercy, Truth, and Love." He was especially struck by the final verse.

Unfailing Comfort, heavenly Guide,
still o'er thy holy Church preside;
O shed thine influence from above,
Spirit of mercy, truth and love.

He noted that Josh sang with great exuberance—he did have a beautiful voice. Tom only wished he shared those sentiments, that some divine being was watching over him and protecting him with unfailing comfort. Yet feeling the warmth of Josh's body against his did provide some solace.

That feeling did not last long, however, once Josh and Tom sat down to brunch. Josh obviously had something on his mind. He talked cheerily about the service and how he enjoyed being free from the Catholic menace, as he called it. He told Tom that he had been confirmed in the church at Easter, a decision he confessed he had not told his mother. "She's disappointed with me as is."

Tom refrained from asking questions because he could again sense a "no trespassing" sign.

Nevertheless, Josh did reveal more. "You see, my father started the insurance firm but died quite young, leaving it to my mother and my brother and me. It has been a very difficult arrangement. I had originally trained to be a chef, but that didn't work out, so I ended up trying to sell insurance. Since I've been in Florida, life has been very good, especially since I have been principally on my own. But the family dynamics has been very difficult. And my mother is suffering from Parkinson's disease and is in failing health. We're going through a reorganization right now, which means I have to return to New Hampshire. In fact, it might be permanently." Tom's heart sank.

"I'm really sorry," Josh continued. "I thought I had finally met someone who I could develop a relationship. But that's probably not to be." Tom thought he saw a tear in Josh's eye.

"You don't know how sorry I am to hear you say that. I had that same sense that there was something really good here. Seems to be the story of my life." They ate the rest of the meal in silence without the discussion of music or books that seemed to cement their growing relationship, now clearly almost at an end.

In fact, for the several weeks, they exchanged almost nightly telephone conversations in which they discussed books, films, and the arts in general. For the most part, they agreed on just about everything except some sensitive topics: Josh preferred the post-Impressionists, and Tom the Impressionists: Josh, Prokofiev's *Romeo and Juliet*; Tom, Tchaikovsky's *Swan Lake*. They also shared two dinners. At the last, Josh said he would be leaving Orlando soon.

Tom received a long letter that week in which Josh said goodbye. His mother had the problems with ill health, and he needed to get to Portsmouth as soon as possible. He signed the letter "Love, Josh." That hurt even more. The same week, Jeff and Tom drove Toby to the airport to board his flight to London. "Not a good week," observed Tom. "Josh—and now you—deserting me."

"It's only to the end of August. Then I have to get back to my cheery students at Winter Park. And you'll see me before that."

"What do you mean?"

"You have a ticket to fly to London with Jeff my last two weeks at Oxford."

"That would be great, but I can't afford that."

"Already paid for. And it's nonrefundable, so you have to use it."

"You paid for it?

"Wish I had. No, it's a farewell gift from Josh. He had planned to come over with Jeff but couldn't because of his family's business. So he bought it for you. Said Jeff is too unstable to travel alone."

Tom tried to find Josh's phone number but failed to locate it; he then realized that Josh had not given his number in Portsmouth. He tried to call the insurance company in Portsmouth but was told that Mr. Simmons was not available each time he called. Jeff insisted he did not have his private number there. Tom wondered if Josh had deliberately erected fences between them. Finally, Tom wrote a long letter, thanking Josh for the ticket and telling him quite sincerely how much he missed him and how he would treasure the short time they had together. *And I never had sex with him*, Tom thought ruefully. Yet it was really a first. He had connected with Josh intellectually and even emotionally, but not physically. *Not the normal gay sequence*, he thought.

Tom wrote several other letters but received no reply. He concluded that Josh did not want to hear from him again. Only at the middle of August, just before Tom was to leave for England, he received a short note from Josh, who apologized for not returning his letters and explained that he had a great deal going on. He also wrote something cryptically about things to decide.

Tom had himself been incredibly busy. He had taken on extra shifts at Jordan Marsh because they were short-staffed. He also worked part-time at Ivey's for a few weeks. He did not go to the Parliament House or the Hammer, because he was trying to save money; and truthfully, he was just too tired. He only had time to visit his parents twice the entire summer; and when there, his mother kept up the refrain, "Tom, you look exhausted. You're overdoing it."

Tom was very ambivalent about going to England. On the one hand, he could not afford it, even if the ticket was a gift. On the other, he really needed a change of scenery. Finally, he informed his supervisor at Jordan Marsh that he needed to take two weeks off for family issues. The manager was not happy because the end of summer was a busy season with back-to-school shopping. That comment saddened Tom, since he knew he was not going back to school, probably ever.

Tom and Jeff flew to Atlanta and then across to Heathrow. Tom had the window seat and looked out over a land he thought he would actually never see again, although he had taught courses on English literature for years. The neat, green quilt work of the landscape fascinated him. He remembered seeing Ireland from the air, which was very similar although not as populated. But the intense green was the same. Once they landed, they took a bus to London and then a bus from Victoria Station to Oxford. Tom and Jeff were so jet-lagged that they both slept until the bus stopped on High Street. Only once did Tom note that the bus was driving on the wrong side of the road. They woke when Toby started banging on their window and yelling, "You need to get off."

They clambered off the bus and retrieved their luggage from underneath. "If you hadn't woken up, you'd have ended up at the Oxford train station and had to lug your luggage all the way up here. Good thing I waited for you."

Tom looked around in amazement. He felt as if he was is a different planet, let alone a different country. He gazed up at the tall towers of the various colleges and marveled at the sight of students wearing their academic gowns rushing off he knew not where. "Do you want to see my digs first or go to the B&B?"

They voted for the latter, and so they climbed into another bus, a local one that drove out of the center of Oxford. Toby paid the fares for all of them in a strange coinage, which made no sense to Tom. "The coinage is pretty much like ours since they decimalized," Toby explained, showing them the various coins. "In the old system, twenty shillings in a pound, twelve pence in a shilling There are also farthings and ha'pennies. I had to learn that so I could understand English money before decimalization."

"Bet that made your day," Jeff observed.

"Here we are," and Toby instructed them to get off the bus. Tom hoped this would be the last time he had to move his suitcase in a while.

The B&B, called Victoria's Rest, was a rather tawdry place. The lounge had several high-backed seats with arms covered with a lace antimacassars. Tom was glad he knew the coinage since he felt as if he had travelled back to the age of Victoria. The room was serviceable enough with two rather small and quite lumpy twin beds. Jeff looked around the room and asked where the bathroom was. "These places don't normally have private bathrooms. There will be one down the hall, which you will share. *En suite*, as they call them, are rather rare." Jeff grumbled, and Toby later told him privately that they could have stayed at the Randolph Hotel, but he decided it would be too expensive for Tom. Toby said he would let them rest and see them later in the afternoon.

Jeff got undressed and started to walk toward the door, until Tom reminded him that perhaps wearing a robe would be more appropriate. Jeff came back almost immediately and said the bathtub—there was no shower—was filthy. He said he saw the woman who had checked them in, and she said she would "tidy it up." They both bathed and promptly fell asleep until awakened by Toby's knock on the door.

They took another bus back into the center of Oxford, and Toby played the tour guide of a city that he now knew very well. He had acquired a pride of place. They ended the tour at Exeter College, where he took them up to his "digs." "It's in the more modern section, not like the older ones some of the students in the program got. One had the room that Tolkien had as an undergraduate." Toby's room was actually quite large with a pleasant study area. "And I have a scout who makes the bed every morning and cleans the room." But he pointed out that his room was also not *en suite*. He then showed them the chapel, the Burne-Jones stained glass panels, and the dining hall. "If you sit on the back row against the wall, you have to climb over the table," Toby, the tour guide, pointed out. "I normally eat here, so I'll show you some good—meaning cheap—Chinese restaurants and tandoori takeaways."

The next morning, they continued their tour of Oxford. They got lunch in a large market near the center of Oxford, "near the Carfax," the knowledgeable Toby pointed out. After lunch, Toby asked Tom for a big favor. "Would you mind wandering around town a little this afternoon so that Jeff and I can go back to your room and have some private time together."

"Oh, you mean to—" Tom started to say in a loud voice. Toby had begun to climb under that table. "Of course, I don't mind. Where's the closest bookstore?"

"The best one is Blackwell's, on Broad Street. I'll point you in the right direction. Then we can meet outside Exeter around five."

"Make it six," Jeff suggested.

Tom had no trouble finding Blackwell's, which at first seemed like a small shop, until he discovered it opened up in the back with several floors of wall-to-wall books. He found the literature section and began collecting an armful of books, until he realized that he would not be teaching English literature ever again. Why bother? So he put many of the books back, but kept one on the study of fate in the novels of Thomas Hardy and an analysis of Virginia Woolf's *Mrs. Dalloway*.

He was glad he had come to England with Jeff, but he knew that reality faced him once he returned to Orlando. A wave of depression swept over him as he stood amidst the books in Blackwell's. He looked at the Woolf book and thought about Septimus. Like him, Tom felt haunted by the past, what might have been. Like Septimus, he had become a shell of the person he had been and nothing to look forward to. But unlike Septimus, he did not plan to hurl himself out a window onto the spikes of an iron fence.

When he met up with Toby and Jeff again, he now had four books in his bag, which Toby stored in his room. "Let's go to Brown's for dinner," Toby suggested. "Man cannot live on tandoori takeaway alone. Then I suggest a visit to my favorite pub."

# Book Four

## ALLEGRO MOLTO VIVACE

# Chapter 1

"So are you going to show us the nightlife in beautiful downtown Oxford?" Jeff prodded. "You said there's a gay pub, for instance."

"As a matter of fact, I'm taking you to a lovely pub here that caters to folks like us."

"You mean there is a real homosexual bar in Oxford?" Jeff asked in amazement.

"Sure is. Would I lie? There was one guy in the program who was drop-dead gorgeous. And of course, I knew he was straight. Well, one evening I walked down to the pub, and there he was, big as life. And obviously a lot of other guys thought he was a hunk since he was surrounded by gawkers."

"I'm surprised there is an openly gay pub here," observed Jeff. "England's pretty conservative, isn't it?"

"Well, Wilson is Labour and has made some gestures to the gay population, but nothing that goes very far. But they tend to leave the pub goers alone as long as we behave ourselves."

"That's bunk."

Having completed their dinner, the trio walked down Woodstock Road to the Carfax, past the giant gate of Christ Church College with Tom Tower aglow, and then down Paradise Street to The Jolly Farmers. The pub was crowded and animated. Jeff went over to the bar and bought two pints of Guinness and a gin and tonic for Tom. "Always the outsider," Toby commented.

Jeff suggested that they walk around the room to see if they recognize anyone.

"Oh, come on, I doubt if anyone from Orlando other than us are going to be here," Tom observed knowingly.

"You can never tell," Jeff replied.

They walked to the back of the pub, and Tom gasped. "What are you doing here?"

"Can't a fellow get a drink at a nice pub if he wants?"

"Wait a minute, is this a setup?" Tom demanded.

"You might very well think that; I could not possibly comment," Josh replied.

"So you just happen to be at a pub where we show up?"

"Actually I don't care about the other two—sorry, guys—I came to see you."

"Couldn't you wait until I got back to the States?"

"Not at all. But I'll save that until tomorrow."

The four found a table and talked about Oxford and what they planned to do tomorrow. "I will tell my tutor that I have to miss the tutorial tomorrow."

"Will you get in trouble?" Josh asked.

"No, I'm a star student," he grinned.

"Brownnoser."

"Where are you staying?" Tom asked Josh.

"At the Randolph Hotel."

"How swanky."

Tom looked at Josh, who understood the look. "Not until after we've had our little chat tomorrow. All shall be made clear."

They reached the Carfax and split to go their separate ways. Josh walked up the street past St. Mary Magdalen and the Martyrs' Memorial, two waited near the Carfax for the bus to take them down Iffley Road, and the lone scholar strolled up Turl Lane to the entrance of Exeter College, hoping the porter had not yet locked the gate.

# Chapter 2

The four met at Brown's for breakfast. Josh let it be known that he wanted to be alone with Tom; and although Toby and Jeff had anticipated an adventure, perhaps a trip to Blenheim Palace, Josh said it would have to wait until tomorrow. "I've been there years ago, and it is really pretty ugly. I think Voltaire described it as '*une gosse masse de pierre, sans agrement et sans gout*'" in perfect French.

"Translation please," asked Toby.

"A great pile of stone without harmony or taste."

"Sounds like fun," Toby joked.

"I'd like to be alone with Tom for a while this morning," Josh began. Toby began snickering. "No, not for that, smut brain. We need to talk over some things, that's all."

Toby thought of another smart comment but decided to hold back. Tom began to get nervous about the drift of this conversation.

"Okay, we'll wander off. I'd like to see some of the other colleges," Jeff offered.

"And the undergraduate males," Toby added.

Josh and Tom walked silently to the Randolph Hotel, thence to the parking garage, where Josh had left his rental, a Land Rover in British racing green. It seemed the quintessential means of transportation for an English country gentleman.

"Where are we going?" Tom finally asked.

"To another pub, the Trout. It is quite famous."

They drove a short distance out of Oxford and parked in a lot near the river. "We'll walk from here. I understand from the porter at the hotel it's a lovely walk." Tom obediently fell in line. They walked slowly along what probably had been a towpath for several minutes in silence. Then Josh broke the tension. "I've been doing a lot of thinking this last month and have made some important decisions which I hope you will approve."

"I'm not sure why I have to approve," Tom said hesitantly.

"Because they involve you intimately." Tom just listened. "You know that I had a very bad experience with the Catholic Church. I could never go back. But I have found a new spiritual home. I never lost my faith, just where I would practice it. I never lost God."

This God talk made Tom just a little uneasy since he never thought in those terms. He had gone through the rituals but rarely contemplating their meanings.

Josh looked over a Tom and saw he was attentive but somewhat uneasy. "I know you aren't deeply religious in the same way I am. But I've never heard you wax eloquent about being a committed atheist either. So I assume you can at least tolerate my religious enthusiasm."

"Actually I admire it. I'm just more indifferent, if anything. Certain things do strike a chord with me, particularly the music. One reason I'm pretty cool on the Catholic church is the terrible music. I really enjoyed the music when we attended the Episcopal cathedral in Orlando. It was so different."

"I'm glad you said that. Perhaps we have something to build on."

Tom gave him a puzzled look but knew more would be revealed.

"I had to spend time in New Hampshire because the family had gotten an offer to sell the business to a larger firm, which is buying up smaller outfits. I suppose so they can jack up prices. Anyhow, we actually had a fairly amiable family discussion. Probably because we all had to agree to the deal. So we sold and slipped the receipts into our pockets. I am now quite independently wealthy. You may officially marry me for my money." They both laughed, but Tom had no idea where this conversation was headed.

"So I've decided to become a priest."

"What! You can't marry me if you're a priest."

"Not if I became a Catholic priest, but that, of course, is the furthest thing from my mind. And anyhow, we can't get married because it isn't legal for two men to get married."

"What if I went through a sex change operation?"

"Then I'd totally lose interest. Wrong plumbing. No seriously, I found a spiritual home in the Episcopal Church. It has the sanctity that I thought existed in the Catholic Church but doesn't now. I had hopes that John XXIII would bring about major reform to the church, but it has been lost. Paul VI seems well-meaning, but he's been overwhelmed by the conservatives. I took heart with the Berrigan brothers, but they were crushed. Look at how the Orlando bishop treats those wonderful nuns working with the migrants in Apopka. Not my sense of Christianity; not my view of what Jesus was teaching."

Josh motioned Tom toward a bench along the river. They sat quietly for a few minutes as boats and swans floated by. Josh was allowing what he was saying to sink in. Tom let it.

"But what I liked about Catholic worship, I find also at the cathedral. And I know that the national Episcopal Church is very involved in social issues. Have you ever heard of Bishop James Pike?"

"Not really."

"Well, he was still bishop of California when I was at Berkeley. He was very controversial, but I had a lot of respect for him. He was opposed to American foreign policy, he was active in the civil rights movement, and he thought women should be able to become priests. A group of women were ordained as priests in Philadelphia last month, so the Episcopal Church has moved galaxies beyond Rome. I always wanted to be a priest myself. When I was a kid, I used to dress up in a robe and pretend I was a priest." Tom stifled the urge to suggest that he was actually dressing up like Marilyn Monroe. Josh must have sensed it because he gave him an I'm-being-serious look. "Well, now I can because I have no family obligations. I told my mother and brother that I had applied and been accepted into CDSP." Tom gave him a puzzled look. "The Church Divinity School of the Pacific. It's the Episcopal seminary in Berkeley. I used to pass it when I would take walks around town. And I also told them that I'm gay, and that I was in love with another guy named Tom."

"Oh, I bet that went over well. You becoming a gay Episcopalian. Did they try to disown you?" He had to digest the last part of that declaration.

"Too late," he laughed. "I already had the money in my bank account. But yes, they said they wanted nothing more to do with me.

My brother called me a pervert. Now at least we know where we don't have to go for Christmas. Come on, it's almost time for lunch."

"Yes, and I can use that gin and tonic to calm my nerves."

They started walking alone the towpath until that reached the Trout Inn. Tom thought it was something Disney would have designed for his park: so perfectly English. It was already crowded; tourists had now taken quite a few tables on the lawn leading down to the river. "Grotty Americans," mumbled Tom.

"No, there's a table over there. A couple is just leaving." They rushed to the table and sat down just as two rather overweight American tourists came loping over. Both Josh and Tom just grinned at them as they grumbled away. "Probably from Bithlo," Tom surmised. Josh went into the pub and brought out a Guinness for himself and Tom's precious gin and tonic, informing him that he had ordered lunch for both of them.

"So I bought a very nice house on Grizzly Peak. You can see the Golden Gate Bridge and the bay from the dining room window. I can drive you to campus before I go to my New Testament class at CDSP."

"My what class?"

"Well, I assume you'd like to finish your master's degree. Of course, you could start a Ph.D. program in English literature."

"Oh my god. I probably couldn't get into Berkeley let alone get a doctorate. But I take it you want me to move out here and—"

"Live with me. I know this sounds fantastic, and you will need time to digest it. But seriously, I have found what I want to do the rest of my life. I want to be a priest, and I want to share my life with you. Now if you don't love me—"

"Of course, I love you. Since we met, I've thought of no one else but you, all summer long. But I thought it was impossible."

"Well, it's not. I don't need an answer right now—although I would certainly love it if you fell into my arms and said, 'Josh, I'll follow you to the ends of the earth.'"

"I would. The offer sounds too good to be true, but I would follow you anywhere." Then Tom paused a minute. "But why me? I'm sure there are lots of more intelligent, better-looking, wealthier guys out there that would be more suitable."

"I don't want to brag, but I have had," he paused, "for want of a better term, suitors. But, kid, they're not you. Can't explain it in rational terms, but there is some chemistry between us that I cannot be without."

By this point, Tom was almost in tears. Then a sinking feeling overcame him. "Oh god, I just can't move out here, much as I'd like to tell Sister Alice and all the others who have made my life crappy where to jump. But I can't leave my parents. They live in Clermont and are increasingly dependent on me to help them out."

"Oh, that's already taken care of."

"I should have known."

"I saw them about a few weeks ago. I told them not to mention any of this to you since I wanted to surprise you."

"You have!"

"I'm helping them move out there. They told me they really hated Florida and had begun looking for a place back in Boston. I convinced them that the Bay Area was every bit as nice." Tom started to interrupt, but he knew he was helpless in all this, which was not at all a bad thing. "I've been looking for single-story cottages near Shattuck Avenue, where the shopping is close by. I found two or three and plan to fly your parents out there to take a look."

"But the expense of housing there—"

"You always seem to raise a problem. Stop it," he said with a laugh. "They'll actually get a good sum of money out of their house because Florida is currently going through a housing bubble. It will burst soon, so they should get out now. I've arranged some additional financing, which they can afford to pay off over a very loooong period. It's worth it to get my honey out here with me. And actually I think your mother is a stitch. She told me that she was so happy that I had come along to save you from yourself."

"I can hear her now," Tom said sardonically.

"So all you have to say is I do. Then you can quit your job, start packing, and share our bed for the rest of our lives." At this point, Tom did begin to cry.

Just then the waiter brought out their lunches and gave Tom a very concerned look. "Has someone died?" he asked.

"No, someone was born anew," Tom replied, wiping his eyes on his napkin and taking a bite of his plowman's lunch. "I really don't need time to think it over. The answer is an emphatic yes. Although you might regret having my mother so close."

That night at dinner, they told Toby and Jeff about their plans. Jeff was jubilant for them; Toby looked quite sad. "I'm going to miss you guys. Who am I going to clown around with at the Parliament House? Who will enjoy Miss P as much as you and I did, Tom?"

"Well, Jeff's going to be there."

"Oh, he's a lawyer. No sense of humor. Doesn't understand drag at all. And doesn't laugh at most of my camp jokes."

They decided that they would celebrate by returning to The Jolly Farmers. Since it was Saturday night, the pub was very crowded. Toby squeezed his way to the bar and ordered a bottle of champagne and four glasses. The barkeep asked if it was a special occasion, and Toby told him that two of his friends had just gotten engaged. Immediately the barkeep rang the bell and announced the upcoming nuptials. "Where are they?"

Toby pointed toward Josh and Tom. The crowd turned and loudly applauded the couple, and the pub donated the bottle of champagne. They finally got a chance to drink once the crowd had finished "For they're jolly good fellows." Tom was so embarrassed that he swore he would never forgive Toby.

On their way home, Josh announced that they were all going to church the next morning at St. Mary Magdalen. "Mass begins at ten. Toby, if you're not there on time, no breakfast and no trip to Blenheim."

At the Carfax, Tom started to turn away. "No, you're coming with me," Josh announced. My room at the Randolph has a nice double bed. If you're game, Tom, that is?"

"What are we waiting for?" as Tom turned in his tracks and started toward the Randolph.

"Just as well," Toby added. So they went their separate ways, all smiles.

The next morning, Tom and Josh stood outside St. Mary Magdalen waiting for Toby and Jeff. "Perhaps they're having another round of it."

"We did," said Josh, "and we made it on time."

Tom looked around and saw how quiet it was at a normally bustling intersection. He marveled at the number of bikes chained to the wrought iron fence surrounding the church. He thought there must be a least a hundred of them. Josh then pointed out the sign hanging from the fence. "Do not lock bikes to this fence."

"Obviously very compliant university students."

Toby and Jeff showed up at the last minute, and they entered the church as the organist was playing. Tom and Josh looked at each other. "Bach," they said in unison.

The procession began with the thurifer leading the way. The organist provided a stirring introduction, and the choir and congregation began singing, "Praise, My Soul, the King of Heaven," the same hymn that he had sung with his parents at the Episcopal church in Clermont. "Ransomed, healed, restored, forgiven / Evermore his praises sing." But it was the final verse, when the choir and organist pulled out all the stops, that really touched him. The sopranos added a descant that filled the church with a glorious, almost heavenly sound.

> Angels, help us to adore him;
> you behold him face to face.
> Sun and moon, bow down before him,
> dwellers all in time and space.
> Alleluia, alleluia!
> Praise with us the God of grace!

Again tears welled up in Tom's eyes. He was never a crier, he thought; he never let his emotions get the better of him. But they had. At that point, Josh reached over and held his hand, in front of the congregation, the clergy, and God.

## Chapter 3

Tom stood at the large window looking out over the bay, the city of San Francisco beginning to light up as twilight fell. The sun had just set behind the ridge, but the sky still glowed a brilliant red that backlit the Golden Gate Bridge. The mist moved like a blanket over the top of the hills and began to flow down the eastern slope. He had never seen anything so beautiful, certainly not in Orlando or Boston for that matter.

Josh moved in behind him and wrapped him in his arms. They stood there silently for what seemed to Tom hours of bliss. Neither spoke a word.

As the western sky began to turn slowly from red to gray, it broke their reverie.

"You saw me at my very worst, at my lowest point. I would have never guessed it would end up here."

"Now we are both at our very best."

The buzzing emitting from the oven timer interrupted their peace, and Josh rushed to the kitchen to retrieve his braised beef tips in wine and truffle sauce. As Tom ate, he reveled in the thought that he would continue to eat as if Julia Child hid in the kitchen.

"I spoke with your parents this morning. I think their decision to get that condominium is actually better than the cottage I found them. Then they would not have maintenance and yard work."

"In all probability, you saved me more work than my father."

"Well, I've invited them over for dinner Sunday. They're my new family now."

He explained that he would begin classes on Monday at CDSP. "I have enrolled in three courses this semester. One is called Introduction to Ministry, and the other two are biblical studies. I'm registered for an introductory course to the New Testament. Here's where I'm really concerned. I have to take Greek!"

"Why not French? You seem already fluent in French."

"Unfortunately none of the Gospels were written in French. All I know right now is the Greek alphabet begins with alpha and I think ends with omega."

"I guess I'll see you then in a few years," Tom laughed.

"No, you'll be busy as well."

"Sounds like you've already planned out my life."

"Well, somebody has to do it. Better me than Toby."

"You're right there."

"I checked with the Education Department at Berkeley, and you could finish your master's degree there. They said they would probably accept most of your coursework from Florida. The school systems out here are very good, and the pay is excellent."

"Well, I really would love getting back into the classroom. I'll happily give up selling shoes."

"You might also consider talking to the faculty in the English department. *Dr. O'Mally* sounds very impressive. You could write your dissertation on George Eliot," he grinned. "The man next door is a professor in their History Department. He thought you would have an excellent chance of getting accepted."

"But he doesn't know anything about my academic background."

"Oh, I just made it up. Now let's have dessert."

After dinner, Tom stood at the window again looking out over the Berkeley and across the bay. "I think the journey is finally over," he sighed.

Josh was still clearing the table. "I know that it was a terrible drive from Florida."

"Actually I wasn't thinking of that journey, although you're right. I thought Texas would never end only to be followed by New Mexico. Unrelenting boredom."

"Well, you'll never have to make that drive again. But what journey were you talking about?"

"I suppose from a good straight Catholic boy from Boston to, I guess, a budding Episcopalian gay man. Well, the gay man is definite. A life journey, which I did not plan for or anticipate. But I'm glad I made it. I'm not sure if it was just luck or fate brought me here."

"Or perhaps God."

"All I know that whatever or whoever brought me here, I am eternally grateful. Otherwise, I wouldn't be standing here looking at the most gorgeous guy in the world who loves me and I love him."

"Well, you're home now. No more travels."

## Τέλος

CPSIA information can be obtained
at www.ICGtesting.com
Printed in the USA
BVHW031741241021
619768BV00006B/148